GENT

MW00463470

Gent
Copyright © 2018 by Harloe Rae
All rights reserved.

No part of this publication may be reproduced, distributed, or transmitted in any form or by any means, including photo-copying, recording, or other electronic or mechanical methods, without the prior written permission of the copyright owner and the publisher listed above, except in the case of brief quotations embodied in critical reviews and certain other noncommercial uses permitted by copyright law.

This is a work of fiction and any resemblance to persons, names, characters, places, brands, media, and incidents are either the product of the author's imagination or purely coincidental.

Cover Design:
talia's book covers

Cover Photographer:
lindee robinson

Cover Model:
travis bendall

Interior Design & Formatting:
christine bogford, type A formatting

This book is dedicated to Jacquelyn, Megan, and Shauna.
I couldn't manage without these Hotties.

PLAYLIST

"Another Night in the Life of a Small Town"—Tim Culpepper

"Parallel Line"—Keith Urban

"Noise"—Brandon Scott

"Smoke a Little Smoke"—Eric Church

"Drunk Girl"—Chris Janson

"Filthy"—Justin Timberlake

"Timber"—Pitbull and Kesha

"Never Be the Same"—Camila Cabello

"Tequila"—Dan + Shay

"Bad Liar"—Selena Gomez

"Black Mirror"—Sophie Simmons

"Body Say"—Demi Lovato

"Show Me"—Alina Baraz

"Stronger Together"—Matt Lashoff

About GENT

Raven Elliot blasts into town like a wrecking ball—striking and devastating.

With a few simple words, my reliable routine crumbles to dust.

"Is this seat taken?"

I could close my eyes and let her voice wrap around me like a lover's caress.

But this isn't that type of story.

And I'm sure as hell not that kind of man.

She hovers in my space, batting her lashes and smiling shyly.

The glimmer in her sapphire eyes is a promise of peace.

But I'm not falling for it.

And Raven doesn't take the hint.

What starts as a battle of wills, explodes into a turf war.

She stands directly in my path everywhere I turn.

No matter how hard I shove, she won't budge.

Raven seems dead set on driving me insane.

But I was here first.

And I'm not going down easy.

After all, no one ever taught how me to treat a lady.

PROLOGUE

MOVE

RAVEN

AM I CRAZY?

As I cross the Stockton county line, my heart leaps into my throat. I'm not typically nervous, but this is big. Huge, really. Life changing and all that. Moving clear across the state seems extreme, right? It totally is, but this is happening. *Tonight.* I've never visited this city before, but in a few hours, it will be my home. Talk about taking a chance.

I'm worrying myself into an ulcer, and for no reason. Delilah wouldn't steer me wrong, or offer false promises, yet doubt continues to plague me.

What if everyone hates me? Or Delilah decides I suck at baking? What if I make a fool of myself?

This is the type of impulsive decision I was subjected to growing up. My mother made one hasty choice after another, dragging me along for the bumpy ride. The thought stops me cold.

Oh, Lord. Am I acting like her?

The idea makes me sick to my stomach, and I reject it

immediately. She'd never live in a small town, unless there was a damn good reason. Like meeting her next Mr. Right Now. I shudder thinking of her current flavor of the month. They're overseas living in a gorgeous villa off the Mediterranean. He's twice her age with a bank account busting at the seams. My mother swears up and down his money isn't the reason she loves him. Too bad I don't believe her.

Restless energy courses through my veins as I fiddle with the radio. I wish that audiobook had been a bit longer. It was a stellar distraction from the chaos buzzing through me. Getting lost in a sappy romance gives everything a rosy hue. Once they all lived happily ever after, the panic of my situation filtered in. Living in the pages of a love story would be far easier.

My eyes quickly land on the gift from Delilah. The bright pink apron lays spread across the front seat, like a constant presence reminding me of what's ahead. Master Baker is embroidered across the front. It makes me laugh each time, and this moment isn't different. As my giggle dies off, the view from my windshield looks brighter than ever.

I change the station and a slow country tune fills the speakers, calming my racing pulse. This sounds like sweet haven, which is exactly what I need to hear. I'm digging in and grabbing the happy place buried in my soul.

This is my choice. I'm controlling my future. Confidence replaces the doubt as my foot presses harder on the accelerator. I'll finally be planting roots. Everything will go perfectly. Yeah, I've got to stop overthinking this because the time is now. My hands twist on the steering wheel, and I exhale slowly. I've been waiting for this my entire life. I'm ready.

My headlights flash across a sign welcoming me to Garden Grove, and giddy nerves attack my gut.

Their slogan feels like arms wrapping me in a warm hug. I smile and repeat the words silently.

Where everyone belongs.

That sounds just right, like Goldilocks. Ready or not Garden Grove, here I come.

ONE

MA'AM

TREY

"DID YOU HEAR WHAT I said?"

At her question, my gaze shifts to connect with the woman's stare. She's an unfamiliar face, probably lured into town by the specialty shops off Main Street. Sitting closer than socially acceptable, she's almost stuck on me. The bar is crowded tonight, though. I let the proximity slide, but her attempt at conversation is pushing it too far.

I came to Dagos for a few beers after work, not to engage in chit-chat. Usually I won't hesitate sampling fresh meat, gladly gobble up what's being offered, but not today. Try as she might, this chick is striking out with me. I have zero intentions of giving her the quick fuck she's been practically begging for since sitting down.

I clear my throat. "Ma'am, I'm not interested."

"Excuse me?" she says as her eyes widen. "Ma'am? That's what you call a grandmother. Do I look old to you?"

The dial on her annoying meter cranks up a few notches. I'm

not stupid enough to fall into her trap, but still bite my tongue to keep the insults from barreling out.

I quickly scan her pinched face, covered with powdery shit likely meant to hide her age. I was trying to be polite by using a respectful term, but she's clearly not the type. I rub my forehead while blowing out a breath, frustration already building like a storm cloud.

"I mean no offense," I grind out between clenched teeth, "but I'm spending the evening solo. Cheers." I raise my bottle in a lame-ass salute.

The yappy broad huffs and rolls her eyes. It seems she might spit more crap my way, but then her attention darts to a man across the room. She eagerly slips off the stool, nearly spilling her drink with the jerky movements. She glances back at me, shooting daggers from her eyes.

"Asshole," she shoots over her shoulder before sauntering off. *Good fucking riddance.*

I lift the nearly empty beer to my lips, but a burst of laughter interrupts me.

"Wow. You sure know how to pick 'em. How are you still single with suave moves like that?"

"Not you too," I mutter without turning around, recognizing the raspy voice immediately. "Was the entire female race set on driving me fucking crazy?" My chin tilts skyward as I silently ask for patience . . . or a fucking break. Neither will come for me.

"Would it kill you to be nice?" Addison rests her arms against the bar next to me.

I puff air through my clenched teeth. "Most likely. And I was nice. I called her ma'am."

"You know girls hate that," she shoots back. "It's a dig more than anything and makes us feel old. Might as well call her a raging bitch or wrinkled hag."

"Those names seem more appropriate. Thanks," I chuckle

but there's no humor behind it.

"Don't start, Trey. You know I'm right."

"I'm not saying shit. Just thinking I might use those instead."

"You're impossible."

"That's the point."

"What-ev-er," Addison singsongs while glancing around. "Where's Jack?"

"Still at the shop."

"Burning the midnight oil?"

"In more ways than one. Had a rough day."

She tilts her head and gives me a once-over. "You too?"

"Don't I always?"

"Meh, I suppose. You're always a grump so it's tough to tell the difference."

"And here I thought we were exchanging pleasantries."

"You and pleasant will never go together." Addison hitches a thumb over her shoulder. "Running off that lovely lady is a prime example."

I grunt and shake my head. "She deserved it for being so desperate."

She snorts and elbows me. "Why are you such a dick? All that handsome is going to such shameful waste. You need to find someone to treat right."

Peering at Addison, all toned limbs and tan skin, I consider a quick fuck after all. I grip the cool bottle, picturing her soft flesh giving in to me.

"Why haven't we ever—"

"No way. I know that look," she says. "I see you give women those bedroom eyes every Friday night only to watch them turn cold the following morning. I haven't fallen for them yet and I don't plan to start."

Just like that, our breezy banter slams to a halt. Tension strains my shoulders after being cut off. *Again.* What is it with chicks bulldozing me tonight?

Having Addison call me out does nothing to help my mood, but it's no surprise she sees straight through me. Although I've known her since kindergarten, it still pisses me off. Moments like this make living in a small-town suffocating. There's nothing and no one new around here. I know useless shit about everyone from Garden Grove, whether I want to or not.

I roll my neck and restore my typical look of indifference. "I never get any complaints. Your loss, Addy."

Addison shakes her head. "So fucking cocky. I ain't giving you any ass, but how 'bout another?" She asks and gestures to my beer.

I grumble, "That'd be great," without looking back at her.

Addison just stands there so I give in and glance over. Her arms are crossed as she raises a slim brow my way, seemingly waiting for . . .

"Please," I grit. The irritation from earlier whooshes in my ears and I'm ready to get gone.

Right after this drink.

She snickers and says, "That's better. We'll make a gentleman of you soon."

"Don't hold your breath, *ma'am*."

Addison gasps and flames rise in her hazel eyes.

Before she digs into me, I add, "Chill out. I'm just fucking with you. But seriously, get back to work. I'm thirsty."

"You really are an asshole," she says while patting my cheek with more force than necessary. I'm sure she'd love to slap the shit out of me but won't risk getting in trouble for it. She shakes her head and turns away, strutting off to serve other waiting customers.

My eyes lock on her swaying hips, losing myself in the rhythm of her movement for a moment. No harm in looking, right?

Sweet-smelling perfume wafts in as the abandoned stool next to me shifts slightly.

"Is this seat taken?"

The notes are soft but rise above the booming noise in the space. The feminine lilt of her voice snakes around before I feel a twisting in my gut. I quickly shove that fluffy shit away. My jaw ticks while I ignore her heavenly scent closing in around me.

"Don't even bother," I growl loud enough for her to hear.

"Excuse me?"

Disbelief colors her voice and I can't help swiveling toward her. *Holy shit.*

Bottomless blue eyes greet me, sparkling with fierce emotion. The glittering sapphires are hypnotizing, the type of pull any man would fall victim to.

Except me.

I manage to break out of my trance and scan the rest of her features. Golden waves frame her face, the long locks shimmering in the bright lights. Her skin is clear of makeup, giving her a natural glow that I rarely see on the women around here. That caked-on crap always looks like a shield, hiding secrets and truths, like the ballsy bimbo from earlier. Nothing like this stunner in front of me. She's on a whole new level.

She's open to me, hiding nothing at all, which I'm realizing is a huge fucking turn-on. My hips shift slightly to alleviate the sudden pressure rising in my jeans, but it's pointless. My dick is definitely taking notice of all she has to offer.

Maybe I'm not meant to spend the night alone. This newbie is definitely worth changing plans for.

My gaze wanders lazily along her slender figure, outwardly showing minimal interest while my pulse pounds erratically. Why am I having such a strong reaction to her? With an innocent look and a few words, she's screwing with my mojo like a voodoo witch.

What makes her so damn special?

She's just another woman, looking for an easy lay, and I'm the biggest target. This stranger probably heard about me from locals like Addison and came over to try her luck. My body is betraying me by falling under her spell, but I see the threat like a neon sign. I'm not letting her sink those perfectly painted nails into me.

Her flawless face dips into my line of sight, and our eyes clash. I blink and take a clarifying breath as determination to get rid of her barrels through me.

"Listen, babe—"

She holds up her hand like a stop sign and for some reason, having her interrupt doesn't bother me.

"Did you just *babe* me?" Her question is all sass.

"Sure did, sweetheart. Call 'em like I see 'em. Don't pretend to be offended. We both know why you're over here talking to me."

Her face turns an adorable shade of pink. "First, stop with the nicknames. Second, are you for real? What the hell is wrong with you?"

"I don't see any issue. You're the one disrupting my quiet evening."

"What the . . . I mean, seriously? I want to sit down and this is the only available spot. You honestly think I came over here to hit on you?"

Her ridiculous question doesn't deserve a response. My glare matches hers as I silently explain my opinion on the matter. My expression must tell her everything she needs to know.

"Wow, you're an asshole."

"You're the third woman to call me that tonight. Be careful, I might get a complex."

"Aw, poor baby. I'd hate to dent your fragile ego," she snips with a curl in her lip.

"There's nothing fragile about me. Don't worry. I'm hard and solid. Wanna feel?" I ask and pat my abs.

She nods to my hands. "No, thanks. I'd hate for you to rub off on me."

"Does the grease under my nails bother you? Princess is afraid of getting a little dirty?"

"Do you get a rise out of being mean?"

I lean against the bar and cross my arms. "I don't get many complaints. You're not from around here, so I'll fill you in—the ladies love me."

"Pretty sure I saw Barbie McCleveage storm off after chatting with you. She didn't look too satisfied."

"Now who's using nicknames? Jealous much?"

"Hardly," she huffs.

I smirk before checking out her rack, being extremely obvious about it. Pushing her buttons takes away the tension from earlier, replacing it with a surprising ease. Fighting with her is the most nonsexual fun I've had with a woman in a long time. Wonder how she'd react if I called her ma'am.

"All right, all right. You've broken me down. I was set on not having any company tonight, but for you, I'll make an exception. If you insist on standing here, blabbing away, I've got far better uses for that luscious mouth. My place isn't too far away," I suggest while waggling my brows. My behavior is over the top, but what can I say? She's bringing out the best in me.

Her lips part in shock. This stranger just stares at me, and I'm sure she's about to turn away . . . or slap me. Either way, mission accomplished.

But this chick is full of surprises.

She raises her chin and says, "You're pathetic, and I see straight through your bullshit. I've dealt with guys like you my entire life—dime a dozen playboys looking to score. Having a place to sit isn't worth being ridiculed."

I keep my face void of emotion but my blood is boiling. "Why are you still here then?"

"I have no idea." She rests a palm on her forehead, looking bewildered and sexy as fuck. "I don't want to surrender so easily, but just . . . forget it. You're clearly used to getting what you want. I'd hate to be another tally in your win column."

I chuckle, the sound dark like a rumble. "No truer words. I'm a fucking winner. Since you're not interested in my *cocky bullshit*, let's make a deal. I was here first so go find someone else to harass."

A dimple dents her cheek as she smiles, but the expression looks weak. The fire in her eyes extinguishes as she mutters, "A real man wouldn't hesitate before offering an empty seat to a lady. My mistake."

I'm the one forcing her away, but for some messed up reason, the distress creasing her face is a punch to the gut. So, I offer some parting words for her to remember me by.

"I never claimed to be a gentleman, Princess."

TWO

NEWBIE

RAVEN

I GIVE THE ARROGANT ASSHOLE a final glare, but there's no heat behind it. As I turn away from the bar, my shoulders sag, and all the adrenaline pours from my limbs. It's usually difficult to get my feathers ruffled, but that guy managed to push all my buttons in a few short minutes.

But damn, he's super sexy. All those dark features highlighted by a tan complexion. His soulful brown eyes shot straight through me, daring me to look away. I bite my lip and think about his huge hands covered in grease. He has no idea how dirty I could get with him. Too bad he had to ruin it all by opening his mouth.

Good riddance.

Taking a few shuffled steps is all I manage in this packed place. This type of crowd isn't what I expect from a tiny town, but Delilah did mention extra traffic during the summer months. Thinking about her makes me realize she should have been here by now.

I glance down at my phone to check for any messages, but

find none. She's already twenty minutes late, and I'm not sure what the hell to do now.

Delilah managed to convince me that moving to Garden Grove was a great idea, but doubt is sinking in like a ton of lead. My hopes of a happy housewarming are quickly being dashed. She promised everyone was so welcoming and kind, that I could wait here and make a crew of friends while she finished up at work. In the short time I've been here, there's only been trouble and disappointment.

I'm attempting to distance myself further from the bar when Delilah makes an appearance. She weaves through the throng like an expert, beelining straight for me. In the next breath, I'm wrapped in a fierce hug.

"Holy shit, Rave. Sorry I'm so late," she huffs into my ear before pulling away.

I shrug, feigning nonchalance. "It's fine."

Her green eyes pierce me, slicing through my lie like butter.

"What's wrong? Why is your face so red?"

"Nothing. It's really warm in here," I explain while fanning myself.

She quirks a brow, waiting for me to spill, knowing I'll fold easily enough. It only takes a few moments for me to crack.

"Ugh, okay. I got into it with a dude over a stool. Not a huge deal. We settled it, and I moved on." I give her a smile, but it's forced. "Tell me about your day. What kept you late at the shop?"

Delilah shakes her head. "You're so not off the hook. A stool? Why aren't you sitting down? There's an empty spot right over there," she says and points over my shoulder.

I twist slightly to glance at the bar, and frustration bubbles back to the surface. "Yeah, about that. I already tried, and that seat is reserved for assholes and those willing to deal with one. Found that out the hard way," I mutter.

"What do you mean? No one is reserving it."

I exhale loudly. "That guy," I gesture to the hostile stranger, "has plenty to say on the matter. You can go ask him. I'll stay here where it's safe."

"Do you mean Trey?"

"How do you expect me to know? I'm new around here. Remember?" My tone is harsher than she deserves, but I'm ready to be done with this line of questioning.

Delilah's forehead crinkles as she gages my expression. "Um, who crapped in your Cheerios?"

"I already told you. Can we go somewhere else? All I want is somewhere to relax after my long drive. This isn't helping."

She laughs, tipping her head back and really belting it out. "Girl, you're all fired up. I've never seen this side of you. I kinda like it." Delilah winks at me. "But seriously, you can't let that man bully you. Trey is a real shithead, filthy to the core. I've known him since the sandbox days. Let me handle this."

Delilah grabs my hand and starts dragging me toward him. I dig my heels in, but it does little use. I shout protests at her back, but she plows forward, dodging huddles of people in our path. My friend is stubborn as a mule and protective like a mama bear. This Trey guy is about to get an earful.

His broad shoulders come into view, and I stumble slightly. As a last-ditch effort, I try yanking free of her grip, but it's useless. We're confronting him, right here and now.

With all the confidence in the world, Delilah hops onto the vacant seat and roughly taps his bicep. "I hear you're causing problems for my friend, Trey. That's not super neighborly. We all know you swallow a pint of piss and vinegar each morning, but would it kill you to be nice for five seconds? This stool is wide open, and all she wanted to do was rest her sweet ass while enjoying a brew. But no, you had to chase her off like a rabid guard dog."

Trey slowly turns and scowls at Delilah's finger pressed into his arm. He cranes his neck to glare at me before addressing my friend. "You about done running that loud mouth of yours, D?"

I gasp, but Delilah just grins as if he's amusing her. "That's not my style, and you know it. Now, you about ready to apologize to Raven?"

He snorts and rolls his eyes. "Dramatic as ever. There isn't anything I'm sorry about so that'd be a hard no." Trey looks back at me before adding, "Or do you need it to pad your fragile ego?"

When he tosses my words back at me, they don't register. My brain is short-circuiting at the worst possible time. The moment his caramel coffee eyes sear into me, I lose my voice. That didn't happen earlier, and sounds cliché as hell, but *for real* his dark stare just stole my ability to talk. My only excuse is that I'm wrung out and beyond exhausted. I can only blink and gape, unable to string a sentence together. Shame stings my cheeks, but I don't drop my gaze.

Of course, he takes advantage of my silence.

"Cat got your tongue, Princess? My offer from earlier still stands if you need some help loosening it."

"What?" Delilah snaps. "What happened earlier?" Her eyes dart between us but eventually settle on me. "Rave?"

I clear my parched throat, more desperate than ever for a drink. "N-nothing. I already told you. He's very territorial of his space, and I made the mistake of barging into it."

"For the love of all that's holy. What did he say?"

I shake my head at her question, not willing to delve into more details. Delilah must see the desperation on my face because she doesn't force the issue. "We'll discuss it later. But for now, don't show weakness. He feeds off it. When Trey pushes, just shove harder." She demonstrates by digging her finger deeper into his muscle. He shakes her off and shifts away, apparently done with the debacle.

Delilah waves before blowing me a kiss. "Vodka soda with a lime?"

"Sounds delicious," I say with a smack of my lips.

"Can you two hens cluck somewhere else?" Trey grumbles. Delilah rolls her eyes but doesn't react further so I choose to ignore him as well. When he realizes we aren't moving, Trey barks, "Forget it. I'm done here anyway. Try not to drive everyone else crazy tonight." He mumbles something about three strikes before slipping off the stool and disappearing into the crowd.

The air instantly feels lighter without him around, and I sigh with relief. Delilah pats his abandoned stool before saying, "Take a load off. About damn time, right?"

I gladly sit and swivel toward the bar, more than ready to turn this evening around. "Is that guy for real? I've never met anyone so rude yet forward at the same time."

"Unfortunately, yes. Trey has always been a hot mess, emphasis on the *hot*."

"Ugh, yeah. He's way too good looking to be such a prick," I agree.

"That's why Trey is extra dangerous, like a triple threat. He's bad for your heart, mind, and soul. His touch is a permanent stain you'll never get out."

"Sounds like you're speaking from experience," I say with a raised brow.

Delilah snorts. "Hell to the no. Are you nuts? All of us local gals know to stay the hell away from him and have been since middle school, whether he's good looking or not. My friend, Addison," she lifts her chin to a woman making her way toward us, "manages to remain civil with Trey, but only because she works here. Can't go around cussing out customers, no matter how terrible they are."

"Who's terrible?" Addison asks as she stops behind us.

"Addy!" Delilah squeals and gives her a squeeze. "My two besties are finally meeting. This is Raven," she gestures to me, "and she just arrived tonight." We exchange smiles and waves before Delilah continues. "Raven had the displeasure of meeting Trey so I'm filling her in on all the necessary info."

Addison cringes. "Oooh, I'm sorry to hear that. Had I known you were coming, I would have warned you. Trey was in a worse mood than usual."

"He's not always so bad?" I ask.

She makes a seesaw motion with her hand. "He has good moments, like after several beers. Don't ever tell him that. It's my secret against him," Addison says with a smile.

"Bleh," Delilah cuts in. "You're far too forgiving. Trey is never nice to me, especially during a good night of drinking."

Addison asks, "Can you blame him? You two have never gotten along."

"Hey! Whose side are you on, biatch? He just steamrolled Raven."

Addison nods and turns to me. "I'm sorry you had to deal with him. He's kind of an acquired taste. Trey has his reasons, even D can admit that. Tonight he was more vocal about his displeasure too. Normally there's a few women preening for his attention so that keeps him busy. That man can turn on the charm when necessary," Addison says.

Delilah bobs her head. "Pretty sure his social screws are loose, but he manages to get plenty of ass regardless. We get a lot of clueless visitors who only see the handsome face. They fall head first into his bullshit." She shoots me a wry grin.

"So, what'd he say to you? Was he a total douche?" Addison asks.

I blow out a breath, expelling the negativity. "I asked if anyone was sitting in the empty chair next to him, and that set off a chain reaction. He called me a bunch of nicknames that fired me up, then told me to get lost. While my head was still spinning, he propositioned me. I'm still trying to figure it out. Why are the hottest guys always the biggest assholes?"

They hum and nod, studying my face.

"Why are you looking at me like that?"

They share a glance before Delilah answers. "It's for the best you got that interaction taken care of. Now you know to steer clear. I've had a few friends stay with me from outta town and they've fallen for his shit. That won't happen with you. I won't let him chase you away."

I scoff. "No effing way, thank you very much. I'm not a starry-eyed virgin."

Delilah laughs. "Oh, I know. But you're too sweet and always look for the good in everyone. Trey is the worst of the bad boys. Don't bother searching for something that isn't there, alright?"

"What she said," Addison adds. "Okay. Enough Trey talk. Whatcha drinking? Champagne to celebrate? I've got just the thing to start a girl's night right. And I'll be off in less than an hour so get ready."

"Yay, bring on the booze!" Delilah exclaims.

I join in with, "Bring the bottle!"

"Yes! Now we're talking. I'll be right back with all the goodness," Addison says before dashing away.

Delilah scoots her stool closer to me. "So, how was the drive?"

"Ugh, long and boring. I was listening to a steamy audiobook, so that was fun at least."

"You and those romance novels. Still thinking of publishing something?"

My heart rate spikes at the thought. "Maybe one day. I'm not so sure about all that anymore. I love writing, but letting people read my words? It might all be part of a crazy pipe dream."

"Fantasizing is a great use of time." Delilah nudges me, and we both laugh.

"Why do you think I read all the smut?"

"Gosh, I've missed this. I'm so glad you're here, Rave. You're going to love working at Jitters. The owner is a tad bitchy, but you'll get used to her."

I shake my head. "You're a dork. It's crazy amazing that you've got your own shop. Obviously, I'm the first in line to work for you. What else would I use my Communications degree for except baking and pouring coffee? Plus, this town is adorable. I'm happy you convinced me."

"If you wanna sell erotic novels next to my coffee beans and muffins, I won't stop you. Jitters can be yours too."

"Ah, thanks, boss. We'll see what happens. I haven't written anything exciting in a while. You're giving me a new challenge. I'll be too busy mastering the fine art of cupcakes and pastries."

Delilah smacks her lips. "Sounds delicious. I can't wait to be your taste tester." She leans closer and wags her brows. "But If you need inspiration for the dirty stuff, let me know. There was this hot cowboy around a few weeks back. Lawdy, my lady bits were pleased. You can write a whole book on our sexcapades."

I giggle, but envy stings my skin. I've never experienced anything wild like that. Maybe that's why I like to write about it.

Addison shows up with our bubbly. She has shots too. The short tumblers are brimming with some fruity pink concoction they've coined Slippery When Wet. Seems extremely fitting.

I clink glasses with Delilah, making a toast to friendship and a blissful summer.

After downing the sugary liquid, we order another and brainstorm filthy names for menu options at Jitters. My favorites so far are Afternoon Delight, Muff Diver, Doctor Pecker, and Morning Screw. My hostile encounter with the surly anti-gentleman floats away as I get lost in plans for the future.

And just like that, the unfortunate beginning to my evening is forgotten.

THREE

TROUBLES

TREY

IT'S A SLOW MORNING AT the garage, which is typical around here. My schedule is booked with annual tune-ups, new brake pads, and flat tires. These tasks have become second nature, ingrained in my system like breathing. Makes the time fly by fast.

There's nothing better than getting covered in grease and grime, proof of a successful day. Each smudge on my coveralls is a badge of honor. Spending hours doing something I enjoy always feels like a gift, and there isn't much I cherish. Geeking out over foreign parts or finding a more efficient tool are perks I'll never take for granted. Plus, cars make the best companions since they never talk back.

My hands move automatically as I reach for the wrench and tighten a loose bolt. Then I tweak the battery's wire connection and replace the safety caps. Straightening from under the hood, I stretch while taking a deep inhale. The shop smells like rubber and oil, exactly as it should. The air is musty and stale, but to me, it's the sweetest scent.

For some reason, the scent of a certain flower perfume from a particular blonde broad comes to mind.

I shove that thought away with a harsh scrub along my forehead. That chick, Raven, is still screwing with my mind days later. Why do I find it sexy that her name contrasts with those fair features? She's a puzzle I don't have time—or patience—for. At least I haven't seen her since the night at Dagos. Another bristled conversation with her might toss me over the edge of sanity. There's something about her light features mixed with that sass

Fuck, she was hot.

Raven brought out the worst in me, which is really damning evidence of her impact. I'm not a nice person—my attitude is shitty at best—yet she managed to drag me lower. I'm fucking furious that she ran me out of the bar, but I'm more pissed at myself for giving her the power to do it. Sweat dots my brow as the temperature seems to skyrocket. I use my rag to wipe away the heat but my skin keeps burning.

I can't stop obsessing over her vibrant eyes. The color will surely haunt my dreams. If I wasn't such an asshole, I would've let her sit down just to stare at the light blue swirling into dark navy.

Jesus, I sound like a whipped pussy.

I shake off the disturbing feeling and concentrate on the list of jobs parked in the lot. They're my priorities, not some newcomer who will be gone by Sunday.

Jacked Up is my uncle's shop, his pride and joy, and it has become mine too. I've been working here since my arms could reach under the hood. My eyes refocus on the Chevy's engine in front of me, a complex layout most people don't take the time to understand. I've spent years buried in pistons and valves, studying the mechanics that turn individual parts into a collaborative machine. If I make the smallest mistake, the car won't run right. Even the most common problem can cause a fatal accident.

I'm all too aware of the tragic possibilities, and not just because of my occupation.

When my uncle's hand claps my shoulder, I startle more than normal. Getting lost in the past always has that effect on me. I release a rusty breath while freeing myself from the lingering ghosts. My chin lifts in greeting, but I wait for him to break the silence first.

"What's up, kid?"

I'm twenty-three, but Jack still considers me a snot-nose punk. In most ways, he's not far off.

I shrug. "Almost done with the 30,000-mile maintenance for Marla. Then I'm getting started on that 2016 Ford's rotation. After that," I wave toward the lot, "whatever's left."

His forehead wrinkles. "That's all fine, but I mean, what's going on up here?" Jack taps my temple for emphasis.

I jerk back. "The fuck?" We rarely talk feelings. As in never.

"You've been acting strange lately. Could it have anything to do with your Friday night at Dagos?"

Damn small-town gossip.

I lean against the car's bumper and meet his eyes, the same caramel shade as mine. "Since when do you care about the rumor mill?"

"I can't ask about trouble you're causing?"

"Aren't I always?"

Jack's fingers rake through his shaggy hair. "Greyson told me your reaction was extreme to a new girl."

I grunt. "What the hell does he know?"

"Considering he grew up with you, I'd say a lot."

"There were a few chicks I argued with. Not sure which one you're referring to." I'm lying straight through my teeth.

His nostrils flare with a heavy breath. "Think about it, Trey. This time sounded worse than usual. What happened?"

"You assume it's my fault?"

"Isn't it always? You're acting like I haven't spent the last twelve years raising your ass. Tell me about her."

My muscles bunch at the mention of Raven, an instinct I can't control. My uncle laughs.

"Fuck, she already got her claws in you." It's not a question.

I scoff and cross my arms tight over my chest. "Ha, I thought you knew everything? No woman gets under my skin. You trained me well."

"Ah, shit. That makes me feel like the worst role model ever. I should have done better by you, for your parents' sake if nothing else."

I give him a blank stare. This guy is my idol. He's everything I've always wanted to be. Hearing him say this crazy shit makes my head spin.

"Are we really having this conversation right now? What twilight zone did I get dropped into?"

He punches my arm. "Knock it off. I'm serious. You've grown up proud and strong but rude as hell. I didn't think much of it considering all that's happened. You're still young and can get away with it, but eventually that shit gets old."

"Have you looked in a mirror lately, gramps? Where do you think I got my manners from?" Only eleven years separate us, making Jack more of a brother than anything. But I like giving him shit whenever possible, especially when he's blasting me.

"Oh, fuck off. I might be a grumpy bastard, but I'll always offer an available seat to a woman. Hell, I'd give up my own spot in a heartbeat. I'd rather swallow razor blades than watch a lady stand around while I sit. I might have taught you a lot of stupid garbage, but that didn't come from me. What is wrong with you?"

My temper flares and grows with each of his words. "Where is this all coming from? Why are you suddenly shoving advice down my throat?"

"I've always been proud of you, Trey. I hope you know that. Working beside you each day, watching your talent shine, seeing the love for this shop in your eyes . . . that all makes me feel like I did alright. But when I hear two biddies yammering away about you cussing out a girl, just for trying to sit down at the bar?" His bellow vibrates through me when he asks, "How can I be happy about that?"

He's right. I know that like an indisputable fact. But backing down has never been my thing.

"Save the lecture, Jack. I'm not a child you need to scold. The situation was handled, end of story. There's nothing for you to worry about," I growl.

He scratches his scruffy jaw. "Oh, yeah? It'd be nice if I could actually believe that. You've got the entire town buzzing like pissed-off hornets. Why didn't you just give that girl a chair?"

"Because I was in a bad fucking mood and she was the final straw. Am I not allowed to have a peaceful night to myself? I'd already dealt with too much female drama and didn't want to sit around listening to more. She caught me off guard, and that really pissed me off. She was too damn tempting, and I'd had enough. Happy now? Was that enough sharing for you?" I give far too much away, but it's too late for regrets.

I comb through my hair before yanking on the ends. It's not even noon, and this day is already shot to hell. A loud groan rips from my throat as the frustration boils in my gut. A desire to punch the Chevy's grille burns my hand. I'm mad at Jack and Raven and all the damn gossips in town.

Fuck.

"Hey," Jack murmurs while resting a hand on my back. "We're all good, Kid. Calm down, huh?" I shake him off. My eyes meet his, and as I study him, he appears older. Jack's face is creasing with strain as he tries talking sense into me, like he's been doing for more than a decade. He was far too young when he got saddled with sole custody of me. Who wants that type of responsibility at twenty-two? Yet he didn't think twice before signing the papers and taking me in. And how do I repay him? By making his life a struggle.

I really am *an asshole.*

He reaches for me again, and this time, I accept his peace offering. "No use getting all bent outta shape, Trey. We're just having a respectful discussion. I didn't come out here to start a fight. Just try being respectful, especially around newcomers. You never know what they're in town for. Maybe she needs her car fixed. How do you think it'll go over when she sees you behind the counter after what happened at Dagos?" His all-knowing stare bores into me, hammering the point straight home. "But seriously. If the chick is smokin', that's more reason to have her sit by you. I feel like there are pieces missing to this picture."

"I don't sleep with every woman who shows interest, regardless of how appealing she is. Plus, Raven made it clear she wants nothing to do with me. Not that I would have done anything. Can we stop talking about this now?"

When a smirk curls his lips, I realize my mistake. Another frustrated groan escapes me.

"Raven, eh? You know her name? What else aren't you telling me, Trey?"

"Nothing. End of story. I only got her name because Delilah kept repeating it while demanding an apology. If I ever see her again, it will be too soon." The words hold no truth, but Jack doesn't need to know that. I wouldn't mind getting another look at Raven, so long as she keeps her trap shut. "No happily ever after for this guy. I'll be a bachelor all my life, just like you."

Jack sighs, regret clinging to the sound. "You don't know it all, Trey. Think I actually planned to spend my life alone? Nah. I had a girl once, *the one*, but she got away. We were too young, and I treated her badly. When she left for school, I didn't stop her. I was way too stubborn, and my wounded pride wouldn't allow it. She wasn't willing to stay without a promise of more. I didn't give her what she needed."

He rubs at his eyes, looking more weary and worn than I've seen in a long while. The snarky response waiting on the tip of my tongue dies off. Jack has always been a solid pillar for me to lean on. Witnessing this side of him is a shock to my system. I wait silently while he seems to gather his thoughts. His voice is low and almost hoarse when he continues.

"Life happened, and you came to stay with me. Don't think for a minute you held me back from chasing her because I wasn't going anywhere regardless. I planted deeper roots, opened the shop, did my best raising you, but never forgot her. I've done alright, sure. Could I be doing better? Absolutely," he mutters with a sad smile. "Being an ornery old goat ain't all it's cracked up to be. I'm sure you don't care, but that's a life lesson worth listening to."

I let his words sink in, confusion clouding my thoughts. "Why are you telling me this now? Not sure I understand the point."

"Because of your girl. Raven."

My arm slashes through the air. "Oh, hell no. She isn't my anything."

"Uh huh. I said the same thing once. Damn, it really is like looking in the mirror sometimes." Jack squints and tilts his head.

"Knock it off. I'm nothing like you in that respect. I have no interest in finding *the one*," I lace the words out with extra venom, "or believe she even exists. Just no."

"You're such a shit, Trey," he says with a smirk. "Don't end up like me. I'm trying to give you advice."

"And I'm telling you to take a hike."

"Where did I go wrong?"

"I lost track years ago."

He chuckles. "At least you've got a bit of humor left. But seriously—"

"Can we drop this yet?" I interrupt. "If I try to be less of an asshole to women, will you leave me alone?"

"Fine, just stop burning bridges all over town, yeah? It's bad for business. You represent our brand so if nothing else, think of that."

And that's when his spiel sinks in and strikes a chord. I'd never purposefully cause harm to the shop. "Yeah, all right. I'll do better."

"Even when the girls are driving you crazy?" He pushes further.

"I get the message," I snap.

"Good. I'm glad that's settled." He taps the car's frame. "Now, stop slacking off and get back to work."

FOUR

MATCHMAKERS

RAVEN

THE BELL OVER THE DOOR chimes, signaling another customer. The folks of Garden Grove are jonesing to cure coffee cravings, which makes the perfect slogan for Jitters.

I have no complaints about the steady flow of traffic. The consistency keeps my mind occupied so I can avoid thoughts of—

"Oh, my word!" The woman in front of me exclaims. "You're just the prettiest thing! All the bridge club gals have been in a tizzy since you moved in. I had to come meet you for myself." This lady appears to be my grandma's age, but far more fancy. Her bright purple hat and matching jumpsuit says it all.

I smile as my cheeks heat, uncomfortable as others in the store turn to stare at us. "Uhh, thank you. That's very nice of you to say. This is such a wonderful place to live, and I've already met so many wonderful people. Delilah is a lifesaver for letting me work with her."

She grins back and offers her hand. "I'm Marlene, and it's a pleasure to meet you . . ."

"Raven," I finish for her while accepting the proffered greeting. "So, you're here to stay?"

"Yes, ma'am. Not sure D could get rid of me if she tried."

She waves off my pleasantries. "None of that. Call me Marlene. We'll get to know each other well. I'm the town's social butterfly so everyone's business is mine. At least I like to think so," she explains with a wink.

I chuckle softly, her spunky personality lifting my spirits. "Unfortunately, you won't find anything too exciting about me. Just the typical single girl story here."

"There's no man in your life?"

"No, afraid not. But that's alright." I smile while explaining, "I graduated college last month and need to decide where my life is headed. All those boring adult decisions."

Marlene hums. "Back in my day, finding a husband was the greatest priority for a young lady. I know several strapping gentlemen who would love to take you out."

My stomach knots at the idea of being set up on numerous blind dates. I grip the counter and clamp my jaw shut, unsure what to say. The lack of control terrifies me but turning down her friendly offer is almost as scary. Thankfully Delilah swoops in and rescues me.

"Oh, Marlene. Give my girl some space. Raven is far too nice but I'll tell you the truth—she's not interested."

This time, my entire face sets on fire as both women look at me. I cover my bubbling nerves with a laugh and find my backbone. "Delilah's right, blunt as she might be. I'm still settling in and definitely not ready to date yet. I appreciate the offer though."

Marlene pops my confidence when she asks, "Does your refusal have anything to do with Trey Sollens? I heard you two shared words and it wasn't pretty. Hopefully he didn't scare you off men forever."

My eyes squeeze shut at the mention of precisely who I've

been avoiding thinking about. Why did she have to bring him up? I'd been doing so well too. With a sigh, I tell her, "It was just a minor misunderstanding. Nothing to worry about. To be honest, I'd forgotten all about it until now." I internally roll my eyes at the pathetic understatement.

"And you know exactly what you're doing, Marlene," Delilah adds. "Stirring the pot and sniffing around for dirt. It was just the standard snit where Trey is involved. No harm was done so enough gossiping about. Now, what can we get you to drink?"

With that, the subject is dropped and Marlene orders her cappuccino to go. I give her the bright teal cup, thank her again, and promise we'll chat soon. She purses her lips while giving me a final onceover.

"Think about what I said, Raven. Nice guys don't stay unattached for long." Marlene waves before strutting out the door.

"Nice to meet you," I call out to her retreating form.

"Glad that's over," Delilah huffs.

"She's a bit pushy, isn't she?"

"You can say that again. But don't mind her. Marlene's probably the sweetest of the matchmaker bunch."

I lift a questioning brow, and Delilah explains, "They're a group of nosey old ladies. With nothing better to do, they spread rumors between teatime and try to pair up the singletons. Real old school views, like the only goal in life is getting married and having babies. So progressive," she drones.

I laugh at her haughty expression. "Every small town has them, right?"

Delilah spreads her arms out. "Welcome to Garden Grove, where vultures and buzzards are always circling."

"And drinking coffee," I add.

"Ah, yes. We all love the java."

"Does this place ever slow down? I swear it's go, go, go from open to close."

"Isn't it great? Talk about supplying the ultimate demand. Opportunity was practically banging down my door when I moved back from school."

"I'm very impressed. You've built a very booming business. And not everyone could pull it off. I mean, you've created a very comfortable and relaxing environment. All the cozy furniture and chic details make it a home away from home. I love all the different mugs too," I tell her with a grin. "Plus, the place smells divine all the time. If we brought in a bed, I'd sleep here."

She loops her arm around me. "Thanks, Rave. That means a lot. Having you here makes all the difference. Graduating early was fabulous, but leaving you behind was tough. I consider it a blessing in disguise that your mom took off overseas."

My forehead pinches tight. "Ugh, I wouldn't have moved closer to her regardless. You know I can't handle husband number three."

"Right, right. Sorry about bringing her up. But speaking of people we're not talking about . . . I saw your face when Marlene brought up Trey. Is that situation still bothering you?"

I scratch my temple. "It feels more like a loose end, and I'm terrible about letting things go. He got under my skin, and I don't know why. It's not like I want to know more about him or anything." Well, I do but Delilah will take my curiosity as romantic interest.

There's a nagging in my brain that won't shut up. Trey represents an incomplete storyline and I need more information to finish his chapter. I've tried blocking him out, but it's useless. Each time I pour a cup of coffee, I'm reminded of his eyes. Considering I'm working at a café full time, that's a lot of damn reminders.

"Right," Delilah drawls. "The gears are spinning so fast, there's steam coming out of your ears. What's eating you?"

I take a deep breath and decide to just spit it out. "Can I ask you something without getting a pile of grief for it?" She lifts a brow, and I know her answer. It doesn't stop me. "Tell me more about Trey."

Delilah startles from my blurted statement. "I'm sorry. Can you repeat that? It sounded like you want to know more about the guy we were never going to speak of again."

That's a pact we settled on after too many shots at Dagos. Looks like I'm going back on my drunken word. Fancy that.

I roll my eyes. "I know what we said, but it's driving me crazy. He got the final jab and made me feel foolish. I stood there like a moron while he beat me down. I mean, why is he so mean? I can't get past someone being naturally nasty to the bone without reason."

"Didn't we already go over this?"

"Kind of, I guess. But there's gotta be more to Trey than a shitty attitude and man-whore tendencies."

"Are you sure about that?"

"Yes?" My faith in this argument is slipping.

The bell chimes, and our conversation halts as we serve the customers. While I'm filling their order, the need to know flares like a festering wound. Now that I've asked, there's no shying away. Once the couple is out of earshot, I turn back to my friend.

"You've known him forever. He's always been mean?"

"Well, he definitely got worse after his parents and sister died." She sucks in a sharp breath. "Shit, I shouldn't have said that. Not that you wouldn't hear elsewhere soon enough."

"They all passed away?" I whisper.

Delilah nods. "A ways back, over ten years ago in a car accident. It was just a typical day. Trey was playing baseball at the park with some friends. Jack had to deliver the news. It was fucking horrific."

My heart leaps as my own past vibrates through me. Unfortunately, I know the debilitating pain of losing a parent. I understand how fast life can be taken due to someone else's careless mistakes. With a few crushing words, I soften toward him. We're linked through mutual tragedies.

"Sadly ironic, right? I'm sorry, Rave. It's not my story to tell and I shouldn't have said anything. He's still an ass no matter what," she murmurs while rubbing my back.

I lift my gaze to hers. "But he has reason to be."

Delilah's lips twist. "Don't go feeling sorry for him. It won't do any good or earn you any brownie points. That man is sour and surly."

"Maybe he needs a friend. Someone in his corner," I suggest quietly.

"You're so sweet, Rave. He'd eat you alive. Trust me. Even before they died, he was a hellion. What Trey experienced was horrible, but we've all tried reaching him. He doesn't want help or sympathy or anything from anyone. Well, except sex." She holds her hands out defensively when I scowl. "Okay, okay. I've struck a nerve. But please don't give him excuses for being a jerk because of this. We've all let Trey's shit go because of the accident, but it's only enabling him. He's going to spend his life alone, just like his uncle."

"What do you mean? Who's his uncle?"

"Jack Sollens. He owns a garage on the outskirts of town. That's where Trey works. Jacked Up Repairs," Delilah boasts like a commercial. "He's a decent enough guy but a chronic bachelor. I've never seen him on a date but he gets plenty of attention. Jack is super sexy, especially for a man in his thirties. That family has some great genes. He took Trey in after . . . you know. Ugh, you're turning me into a gossip like Marlene." I elbow her, and she yelps. "What? I speak the truth. I'm airing out all their laundry."

I shoot her a wry look. "Oh, give me a break. I didn't have to twist your arm too hard."

"Riiiiggghhhht." She drags the word out. "Pretty sure you were digging for information on Trey not five minutes ago. The Jack stuff was a bonus."

"Because it was bugging me. Now I know. Case closed."

She crosses her arms. "Uh, huh. Easy as that?"

"Yes. I feel better. Next time we have words, I'll be better prepared."

"Oh, you're planning ahead? Don't put yourself in his path on purpose, Rave."

I wave off her concern. "I won't. But Garden Grove is tiny so we're bound to bump into each other. Turns out we have something in common, like kindred spirits."

Delilah groans. "Girl, you're asking for trouble. He doesn't like talking about it at all. Pretty sure the topic is an automatic trigger to a deeper layer of asshole-ness. But I can tell you've already decided. Always trying to be the balm and smooth shit over. Don't say I didn't warn you."

"There's a point to be made, that's all."

"And you're going to tell him how it is?"

"Maybe," I say. "If I see him again."

"You're impossible."

"But you love me."

"That I do. Are we moving on? Can we talk about tonight?"

I squint at her. "What are you scheming?"

"It's Saturday, which means time to go out. Maisey will open tomorrow so I don't have to be here until noon. That means party time!" She claps, bouncing on her toes. "We can head over to Boomers where there's a decent dancefloor. We've gotta shake what our mamas gave us!"

A few customers glance our way at her outburst, but I just laugh. "You're lucky these people love their coffee or they'd run away scared."

"Puh-lease. This town would be lost without me. Not to mention boring," Delilah sing-songs. "Only two more hours before quitting time. Then we'll pre-game at Dagos. Addy is working the early evening shift so she can come out with us too."

"Oooh, good. She's awesome. Maybe we can convince her to

come work here instead of the bar."

"Nah. I've tried. She makes too much money there. I can't afford her ass."

"Tips from drunk guys are a beautiful thing."

"Right? But owning my own business is better. She can deal with those slobbering jerks."

I smile at Delilah and bask in her obvious happiness. My heart soars at witnessing her success surrounding us. It masks the disappointment constantly dragging me down. Then again, I'm only twenty-two; I have plenty of time to figure out my career goals. For now, working at Jitters is enough.

Delilah wags her brows at me. "Oh, by the way. I've got a killer dress for you. It'll be perfect for tonight."

"Should I be worried?"

She winks. "Absolutely."

FIVE

TEMPTATION

TREY

I'VE BEEN AVOIDING DOWNTOWN SINCE my chat with Jack, but there's no real escape. Even though I can't hear them, the gossips are whispering about me. Spreading garbage they don't know shit about. I should be used to it by now, but their pitying stares are like acid in my veins.

Poor, screwed up Trey.

He can't help being an asshole.

He'll get over it eventually.

Fuck that. This is just me, the way I've always been. These people need to get a damn life and stay outta mine. I'd think talking about me all these years would get boring, but there's always something new to blab about. I was damn surprised to discover the insignificant incident with Raven resurrected their interest. Marlene and company must be lacking for better drama to spread.

That fucking new girl is creating chaos, and she's only been around a week. By staying away, I'm letting her win. Garden

Grove is my town, dammit, and I won't be chased away by bullshit rumors. Whatever Jack heard about Raven and me is bogus. If anyone dares to ask, I'll set the record straight.

Being cooped up at my house has left me more agitated, which isn't good for anyone. The urge to hit something twists through me, and I flex my hand. The sting from my busted-up knuckles is evidence that I've already been beating the bag too hard. The extra workouts haven't curbed my frustration in the slightest. If anything, the additional exercise has me keyed up for another release.

Which leads me straight to Dagos. I park my Ford pickup in front of the glowing windows and blow out a breath. A warm breeze whips through the truck's open door, a reminder that summer is in full swing. Even after sunset, the temperature is oppressive and suffocating. My shirt clings to me as I walk in, more than ready for the cool blast of air conditioning.

Agitation curdles in my stomach as a few people watch me enter. I ignore their eyes. I lift my chin at Greyson, the bartender on shift tonight. As I settle on a stool, he ambles over and wipes the countertop in front of me. He gets straight to the point, which I appreciate.

"Hey, Trey. Want the usual?"

"Yeah. A bottle would be great."

He pops the cap and slides the beer over. "You just missed the new girl."

So much for no small talk.

I offer a grunt in response, not wanting to discuss Raven. Greyson keeps blabbing away, unaware of the heat rising up my neck.

"She was dressed to kill. Or fuck. Not sure which. Either way, smokin' hot."

My teeth grind together. "And I care because?"

He shrugs while pouring a draft. "Thought you usually enjoy

the newbies. Anyway, whoever ends up with her tonight is a lucky man."

Not sure why I'm feeding into this but, "Thought you said they already left."

Greyson nods. "Yeah, from here. She's with Delilah and Addison. They stumbled over to Boomers."

Fuck, they're going to dance. Probably looking for some nice guys to buy them drinks and treat them sweet. Raven is sure to get plenty of attention. But who the hell cares?

I scoff. "Good for them." With that, I'm putting an end to the subject.

Yet I can't control the pang of desire rushing through me. What do I want? Fucking Raven would be great, but unlikely. So, then what? I'm not gonna trudge over there and watch her shake ass, no matter how fine it is.

I glance around the room, searching for a distraction. The bar is fairly empty considering it's Saturday night. Some regulars are shooting pool along the far wall. A few more folks are scattered about the space, keeping to themselves.

"Where the hell is everyone?" I ask Greyson when he comes back with another beer.

"Boomers has some swanky cover band playing. Everyone dashed over there by nine o'clock."

"Fucking figures," I mutter.

He leans closer. "What's that?"

"Forget it."

"Suit yourself, Trey. But I won't be offended if you wanna go over there."

"I'll take my chances and stick around, but thanks."

"Or you can follow the masses. Find yourself some company because there isn't any here." And Greyson isn't lying about that.

I peel at the bottle's label while playing the options in my mind. Going home to sulk isn't happening. I refuse to tuck tail and leave so soon. My knee bounces wildly as restless energy swims through me. Another round at the gym might be helpful. I can stay here and silently stew in the misery of my current situation. Otherwise I've gotta suck it up and check out the action at Boomers.

A groan rumbles from my chest as the possibilities ping-pong around. Under normal circumstances, I'd eagerly follow the crowd for a chance to get laid. Running into Raven makes everything more complicated . . . and I hate her for it.

After downing half my beer in one gulp, I'm determined to man the fuck up. She's just a chick, and I've dealt with her type countless times. Raven wants to be the talk around town, another dramatic diva to stir up trouble. She can have the spotlight. I prefer being ignored, sneaking off unaffected with my dignity intact. If I happen to have a hot hookup on my arm, that's even better.

It's been several weeks since I've gotten laid. A large portion of my recent frustration is of the sexual variety. After tonight, that shouldn't be an issue. This will be my reset button.

"Another?" Greyson asks and motions to my bottle.

I shake my head. "Nah, I'm gonna check out the band."

He laughs. "The hell you are."

"If I happen to find some company over there, even better."

"Play on playa. Best of luck."

I knock on the wood ledge. "Don't need it."

Without a backward glance, I'm off the stool and striding outside. I roll the strain from my shoulders as the dense heat envelopes me. Driving would provide momentary relief, but Boomers is only a few blocks away. I jog across the street before hitting the sidewalk, thankful for the lack of traffic. Loud music vibrates off the walls as I near the brick building. If I didn't already know, the noise would be a dead giveaway to the concert inside.

As I push through the double doors, it's like entering a different world. This place typically turns into a dance club on the weekends, but tonight is something else entirely.

What the hell did I get myself into?

On the brightly lit stage, the band belts out a popular country song, and the sound is deafening. Apparently, this show is drawing people in from several towns over. Bodies are packed in the dark room, so many it's impossible to count. Thick smoke and fog coat the air, which makes visibility even harder. I rub the sting from my eyes before pushing toward the bar.

Out of nowhere, a tornado of blonde hair and flailing limbs crashes into me. I reach out to hold her steady as she stumbles again.

"Shit. You okay?" I yell over the racket.

She wobbles in my grip before standing upright and spinning around. Ice floods my veins and everything around us slams to a stop.

Raven.

Fuck. What are the chances?

Pretty damn good considering the size of this town and my shitty luck. Regardless, this seems like a far-fetched stretch. I yank my hands off her smooth skin as if the touch suddenly burns. Another curse flies past my lips as I get a look at her outfit . . . or lack thereof. The sorry excuse for a dress is just a scrap of red material, a bright signal for trouble. My gut clenches as I glare into her glassy eyes.

"You hounding me, Princess?" I growl in her ear.

"Why do you insist on calling me that?" Raven jerks away, only to topple back into me.

"How much have you had to drink?" Not sure why I'm asking—she's obviously had plenty.

Raven holds up her thumb and pointer finger, indicating only a pinch. She squints at me and tilts her head. "Crazy running into you here. This place is packed."

I roll my eyes. "Yeah, real great. Where are your friends?"

"Why do you care?"

"Because you're alone in a massive crowd. Don't know where you're from, but girls around here tend to travel in packs." And for some stupid reason I don't want her wandering into the wrong hands.

Raven jabs my chest several times. "I'm from here now. And you better get used to it."

I grab her wrist and yank her closer. "Didn't you learn not to poke the bear?"

Her unfocused gaze morphs into blue flames, threatening to incinerate me. "Oooh, big scary furball. I've heard all about you. There's nothing to be afraid of."

I'm sure she's heard all sorts of shit, most of it bull. The urge to shake some sense into her rattles through me. Raven needs to stay the hell away from me. Yet I don't let her go.

She peers down at my grip on her arm. I'm about to snarl something nasty about her getting dirty until she swipes along my torn-up knuckles. The tentative touch is an electric surge to my system.

"What happened to your hand?"

"Fighting."

"With who?"

"Myself."

Raven's focus jumps to my face. "You're hurt. Why'd you do that?"

"Better than breaking someone's nose."

She smirks. "I don't believe you'd actually harm anyone."

I bark out a sharp laugh. "Well, you're dead wrong."

"Does attacking others make you feel better, then?"

Red flickers on the edge of my vision. "You shouldn't test me, Princess."

"Why's that?"

"Because I'm not a nice guy. I won't hesitate to wreck you. That's what gets me off."

She squeaks, "On purpose?"

Frustration is coiling tight, strangling any patience I have remaining. "And I won't be there in the morning to put you back together."

"Wait. Are you talking about sex? Or in general? I'm confused."

A rumble rises from me as I snap. Tugging her hips into mine, I let her feel exactly what I'm referring to. Raven gasps and wiggles, which gets me harder. Her luscious tits are pressed tight against me, and the mounds look good enough to eat. I'm tempted to take a bite. Toying with her couldn't hurt, and I could use a little fun.

I lean down to murmur, "All night long, Princess."

She sputters. "Wh-what?"

"Don't look so shocked. You're pitching tents wearing that. Pretty sure we're here looking for the same thing."

Raven looks down before glaring at me. "This is Delilah's dress. Everyone seems to love it."

"Can't imagine why," I scoff. "The dense act doesn't work for you, Princess."

"Ugh, you're a jerk."

When she tries pulling away, I drag her to the nearest corner, cloaking us in darkness. I cage Raven in, effectively pinning her to the wall with my lower half. Her sweet scent seduces me, and I'm getting higher with each inhale. The floral perfume invades my airway, and all I can do is breathe her in. Why must she smell so damn good?

"Do you want me?" I murmur close to her mouth.

"In your dreams," she snips.

I grind into her, pressing my hard against her soft. In this inebriated state, she doesn't hide her reaction. Raven's head rolls back as she bites her lip. I'm toying with her, hoping to provide a sliver of the torture she's giving me. When her fingers dig into my biceps and tug, I know she's feeling it. That's my cue to back off. I might be an ass, but there's a limit, even for me. I'd never take advantage of an intoxicated woman. Screwing with her mind is enough for now.

"That's what I thought, Princess," I taunt.

Raven immediately snaps out of the lustful haze. "Asshole."

"That can be arranged."

She sucks in sharply and her eyes widen. Her shock is amusing so I take it one step further. "I'd never deny some backdoor action."

Raven's jaw practically hits the floor. "You're something else, Trey."

"And you love it. Otherwise you'd be trying to get away."

She seems to take stock of our situation, but still doesn't move. "I've been drinking and can't control myself."

"Oh, yeah? So, this is typical for you?"

"You're twisting my words!" Raven spits. She pushes against my chest, and I back off slightly, giving her some space. "I'm done with this conversation."

A flash of disappointment strikes me, which means it's definitely time to go. I separate from Raven completely and rub at the tension building in my nape. I clear my throat, confused by the tightness gathering there. "Do you need—"

From out of nowhere, Delilah screeches, "Cheese on a cracker! What the hell is happening here?"

My attention shoots toward the sudden interruption. I cringe and cover my ears; her pitch is high enough to leave dogs whimpering. "Jesus, D. What the fuck is with the hollering?"

"Oh, no. Nope. Don't you start with me, Trey." Delilah's sights land on Raven. "And you! What the hell? I thought you were just going to the bathroom."

"Uh, well . . ." Raven stutters.

Delilah doesn't wait before coming at me again. "This place is packed with available pussy, Trey! You can have any girl in this damn bar, but not her. Didn't I already tell you that?" She wags a sloppy finger in my face.

I tuck my chin and take a deep breath, allowing the irritation to wane slightly. When I raise my eyes again, she's shooting daggers at me.

"I wasn't gonna do anything. Just messing around."

Delilah scoffs. "That's all it ever is with you, right? Well, go screw around with someone else."

"Hello? I'm still standing here." Raven announces.

I ignore her and address D. "You got this?"

"Yes, I have *her*. She's not a thing, Trey."

I'm well aware, fuck you very much.

Instead I say, "Whatever. Good luck with all *that*."

Raven huffs while Delilah snips, "Gee, thanks. Have fun with your next victim."

"Gladly." I offer a middle-finger salute.

What a waste of time. But the night is still young. I stride away wearing a smirk.

Time to get laid.

SIX

REGRETS

RAVEN

AS I CRACK MY LIDS open, the morning light stings my dry eyes.

"Ohhhh," I whine pitifully while clutching my pounding head. "Why did I drink so much?"

Delilah moans from the other room, echoing my pain. "You're not the only one. Pretty sure my skull is splitting open," she croaks through the thin wall.

"Big mistake, D. We're not in college anymore." The words scratch from my parched throat. "Need water."

She staggers into my room clutching two bottles and flops onto the bed next to me. She hands me one, and I greedily guzzle the cool liquid. I sigh at the sweet relief.

"Better?" Delilah asks after chugging her own.

"Much."

"Just wait until we're thirty. That's when I hear the real hangovers start."

"I doubt we'll still be slamming shots on Saturday night at that point."

She scoffs. "Speak for yourself. I'm never growing up."

"You're the most responsible twenty-two-year-old I know. Well, most days." I laugh and immediately wince. "Ah, that hurts."

Delilah pats my cheek. "You're so sweet. I appreciate the rave review. But let's talk about you putting me to shame last night. It's probably for the best I stopped trying to keep up. Who knows how we would've gotten home if that was the case."

Blurry memories from the bar flicker through my sluggish brain. I squint against the harsh glare bouncing around the room while recalling most of the evening. There are some definite gaps, though. Especially after midnight.

"I don't even remember getting back," I complain. Unease tightens my chest and a heavy dose of guilt filters in. I shouldn't be so careless, even with Delilah watching out for me. At least there was no threat of being picked up by a stranger. Living off Main Street conveniently places everything within walking—or stumbling—distance. But wait. "Did Trey—"

"Drive us home? Yes."

"Oh, God. Did I almost—"

"Throw up in his truck? Yup," she says.

I scowl at her. "Stop cutting me off. Why would he do that?"

Delilah chuckles. "Didn't give him a choice. After feeling you up, he owed us. There was no way either of us were walking even a few blocks. He was definitely regretting it when you nearly puked all over his floorboards. I've seen that guy ten shades of pissed off, but you about shoved him over the edge."

"Super. I'm never going to live this down."

"Probably not."

"Thanks, biatch. Everyone will catch wind of this by tomorrow. I'll never be offered a ride home from anyone again."

"Trey won't say anything. Your secret is safe. Unless you piss *me* off. Then it's totally going viral," she jests.

"Don't forget about all the photographic evidence I have saved of your drunken nights."

"Raven! You wouldn't," Delilah gasps. "I thought you deleted those?"

I wiggle my eyebrows. "I need a way to keep you honest. So, keep filling in the plot holes and I'll let it slide."

"There isn't much to it. I strolled over and told him it was time to go."

"Just like that?"

"Of course not. Trey put up a fuss, but one look at us and he could tell I meant business."

"What? Were we really that bad?"

She bats the air. "Nah. We were fine. Well, at least still standing. I made it seem far worse. Everyone has their soft spots. Even Trey." She rolls her eyes. "Just like Addy said, I guess. Turns out girls walking home alone doesn't sit well with him."

"That seems odd. Not sure why he'd care about that."

"Right? Not like he's ever stepped up before. Not that I've ever asked. But this is Trey we're talking about. He doesn't do anything unless there's something in it for him."

"So, what was the trade-off? Do I owe you a large sum for cab fare?"

"No, silly. You promised to sleep with him."

"What?" I shriek before immediately flinching. "Ouch, that was loud."

Delilah starts cackling and points at me. "That expression is priceless. Oh, wow. And seriously, Rave? You honestly believe I'd let you trade sexual favors for a measly ride?"

I shove her and get a slice of satisfaction when she almost topples out of bed. "Hey! No need for roughhousing. We're in a delicate state, and I'm just fucking with you. Let's take it down a notch or twenty."

"That wasn't very nice, D. I feel shitty enough as it is."

"Aw, I'm sorry. But not really. You totally deserve it for nearly giving me a panic attack. If you'd barfed, guess who would've cleaned it up? Definitely not Trey." She shudders and sticks out her tongue. "You know I hate anything to do with vomit."

I cover my burning face. "Why don't I remember any of this?"

"Maybe because you drank away the sexual frustration with a bottle of booze? Once Trey scampered off, you decided more drinks were needed. *A lot* more. And who was I to say no?"

"Such a good pal," I mutter. "Effing Trey."

"You didn't seem too unhappy with him. Probably would have been screaming his name all night if I didn't step in."

I grumble, "Yeah, right. I wouldn't have done anything."

She turns to face me. "Rave. You were practically climbing him like a tree. Or maybe a pole would be a more appropriate example in this case."

I toss a pillow at her before we crack up. "Why didn't we call an Uber?" Delilah gives me a blank stare. "What?"

"Oh, my sweet friend. Where do you think we are? Those apps are useless in Garden Grove. You walk or find a ride. Hence me hailing Trey. He was plenty pissed. You should have seen his face when we wobbled over. Too bad you can't remember the steam coming outta his ears. We totally cock-blocked him. It was hilarious."

My stomach squeezes tight. "Shit, that's bad. I'm really embarrassed."

Delilah rolls her light eyes. "Why? He's the one who should be ashamed. The girl he was chatting up was gross. We did him a favor."

"If Trey didn't already hate me, he officially does now."

"You say that like it's a bad thing. Who cares?"

"I do!" The words are a wail. "I hate it when people are mad at me. Even if they're the enemy."

"Meh, you'll learn to live with it." She snuggles deeper into the pillow.

I shake my head. "I shouldn't have gotten so wasted."

Delilah waves me off. "Oh, stop. Most people were far worse off, trust me. Something about a live band brings out the wild and crazy side. It's alright to indulge every now and then. You just graduated from college, for crying out loud. That's the best reason to let loose, and you've definitely earned it. Don't beat yourself up, Rave. We're respectable ninety-five percent of the time," she snickers. "But yeah, you were acting like a woman on a mission to forget."

"I blame Trey."

She whoops. "See! Now you're getting it. He's the perfect scapegoat for bad decisions."

I sit up slowly and grip my temples. My mind spins while trying to fill in the cracks. There was music and dancing and cocktails and . . . *shit*.

Trey. So. Much. Trey.

The first time we met, he'd been sitting down so I missed how tall he was. Last night, he towered over me with his solid muscles and hard . . . *everything*. A shiver ripples through me as I recall his steel bulge grinding into me. My thighs squirm, and the temperature suddenly spikes as a flush blankets me. I peek over at Delilah, but she's messing with her phone, clueless to my internal struggle against the lust pooling in my belly.

I release a long breath. *Damn.* If she hadn't interrupted, what might have happened? That's a bumpy road to wander, not to mention useless. I tuck my chin and pinch my lids shut. I should have felt intimidated or weak by Trey looming in front of me. All I felt was protected and safe. I wouldn't have given in, though. He's too crass and cold, exactly the opposite of my typical taste. Trey is not the type of guy to get romantically involved with. I huff and smack a palm to my forehead.

There's nothing romantic about him.

He was blunt and honest about that, clearly explaining he'd

wreck me. My heart races as I consider what that involves. But, no. I'm not going there with him—*ever*. Maybe we'll learn to tolerate each other or, by nothing short of a miracle, become friends.

I want to talk to him, have an actual conversation. If given a chance, I could share my story with him. Let him know I understand gut-wrenching loss. Just the notion sounds like a bad plan but the seed was planted when Delilah told me about his family. Putting myself in Trey's direct line of fire is most likely the stupidest idea ever, but my heart tends to lead the way. Even though Trey has been nothing but rude and callous, there's something deeper speaking to me. Perhaps it's his sad coffee eyes or the heavy armor he's dragging around.

Did everyone really turn their backs on him? Letting him wallow and suffer alone? If that's the case, it's no wonder Trey is closed off.

No matter what Delilah says, I find it hard to believe he's happy being the town asshole. I don't know Trey's history other than the secondhand version my friend blurted out. There has to be misery mixed with the madness, right?

I want to offer him . . . what exactly? A helping hand? Maybe a shoulder to lean on? A peek at my emotional scars? I scrub down my face while imaging his reaction. Pretty positive Trey could care less about anything I have to share.

But why did he drive us back? He didn't have to do that. Dammit, I wish those moments weren't trapped in a fog. I'm driving myself crazy with these dead-end thoughts.

A loud snap in front of my face jolts me from the Trey-daze. I shake my head and look over at Delilah. "Why'd you do that?"

She giggles. "Are you gonna survive?"

"Huh?"

"You've been caught in a serious stupor, gazing out the window like the glass has all the answers. What's the deal?"

"Oh," I mumble with a gentle toss of my hair. "I was lost in thought."

"About?"

"Last night. Being dumb."

Delilah rolls her hand in a circle, silently asking for more. I just shrug and she huffs.

"Well, that's cryptic. Better not be about you dry-humping with Trey. Lucky for you, I need some strong coffee before diving into this dilemma. So, for now, you're off the hook."

I ignore her assumption. "*Yes*. Caffeine is needed to restore normal functioning." Hopefully a few cups of java will clear my mind so I can stop obsessing about what could happen.

"How great is it that we live right above the best cafe around?"

A chuckle bursts free from my tight lungs. "It's also very convenient for rolling out of bed and heading straight to work."

"Exactly! This building is my one-stop-shop. Another perk of growing up here. I got dibs when the place went up for rent." She fist pumps. "Boom. Done."

"And it has extra room for your college bestie." I wink at her.

"That's the best bonus yet."

"Aww.," I coo with a pat to her back. "Let's finish this love fest downstairs."

Delilah claps happily. "And then I'm introducing you to the Greasy Spoon. Best hangover cure known to mankind."

"Hence the name?"

"They know who to target. The breakfast specials are the greatest deal too. You'll be addicted in no time."

"I'll need the strength for working in the kitchen tonight. I found a new chocolate-peanut butter frosting recipe to try."

"Freaking yum," she says. "You know that's my kryptonite. The Spoon is about to have some serious competition. Your master baking will turn Jitters into the place everyone stops for their morning fix, whether it be coffee or tasty treats."

I smile easily, my spirits lifting along with my lips. "We make a great team, D. And the adventure is only beginning."

SEVEN

TRAITOR

TREY

I FINISH LOADING THE COUPE onto the flatbed before securing the tow cable. I make quick work of cranking the ratchets until all the chains are tight. After inspecting the binds a final time, I hop down onto the gravel roadside. The car's owner has been waiting patiently and smiles once I'm in front of her.

"You work fast. I like that," she rasps while shielding her eyes from the glaring sun. "Didn't catch your name yet, handsome."

"Trey," I tell her and point to the tag on my shirt. "And you are?"

"Olive."

"Nice to meet you."

She smiles. "Likewise. Are we all set here?"

I nod and lean against the trailer's bumper. "Yup. The garage is about twenty minutes from here. Do you need a lift? I'm assuming you're not from around here," I say while studying her closer. "If you were, I'd know."

"Yeah, I live an unfortunate distance away. Especially in this type of situation. I called a friend, but she's an hour away." Olive bites her lip and plays with the plunging neckline of her shirt. "Looks like I've got some time to kill."

Regardless of having been stranded in the blistering heat, this woman is smoking hot. Damn sure she knows it too. Without being completely obvious, my gaze roams her ample curves and sexy assets. Her tiny shorts show off plenty of leg, including a hint of ass. She doesn't mind my appraisal in the slightest. Instead she bends closer, putting her cleavage in my direct line of sight. This time, I'm not shy about checking out her generous rack.

I scratch along my scruffy jaw. "Is that so? Well, I can give you ride."

She hums. "That sounds . . . promising." Her breathy voice is dripping with filthy suggestions. My stomach tightens as I continue gawking at the endless expanse of exposed skin. Seems luck is finally on my side.

"Damn, babe. I'm supposed to be professional, but you're not making it easy."

Her laugh is all tease. "You don't need to play nice for me. I'm looking for some fun. Or maybe trouble." She steps into me and peers up through lowered lashes. "How about both?"

I clear my throat and focus on Olive's flawless features. She's beautiful and willing. I'm horny and long overdue. But this chick's hair isn't blonde and her eyes aren't blue.

What the fuck?

No way.

My teeth grind as I shove the stupidity away. That Raven nonsense has no place here . . . or anywhere.

I smirk at Olive to mask the bullshit clouding my judgement. "Where to?"

Her expression turns predatory as she moves against me. "Your truck cab looks spacious. Maybe we take a tiny detour on the way to your garage. What do you say?" she whispers in my ear.

How can I say no to a proposition like that? Simple—I don't.

My fingers dig into her narrow hips and squeeze. "Best plan I've heard in a long time." Yet my heart is calling me a liar. I ignore my pounding chest and lead Olive to the passenger door. After getting her settled, I take my time rounding the hood. A few moments alone will put a lid on the chaos swirling inside me. Once I'm behind the wheel, the clarity isn't much better. When the diesel engine roars to life, the rumbling pipes jolt me out of the fog.

The summer heat is screwing with me.

I crank the air conditioning and wink at Olive, who's practically foaming at the mouth. Damn, that's a sight for sore eyes . . . and other neglected areas. But my typical enthusiasm for getting laid is still lacking.

Luckily there's a bit of a drive before reaching any suitable destination. I'll get my shit sorted by the time we get there, wherever that is. My distracted mind flickers through spots we can stop as the tires roll along the empty highway. A section of abandoned warehouses isn't far from the shop and the threat of getting caught there would be minimal. That'd work out all right.

The silence stretches between us a bit longer before Olive breaks it. "So, Trey," she purrs. "Tell me about yourself. What keeps you busy, other than saving deserted women?"

I smirk at her comment. "I definitely enjoy passing the time with beautiful company. Other than that, I run the garage with my uncle. Living the dream."

She leans against the center console and strokes my bicep. "All that manual labor is doing your body good. I can't wait to see what these clothes are hiding."

Her overtness would usually be welcome but in this moment, I'm forcing myself not to recoil. I recall the ballsy bimbo at Dagos a few weeks back and compare that exchange to now. There aren't many connections to make, but I'm finding my reactions similar.

But why? What the hell is wrong with me?

Olive is extremely attractive and definitely my type, yet I'm struggling to get on board. I refuse to give voice to the reason practically blaring inside my head.

This has nothing to do with Raven. No fucking way she's ruining sex for me.

A dry chuckle escapes me. "You'll find out what I'm packing real soon. We'll be at the lot in a couple minutes."

"Why wait? Nothing wrong with getting a head start," Olive suggests. I'm unsure of her meaning until fingers begin walking up my thigh. I jerk slightly, and she snickers. "Easy, tiger. Just a little tease to get us going."

I press back against the seat and adjust my position, but there isn't far to go while driving. With a slow exhale, I defy the resistance hammering into my skull.

"Damn, babe. Diving right in. I like your style." My voice is a rough scrape, which Olive mistakes for arousal.

"Of course you do. Men love a woman taking charge. Just relax and let me play."

I almost choke when she cups me. The truck swerves, but I correct the steering immediately. *"Shit,"* I spit. "Gonna cause an accident."

She laughs, like my discomfort is humorous. There's nothing funny about this shit. Number one reason—I'm not hard. At. All. I repeat—what the fuck?

I'm not the type to panic, but alarm is clogging my windpipe. Good Lord, why is this happening?

When Olive realizes my problem, a pout forms on her lips. "What's wrong? You don't like this?" She continues fondling, giving a lap massage any guy would kill for, but there's no response down there. I glare down at my traitorous dick because this is straight up offensive. Not just to me, but also this gorgeous chick rubbing my junk. She edges closer and whispers, "Maybe my mouth will have better luck."

I almost shudder, and not in a good way. *Fuck*. By this point, there's no arousal pumping through me—period. Even my mind has ditched this idea. Fierce agitation fills me and there's nothing Olive can do to turn my mood around.

Stilling her movements, I grumble, "It isn't you, babe. Trust me, you're doing everything right. I'm focusing on keeping you safe and not getting into a wreck. I'd hate to see a scratch on this beautiful face," I tell her with a quick graze to her cheek. I'm laying it on thick, but damn, this shit is embarrassing.

"Isn't that sweet?" Olive hums and shifts to her side of the cab. "Thanks for worrying about me. I can be patient."

"That's me," I cough to cover my disbelieving grunt. "A real gentleman." I roll my eyes at the window.

How the hell do I get out of this mess?

With my dick on sabbatical, sex isn't happening. I'll get Olive off and be done with this disaster. Later, I'll take out my epic failure on the punching bag.

My cell rings from its spot on the dash, and Jack's name flashes on the screen. A sliver of relief filters in at his welcome interruption.

I grab the phone. "What's up?"

Olive looks at me quizzically. I mouth *my uncle,* and she nods.

"Where the hell are you? It's going on two hours," he gripes.

I glance at the clock. "Fuck, sorry. The car was thirty minutes out, and it took a bit to hook up. We're on the way."

"We?" Jack questions.

"I've got the owner with me. Her ride is meeting us at the garage."

"Ah, all right. I need you to hustle up. We've got three walk-ins waiting, and Shane has to leave by four."

"Got it. Should be there in ten."

"All right, step on it," he says before hanging up.

I toss my phone away and flick my gaze at Olive. "Change of plans, babe. The shop is packed, and I've got work to do. We've gotta head straight there. Raincheck?"

She pouts and mumbles, "That sucks. I was looking forward to seeing you naked. But I understand. We can definitely meet up next time I'm in town."

"Can't wait. You've made this quite an interesting afternoon," I tell her honestly. I've learned a few things about myself that need to be expelled, and damn quick.

Silence surrounds us until we arrive at Jacked Up. I pull the tow into the rear lot since the front is full. A punch of guilt hits me for leaving them in a lurch. Guess it's a good thing my dick wasn't cooperating.

"Wow," Olive breathes. "Your uncle wasn't lying. This place is a zoo."

"No kidding. I haven't seen it this slammed for months. Must be a busy shopping weekend."

She nods. "That's why I'm here. A few of the boutiques have clearance sales for the summer season."

"That explains it." I sigh. "Well, I'll get your vehicle unloaded and into the garage so we can figure out the issue. Hopefully nothing too serious. Once we find the cause, someone will let you know before starting repairs."

"Sounds fair. I'll be busy in town so no rush. My friend can haul me around until you're done. Shouldn't take more than a day, right?"

I peer back at her Toyota. We should have any part required on hand. "More than likely. I'm guessing it's real simple, like worn out plugs. Your car isn't old enough to have serious engine failure."

"Great!" Olive reaches for the door.

"If you go in the lobby, someone will get you the paperwork. Then you're free to go until we call."

She looks back, her eyes sparkling in the sunlight. "It was a pleasure meeting you, Trey. I hope next time will be even better."

"Looking forward to it." But that's a lie. I'll never see this woman again. I offer a short wave and she strolls away.

I jump out of the truck and head toward Jack, who's waiting by the first stall.

"I can see what held you up," he chuckles and gestures to the entrance Olive passed through.

Shrugging off the earlier irritation, I meet his stare. "Sorry for the delay. Nothing happened with her though."

Jack tilts his head and quirks a brow. "Good. It'd be bad for business if you left her in a snit."

"Yeah, yeah. I've heard it before."

He knocks on my temple. "And I'll keep telling ya until it sticks." Jack points to a blue sedan. "Get to work on that Focus. The valves are shot. Might wanna check the oil pump too. She'll be in tonight for pick up." I'm already walking before he's done so any underlying meaning escapes me.

"Got it," I call over my shoulder. My shoes pound over the concrete as I jog toward the Focus. Hopefully this won't take long so I can knock out another job before Shane leaves.

When I wrench open the door, a familiar floral scent accosts me. Raven strikes again. I glare at the clear sky, wondering what I've done to deserve this torture. I laugh at my own stupidity because that list is endless. But still. This is straight up cruel.

I settle behind the wheel while attempting not to inhale. I give up after a few moments and take a deep breath. The fight within me melts away as I drink her in.

Dammit, she smells so fucking good.

My palm slams on the center console as I curse the wicked witch for casting spell on me. But I won't let her defeat me. She might have won this round, but the war is mine.

Game on, Raven.

EIGHT

FAULT

TREY

I HEAR RAVEN BEFORE I see her, a sacrificial lamb willingly wandering into the lion's den. She taps the service bell on the lobby counter. I ignore it. We're doing this my way, which means she comes to me. I bask in the comfort from my surroundings before shit hits the fan. Oil and grease permeate the air as I roll from underneath her car. The main repairs were done hours ago but after everyone left, I checked the brake lines. Gave me something to do while waiting.

"Hello?" Raven calls from the doorway.

She can't see me so I let her wait a bit longer. I spend a few extra moments wiping my hands before pushing the creeper away.

"Jack? Is that you?"

I step around the car, coming into view. "Sorry to disappoint, Princess. You get to deal with me." The hitch in her breath makes my dick twitch and aggravation plows into me. My body's reaction is stupid strong to this chick. She makes a tiny noise and I get semi-hard, go fucking figure. No time for that now.

Raven attempts a smile, but it's forced. She steps into the garage, unaware of the danger waiting for her. "Hey, Trey. I'm glad to see you. Last weekend was, um," she stutters while her gaze bounces around the space. "That wasn't my finest moment. Delilah filled me in on the missing pieces and seems like I owe you, well, uh . . ."

"Spit it out," I growl. "Already been waiting long enough for you."

Her blue eyes snap to mine. "Ugh, stop rushing me. You're making me nervous."

I almost laugh at her flared nostrils and flushed cheeks. Glad I'm not the only one affected. "Oh, yeah? What am I doing that bothers you?"

"You're so intimidating. You know it too, which makes it worse. But you still don't scare me. More like, fascinate," she says with a tilt of her chin.

"That makes me sound like a fucking freak on display," I grit.

She combs her fingers through that long blonde hair. "You're twisting my words, dammit."

My patience fades to nonexistent. "Get to the point."

"Thank you, all right? I appreciate you driving us home. D said she interrupted you, and someone . . ." Her voice trails off.

Raven reminds me of the reason for all my recent frustration. I prowl forward, getting into her space. "And what? You're gonna make up for it?" I expect her to shy away, but she stands her ground. "Because that doesn't sound so bad, Princess. You've cockblocked, turned my dick against me, and flipped my life upside down in a few short weeks."

She squints. "Huh? All I'm offering is an apology and my thanks. What happens with your body isn't my fault."

A storm brews in my gut, spinning faster as I stalk closer. When I press against her, Raven bumps into the car and gasps. I have her pinned, and this position gives me all the power.

"Admit it," I whisper against her jaw.

"Wh-what?"

"You want my filthy hands all over you."

She blinks rapidly and appears to recover from the shock of my proximity. "No. That's not why I came."

"Yeah, well, I was gonna stay the hell away from you. Plans change. My dick wants to fuck you. Maybe if I give in, you'll finally get out of here." I tap my temple. "I want you outta my head."

Raven struggles against me, but doesn't get far. "I never asked to be there. That's crazy. I'll take my car and go."

"That's not much of a cure, Princess. I'll probably see you tomorrow, and the cycle will start again."

"What do you expect me to do?"

"Are you listening? Thought I was being clear. This has nothing to do with emotions."

"I'm not sleeping with you."

"Oh, really? Because it's obvious you want me. It's clear in the way your thighs tremble when I'm close," I mutter while stroking up her leg. "Or the rapid rise of your chest," I blow out across her tits. "Can't forget the blush covering your sweet cheeks," I say with a gentle touch to her silky skin. "Even without all those not so subtle cues, your eyes are the window to your hungry soul. You're starving for me, Princess."

Raven's lids are hooded, hiding her glazed sapphires. "This is a wicked game you're playing, Trey. I want no part of it." Her husky voice gives her away.

"No? Are you sure? Think about it," I taunt. She shakes her head and remains silent. She bites her plump lip, and fierce desire slams into me. She makes me hard with a simple move. "Delilah isn't here to save you, Princess. Who's gonna rescue you this time?"

She releases a long exhale. "I can take care of myself."

Raven is strong, that's for sure. Too bad I have to break her.

"I'll make you feel so good, baby. Fighting is useless." I grind into her, and she moans softly. "See? You're pent up too. We can help each other."

"And what happens tomorrow?"

I shrug. "You'll be outta my system. We move on. Problem solved."

Why is that so hard to understand?

"I don't like the sound of that."

"What do you suggest?"

"How about a truce? We can be friends."

Is she serious? One glimpse at her hopeful face gives me the answer. My lust cools as doubt threads through me. Maybe I'm taking this too far. For a moment, I consider accepting her offer, and a foreign feeling settles in my chest. Is that compassion?

Shit, I can't think straight. She's destroying my sanity.

"Are you all right?" She asks it softly. "You're looking a bit green."

Makes sense since my stomach is churning. I cover the discomfort with a smirk. "Sweet of you to care. Wanna be my naughty nurse?"

Raven laughs. "Wow, good one. Not gonna happen, buddy. You see my desire? Well, I notice you, the *real* you hidden beneath all the crap. I'd like to know him. Maybe we'd actually get along."

This conversation is going nowhere fast.

"You're fucking stubborn." I rub my forehead. Her denial has frustration bubbling back to the surface.

"Because I won't have sex with you?"

"Along with everything else." Wow. We're bickering, and my lust is dissolving with each pass. It pisses me off.

"Such as?" she asks with a lifted brow.

I grunt with exasperation. "Since you've been around, I can't get a moment's peace. Not to mention my dick has been aching for weeks."

"Because of me?"

"Don't get a big head, Princess." No way I'm admitting the truth to her. For the first time, I'm drawn to a woman for more than her body. It terrifies me. I've got to shake her loose before it gets worse. "My cock just happens to show a particular interest in you. Once we fuck, this stupid infatuation will be gone."

She rolls her eyes. "How romantic."

"Romance has nothing to do with it."

"You think I'm falling for this shit? Trey, no. Absolutely not." She slices a hand across her throat. "I wanna go home and pretend this never happened. I don't wanna fight with you."

I make a sound of disbelief. "Really? Fooled me. Seems that's what you're always setting out to do. Everywhere I turn, there you are. I can't escape."

"That's what happens in a small town. Especially one the size of Garden Grove."

"You an expert after living here all of five minutes?"

"Stop being an ass. I haven't done anything to you."

The dam breaks, and I snarl. "You're ruining my simple life."

"Oh? Because it was so great before?" Raven's mouth slams shut like she spilled a secret. "I shouldn't have said that," she mumbles.

"Why not? Everyone around town knows I'm a worthless manwhore. Pretty sure you found out the night we met. Not like I hide it."

"That's not what I meant."

"Enlighten me." I can only imagine what stories she's heard. This should be entertaining.

Raven glances away before swallowing hard. "I know about your family."

Any control I felt vanishes instantly as lightning crashes in my chest. I set out to destroy her, but with one statement, she decimates me.

"What'd you say?" I hiss through clenched teeth, menace dripping from my tone.

"Your parents and sister. I heard about the accident," she chokes out.

The coldest bucket of water pours over my head, washing away all traces of desire. She made a big mistake bringing them up. My wrath forms like a hurricane, and she's the target.

My expression hardens while an inferno builds inside. "Poor me, right? Save your pity, Princess. And don't bring up shit you weren't here for."

Her lashes flutter and she gulps again. "I understand how it is. Maybe I can—"

My palm slams against the car window, inches from her head. Raven flinches, but recovers quickly. "You don't know shit. My life is none of your business. Got it?"

"O-okay, I get it. But I wanna tell you something."

"Hell no," I boom. "You've said plenty."

"Just fucking listen to me, all right? Dammit!"

I push away from her, needing the distance to clear my head. But I keep her trapped with my gaze. "Can't help running that smart mouth, huh? Am I the only one lucky enough to receive this treatment?"

Her features flash with hurt. I keep pushing forward. "I don't care about whatever you wanna say. Keep that precious advice to yourself."

Raven is getting too close, digging into the hidden crevices I prefer to forget.

"You're not the only one who knows loss, Trey. Trust me, I'm the last one to offer suggestions or pity. I'd love to be supportive, if you're ever interested." Her eyes are shining with care, her forehead creasing with concern, but I call bullshit.

"I haven't—"

"Not interested," I sneer. My hand slices the air. "Save your white picket fence bullshit, Princess. I don't need others to be happy. I've survived this long fine enough."

"I don't believe you."

"Makes no difference to me," I grunt.

"Don't you get lonely? Everyone needs someone."

"Not me. I lost my someones, and they're irreplaceable. Other than Jack, people are just placeholders, temporary and ever changing."

Raven tucks her chin and slowly blows out a breath. "That's really sad, Trey."

"And that's your opinion."

"I hope you'll change your mind."

My shields slam down as I turn to stone. "You're far too smart to be acting this stupid. Just leave it be. I'll never wanna talk about this."

She doesn't let my attitude dissuade her. Raven is determined to squeeze answers out of me. "Call me names all you want. I'm not going anywhere, remember? I'll be popping up all over town, never giving you a moment's peace."

"You're fucking relentless." Exhaustion sinks in and my bones feel heavy. "We done here? I'll drive your car out and have Jack send you a bill."

"Why do you hate me?" She blinks rapidly.

"You represent everything I despise," I tell her honestly.

"Such as?"

"Always with the questions." I rub my neck, the muscles strained. "For starters? Happiness. Commitment. Belonging. Forever. The list goes on just like your inconvenient presence."

"Yet you wanna sleep with me."

My head tips side to side. "I'm horny, and you're hot. Even with those lips flapping nonstop you're a decent catch. I'd love to get into your pants, all night long, without stopping to rest. Bet I could teach you a thing or two, Princess." Raven's jaw drops so I keep goading her. "Like the sound of that? I'd have you moaning in no time."

A blush stains her cheeks. "You have quite the imagination."

"You'll be asking for it eventually. I'll be waiting with a smug smile."

"Don't flatter yourself."

"This is all for your benefit, baby. I don't need to toot my own horn."

Her golden locks shine in the fluorescent light as she leans back. "I feel like we're on a Tilt-A-Whirl."

"You and me both."

She turns me on only to switch me off, and my body aches from the conflicting extremes.

"Who's responsible for that?" I ask.

Raven sputters, "Me? Don't try making me the bad guy."

I wave her off. "Trust me, Princess. We both know who's the villain in this story. Not sure why you're sticking around when the ending is clear."

"Yet you're still talking to me."

"Already made it obvious what I want," I tell her with a grin. How else am I going to escape this hold she's got on me?

"Am I missing something? How do you flip so fast? You were pissed a few minutes ago. Now you're hitting on me again?" Her question is absurd, like this entire debate.

I offer a humorless chuckle. "That's cute. I was barely bothered. You'll have to try harder to ruffle my feathers." Which is a lie. I'm spreading them like wildfire today. This chick rattles my cage harder than anyone, but I'll take that to the grave. I'll never show weakness again.

The air pulses with electricity as I wait for Raven to do . . . something. She just watches me, and it's making my skin crawl. I'm exposed yet fully clothed, and it fucking blows. I clear my throat. "On that note, it's time for you to go."

Raven nods but still doesn't speak. There's so much left unsaid. It's okay. I prefer it that way. She shouldn't be seeking out my secrets, and I need to derail her. Raven needs to understand I don't share personal shit, especially about my family. It's part of what gives me a bad reputation—I never spoke up when people started spreading shit.

I head for her car, and the silence stretches between us. The need to know what she's thinking keeps poking at me, but I ignore it. Pretty positive it wouldn't do much good finding out. Convincing Raven to sleep with me is what matters most. That's the only cure for this crazy illness invading my body. Fucking her will return everything to normal. Otherwise, I'll continue being screwed in an entirely different way.

Raven calls to my retreating form. "I can tell you're hurt. My offer to be friends stands. If you're ever interested." She doesn't see when the hint of a smile hits my lips. I catch myself in the next moment and mask it with shallow arrogance.

"Save the platonic spiel. But when you're ready for real fun, I'll be waiting."

NINE

CRUSH

RAVEN

FROM THE SOUND OF THINGS, or lack thereof, Jitters is finally winding down for the night. Only occasional murmurs reach me in the kitchen as I toss ingredients into the processor. My stainless-steel oasis is a welcome change of pace after a day spent in the hustle and bustle.

But being back here alone has one serious disadvantage.

My mischievous mind roams straight to delicious desires that are *very* bad for me. And I don't mean indulging in extra sugary treats. No, I'd gladly accept those tasty temptations.

While my hands get busy baking, my brain has me leaping directly into Trey's arms. In the days since our last confrontation, I've stopped fighting the inevitable and allowed my imagination to run free. There's no real harm done, aside from my body demanding I accept his proposition.

Yeah, there's that. No biggie.

My interest has been magnified since I saw a crack in his harsh exterior. It was slight and gone in an instant, but I caught it. That hint had flutters wracking my belly and made me a tad light-headed. All from a tiny glimmer. It gives me faith that Trey is far more than he pretends to be.

Splashes of guilt tint the layers of lust as I recall my careless mention of Trey's family. I didn't mean to share my knowledge as part of our argument. I'd only wanted to thank him for the ride, but our conversation escalated beyond reason. Before I knew it, Trey had me pinned and kept pushing until I snapped.

With a soft hum, the mixer churns to life and my thoughts spin watching the smooth cycle. I planned to tell Trey about my dad, but his mood swings held me back. The words were forming on my lips before he went back to hitting on me, and the moment for sharing faded away. He'd probably assume I was looking for pity or sympathy, like he accused me of giving him. I'll tell Trey when he's willing to listen and not slinging insults my way.

I start whipping the frosting, the whisk a blur as my wrist spins rapidly. A heavy sigh escapes as I calculate the numerous batches that need to be made. I can't afford to be so distracted, especially when Delilah is counting on me. Trey and his unpredictable behavior can wait.

"Rave?"

I startle and almost drop the mixing bowl as my eyes leap to Delilah. "Jeezus, you scared the crap outta me!" I exclaim with a palm to my pounding chest.

She snickers. "What were you thinking about? You've got that faraway look going on."

My cheeks heat as visions of Trey flicker before me. I wipe them away. "Nothing much. Just trying to plan for this weekend."

She crosses her arms, staring me down. "Uh, huh. What's your deal lately? I was standing here for several minutes while you kept stirring away. Pretty sure that frosting is blended extra smooth."

Glancing down, I confirm her suspicion. No lumps in sight.

While I'd been daydreaming, my hands were working on auto-pilot.

"Uh." I stammer and search for a reasonable explanation. "I'm a bit frazzled trying to get everything done. I haven't been sleeping well either." Both are true, but not due to the upcoming event.

"Do you need help?"

"No, no. I'll be fine."

Delilah doesn't look convinced. "Well, Garden Graze starts Friday. That's two days away," she reminds me unnecessarily.

I start stirring again, but stop when her brow rises at my movements. "I can't help it. You're making me nervous," I complain.

"Dude, get your head in the game."

I push the bowl away and rest my palms on the table. "Tell me about this shindig again. Talking business will help me focus."

She walks into the room and hops onto the counter beside me. The strong aroma of coffee accompanies her, and I take a greedy whiff. Trey's brown eyes appear in the rich scent, proving I can't escape him. Delilah clears her throat, drawing my focus to her.

"Sorry," I mumble. "Told you I was preoccupied."

She squints at me and smiles. "You're a nut, but we'll discuss that later. So," she starts and holds up her palms, "Garden Graze marks the beginning of summer. Food booths are set up along Main Street, either from restaurants or home-baked goodies. They're not picky about vendors. Pay the fee and you're golden. That allows for a wide variety to please any appetite. City slickers arrive in droves for our traditional festivities that their fancy metropolis doesn't host. This is where small towns shine," Delilah says with a gleaming grin.

"Spoken like a true local."

"Damn straight. Born and raised. I left for college, which was enough big world experience to cure my curiosity. I'm meant to be here, with my people."

I plop my chin on my palm. "Pretty sure I am too."

"Absolutely, Rave. You fit right in. Everyone loves you."

Heat stings my eyes. "You know it's more than that though. After my dad died, my mom couldn't sit still. She bounced us from place to place, always searching for something. Still hasn't found it," I mutter quietly. "Growing up, I never had a house to call home. I didn't bother growing roots or getting attached because soon enough, we'd be leaving again. I've never had that sense of belonging, you know?"

Delilah nods with a soft smile, and I give her one in return.

"Whenever you talked about Garden Grove and your inclusive life, I was jealous. Listening to you describe exactly what I'd always wanted was the biggest tease. Probably explains why you didn't have to try hard to convince me to move here. After only a month, this feels more like home than anywhere else I've lived. This town is a little slice of magic."

She claps happily and bounces in place. "See? You totally get it. This lifestyle isn't for everyone, but I knew you'd appreciate it. Gah, that little story almost made me cry."

I laugh at her pout. "Me too, D. I'm so happy we got stuck together freshman year."

"And now we're roomies again." Delilah squeezes my shoulder. She glances at the abandoned bowl. "So, what's the latest flavor? You still planning to roll out several new recipes for The Graze?"

I nod. "Yup. This is one of them."

Her nose wrinkles. "It looks like grease."

I gasp. "Really?"

"Is that a good thing? I can't tell for sure by your reaction."

A chuckle bubbles from me. "In this case, yes. The entire design will be dark and grungy. I'm calling these cupcakes Dirty Mechanic. It's a blend between black licorice, chocolate, and gingerbread." Delilah gapes, blinks slowly, and doesn't speak. "What?" I ask. "Do I have something on my face?" Her reaction is expected, but I pretend to be clueless for fun.

"Seriously, Rave?"

I shrug. "People will get a kick out of it. They're an acquired taste that only certain people will enjoy. Just like, you know, our favorite town asshole."

"Wow," she snorts. "That's fucking brilliant."

"Right? I was trying to get creative."

"Trey will be flattered," Delilah deadpans.

"Will he be there?" I don't bother masking the hope in my voice.

She rolls her eyes. "You poor girl. Never stood a chance. You might as well sleep with him and get it over with."

My heart skips a beat. "You think so?"

"Have you been waiting for my permission? Your face just lit up like Christmas morning."

I cringe. "It would be nice to know you won't judge me too poorly."

"Are you that hard up, Rave? Slumming it with Trey is a bad idea."

"Or maybe the best one ever."

She smacks her face. "Ugh, you're ridiculous. I was mostly joking, but clearly this is happening."

"He's so hot," I whisper. "My lady bits practically whimper whenever he's around. I can't even handle how gorgeous he is."

"Gross, I don't wanna hear that."

"Oh, whatever. You can admit it. This is a safe space," I say and pat her arm.

"Uh, huh. Sure, he's good-looking, but I'd never be attracted to him. I know him too well."

"Meh, I'm rooting for him being misunderstood." I point to myself. "Hopeful optimist."

"More like hopeless," she quips. "Not sure why I bothered dissuading you in the first place. This was clearly going to happen one way or another," Delilah grumbles. "Trey is such a snake."

"That's not super—"

"D, we were in the middle of a conversation," Addy calls from the hallway. When she reaches the doorway and sees me, a smile lifts her lips. "Hey, Raven! I didn't know you were back here. Is the slave driver keeping you busy?" She strides over to us and leans against the counter.

Delilah snorts. "Hardy-har-har. Rave would have been done by now without all the daydreaming." I flick her arm, and she giggles. "Our girl has a lady-boner."

"Oooh," Addy says, wagging her brow. "Do tell."

"I didn't know this would be a group discussion," I say.

Delilah scoffs. "Puh-lease. Addy knows Trey better than me. Maybe she'll shake some sense into you."

Addison gasps, and her eyes widen on me. "No! You like Trey? When did this happen?"

"I don't know," I mutter. "I can't stop thinking about him. And after our last battle at Jacked Up—"

"Wait. You went to his garage?" Addy asks, and I nod. "Alone?" she adds.

"Yes." My eyes flicker between them.

Delilah says, "I told her not to, but Miss Independent over here wanted to handle her car trouble alone. Sounds like there was another issue under the hood you want looked at."

Addy giggles and offers Delilah a high-five. "Good one."

"You guys act like Trey is dangerous or something."

My friends share a look, and I continue defending him. "He wouldn't physically hurt me. Sure, Trey is a jerk and has a slight temper but he's fairly harmless. As an outsider, I think his behavior is justified to a certain extent."

They wear matching expressions, creased foreheads and pinched lips.

"Seriously, guys. Don't worry so much. It's not like I'm going to fall in love with him. I probably won't gather the guts to do more than make desserts in his honor."

"I think Trey brainwashed her," Addy murmurs from the side of her mouth.

"Wouldn't put it past him," Delilah agrees.

"Ugh, stop. Honestly, I'd really like to talk to him more. There's so much left unsaid, and I want to finish the sentences he cut off. I'd like to tell Trey about my dad, even if he doesn't care. I chickened out after bringing up his family." They both suck in sharply. "I know, big mistake. He made it perfectly clear that topic was off limits."

Addy clears her throat. "Well, maybe you're the one who'll knock sense into him. There's been a few rumors."

"Regarding . . . ?" I prod.

"The regulars at Dagos haven't seen Trey with another woman since you've been around. He'll stop by with the guys for some beers but leave alone. Surly as ever though. I can vouch for that," she tells me. Goosebumps rise on my arms at her explanation, but I smooth the sensation away. Trey's dry spell is pure coincidence, of course.

Delilah slides off the table. "And the plot thickens," she says and wiggles her fingers. "He looked pretty cozy with some broad a few weeks ago, but we put the kibosh on that."

Addy laughs. "I heard about that. The girl went home with Dylan but didn't put out. Sucks for him."

"He's a schmuck," Delilah says and looks at me. "You haven't met him yet but count it as a blessing. Dylan will hit on you relentlessly."

"Ah, fun times. I have enough boy trouble as is. Thanks for the warning," I respond.

"Not like you'll listen," she sasses back.

I roll my eyes. "I've got Trey handled. Or will soon."

"He's going to have a bite of your cupcake this weekend and

be done for," Delilah says. "I wanna watch. Please make sure I'm around."

"You're a bit diabolical. Why haven't I ever noticed?"

Delilah wraps her arm around me. "You've been too taken with my shining personality all these years. I've got a devious side. That's why I'm still single. No man can keep up with me."

"Is that the reason? I was starting to wonder," I tell D.

She sticks her tongue out. "Biatch, you better get back to work. Those cupcakes won't bake themselves. Wouldn't want to disappoint Trey." Delilah looks at Addison. "Her extra special batch is called Dirty Mechanic."

"That's precious," Addy coos. "I'm getting on board with this plan. Even though he's an ass, I want him to have some good. You could be that for him."

I laugh. "Don't go writing a happily ever after. Pretty sure this isn't that type of tale."

"You never kno-ow," she sing-songs.

My chest expands with a deep breath, but I don't let any hope for more float in. If anything happens with Trey, it'll be quick and filthy. There's no doubt in my mind about that.

TEN

BEND

TREY

MY STOMACH RUMBLES WHILE MOUTH-WATERING aromas from The Graze assault me. I haven't eaten anything today in preparation of this feast, and my body is tired of waiting. When I cross onto Main Street, rows and rows of food stands greet me. My spirits lift as I take in the glorious sight spread throughout downtown.

By the looks of it, the festivities are off to a great start. Tables take up the center of the road, and almost all the seats are filled. Lines of hungry customers are formed by the booths, eagerly awaiting their turn. My eyes roam the clustered space and my stomach produces another noisy complaint.

Colorful banners and streamers hang from every available surface, drawing attention to the bustling activities. Not that anyone needs reminding. Everyone's ready to celebrate the summer season, and this event always kicks things off. Pride swells in my chest when locals and tourists swarm Garden Grove. This turnout is damn impressive.

Nostalgia warms my skin as I digest the joy surrounding me. Jack gave me the day off so I could be here. We never talk about it, but attending was a family tradition growing up. Since my parents and Grace died, I've been going alone. These festivals are in my blood. Even though I don't get along with most people around town, it doesn't stop me from partaking in our rituals.

With a deep inhale, I let my gut lead the way. Smoked meat is heavy in the air, and a turkey leg sounds mighty fine right about now. As I seek the butcher's booth out, my gaze snags on the bright pink stand for Jitters. I don't bother hiding my stare. She's like a beacon calling, and I'm tired of fighting against the force pulling me in.

Delilah catches me looking and glares. I smirk before flipping her off. Raven is busy talking to Greta, one of the gossip gals, so I decide to stay away for now. I'll save the best for last.

I find the BBQ Shack and order my grub. I'm about to park myself on a nearby bench when someone calls my name. I turn to find Shane waving from a table, sitting with a few guys we graduated with.

I lift my chin at them in greeting before slapping palms with Shane. "Hey, man. What's up? Been here long?"

"Not much, Trey. We just sat down. Take a load off," he says while patting the empty spot next to him. "You come alone?"

"Yeah, Jack and Marcus are at the garage. Might stop by after quitting time," I tell him before taking a bite. The flavor explodes in my mouth, and I groan. Damn, that's good.

Shane laughs at my reaction, but stays on topic. "They busy today? I could have swung in for a few hours."

I shrug. "Nah, they've got it handled. There wasn't much on the schedule. The entire town is probably here today."

"Right? It's crazy chaos. Everyone is making a killing. The shops have gotta be pleased," he drawls. "I got a burger from Maggie's, but am already thinking about what's next. You're making that turkey look like a solid choice. Sounds like Steve has kabobs grilling and Shawn's dad brought his smoker for ribs. Plus, we've gotta save room for dessert." Shane rubs his flat stomach.

My mind wanders to Raven, and I wonder how their sales are doing. Not sure how many people want coffee or tea with these other options available. As if I'd spoken aloud, Shane clues me in big time. "Have you tried the new girl's baking? Best cookies I've ever had. Word on the street is she made special recipes for today."

Shock streaks through me before my filter can catch up. "Raven?" I blurt. "You mean that girl always with Delilah?" Before looking like a complete tool, I rein it in and smooth my features.

He quirks a brow. "You know her?"

Shit, not really. His words are a reminder of how little I actually know, besides her tendency to monopolize my thoughts. "I've seen her around," I say coolly. "Didn't know Jitters was making food."

"They weren't until recently. You've gotta try her stuff. So damn good." The appreciation in Shane's tone sets off a chain reaction inside me.

The meat in front of me is forgotten as a craving for something far sweeter sets in. A spike of unexplainable jealousy strikes next, but I force it aside. There's no way I'm envious of people eating her desserts. That's utterly stupid . . . but exactly what's happening. This fucking chick is destroying me . . . and I'm starting to enjoy the ruin.

"You okay?" Shane asks, shaking me from my idiotic revelation. "Why'd you stop eating?"

I comb through my hair, fidgeting to keep my hands busy. "All good. Just thinking about shit." He waits a moment for me to elaborate. I don't.

"Gotcha. Well, we're planning on heading to the raceway later. Connors and Holt are going head-to-head for some charity event. One of them will probably break the track record. It'll be a sight to see," he tells me while finishing off his burger.

I find myself nodding. "That'd be great. I don't got shit to do."

It doesn't get much better than watching fast cars fly across the finish line. Burning rubber coats the air as tires peel out while the engines roar so loud my bones vibrate. It's a piece of heaven on Earth.

Shane smiles wide, like I've just made his day. "We were thinking of asking some chicks to tag along. Got any suggestions?"

With a chuckle, it hits me. They always come to me when digging for company. "Need me to round up some girls?"

His expression lights up as his head bobbles happily.

I rub over my mouth to hide the grin breaking through as a plan materializes. "Pretty sure I can find a few. What time you thinking of going?" He prattles off some details, but I'm not listening. My mind is lost in golden waves and sparkling sapphires. Adding Raven into the racetrack equation? Fucking wet dream waiting to happen.

It takes all my control to remain seated after Shane hands me a reason to approach her. My knee bounces in anticipation of walking over to the bright pink stand with the gorgeous dessert maker. The type of sugary treat I'm after isn't a cookie or cake, yet that's a convenient excuse for my eagerness. We want women to tag along tonight and fuck, she's turning me upside down so I might as well take advantage of the ride.

I cut into Shane's stream of nonsense. "All right. I'll message you later. Gonna get to work."

He claps me on the back before I stand. "Yeah, buddy! Knew I could count on you. Is Addison on your list? She might be cool."

I study him while scratching my jaw. "Got a crush?"

Red creeps up Shane's neck, lighting him up like a neon sign. "Uh, well . . . I dunno. Maybe? Doesn't have to be her, or anything. Just, um, a thought. You can decide."

"Yeah, whatever," I mutter dismissively, already losing interest. I turn and weave through the crowd with my target set. My heartrate kicks up as I decide how to play this. For some asinine reason, Raven wants to be friends. That's not happening, but I can use her interest in my favor. I'll take her out and wear her down until she's helpless to resist.

When I see Raven in the booth alone, the burning in my lungs disappears. She doesn't notice me right away so I stand silently, taking in her graceful movements. She's adding something on top of a cupcake when she glances up. Her fingers slip and jab into the frosting, ruining the perfect swirl. I'm about to make a comment when she shocks me silent. Looking directly at me, Raven licks the icing from her thumb, and my cock jerks to attention. As she continues torturing me, I attempt to adjust myself without being too obvious. This is a family gathering, after all. Raven smirks, catching me red handed, so I shoot her a wink. Little witch knows exactly what she's doing.

We continue staring without exchanging a word. Maybe we can get through this without fighting.

Wishful thinking? Perhaps. But I'm determined not to fuck up, at least until later.

I step closer and lean my forearm against the stand's siding. "Fancy seeing you here, Princess. Had no idea you've been busy baking."

She leans closer and whispers, "What gave me away?"

"Smartass," I snort.

"Asshole," she shoots back.

"Glad that's outta the way."

Raven tilts her head. "Uh, huh. What's up, Trey?"

I rock back on my heels. "Just checking out the goods."

"That sounds suspicious."

"Maybe. Or not." I keep my expression neutral, locking down the desire in my gut. For now. "Tell me what you've got here."

Raven starts at the far end of the counter and points to each dessert while listing them. "Mixed berry fruit tart, blueberry scones, key lime cookies, strawberry muffins, and of course," she pauses while gesturing to a fancy tiered setup, "a wide variety of cupcakes."

I take in the impressive display, and my attention snags on a particular detail. "Is that a wrench?" I ask while reaching for a black cupcake.

"Yup. I made those specifically for Garden Graze. They're called Dirty Mechanic."

My hand freezes as her explanation registers. That bizarre pressure is back in my chest and for a moment breathing is difficult. The sensation is happening more frequently in her presence. I rub at the ache and sneak a glance at Raven. She's smiling at me. Not in a snarky way like the local girls do. Her expression is genuine and open, goodness radiating from her. I'm caught in the tide and sinking fast.

Fuck it. Might as well plunge deeper.

"That's . . . interesting. Any specific inspiration behind these?"

"Isn't it obvious? You've left quite the impression. Figured I owed you something in return," she says with a lift of her chin.

My fingers are gravitating toward the frosted dessert again. "Can I have one?"

"Of course. That'll be five bucks."

"For a cupcake? Seems a little steep," I mutter while picking it up.

"They're gourmet and made with the finest ingredients. That's how we get away with charging so much. Plus, they look so pretty."

"Not sure if that's the term I'd use," I reply. She's not far off, though. The thing is decorated professionally with a stupid amount of detail. Not sure why someone would spend this much time on something to eat. I twist it this way and that, inspecting all the angles. The shading and layers are impressive, like a tiny piece of art.

Raven laughs. "It doesn't taste like grease and chrome. I just made it look like something from the garage."

"I'll say. There's even specks of grime on the metal. Almost a shame to ruin it," I grumble as my mouth begs for a bite.

She gestures to the cupcake. "Will you just try it? I'm on pins and needles over here."

"What's the flavor?" I ask, although nothing will stop me at this point.

"Black licorice, chocolate, and gingerbread." My eyes snap to hers as she continues, unaware of the bomb detonating inside me. "They're actually really good. The combination sounds a bit odd, but that was the point. I wanted something unique, like you."

The words are out before I can stop them. "My mom loved black licorice."

She sucks in sharply. "Oh, wow. Um, I wasn't expecting that. Do you like it too?"

My gaze lowers, and I nod, stunned silent. I stuff my mouth full as a means to recover, which has the opposite effect. The rich flavor explodes on my tongue, and a rumble rolls through me. Memories of licorice wheel races in the kitchen slam into me, and my lids slide shut. We would laugh while unwinding the sticky spirals, ribbing each other about who'd win. Sometimes we'd go through an entire bag without thinking twice. I loved those things but haven't had one since she died. Without even knowing, Raven gave me a piece of the past I've kept buried.

When I'm done chewing, Raven holds up another. "More? This one's on the house." I grab it without a word, opening the floodgates wider. Suddenly I'm desperate to have all the good vibes wash over me. I groan again, getting far too much satisfaction from a cupcake.

There's a hitch in Raven's voice when she murmurs, "Hopefully I didn't upset you. I made them as more of a joke than anything. I had no idea that, well, there was such significance to the flavor."

I clear my throat between bites. "Nah, Princess. This is a good thing, really fucking great actually. I'm surprised, sure, but in a nice way. Am I making any sense?" I finish with a rough swallow as Raven wipes her cheeks, affected by my honesty. Her reaction means more to me than it should. Something shifts between us in this moment, like a key opening a rusty lock. It's raw and potent and scares the hell out of me.

I watch her, waiting for the spell to be broken. Delilah does the honors when she rounds the corner into the booth. My guard crashes down, locking firmly in place. The peaceful atmosphere evaporates with her unwelcome presence.

"Look what the cat dragged in," Delilah says. "Took you long enough. Figured you'd be over here first thing, drooling over my girl's sweets."

Raven elbows her and shoots off a glare. "Be nice."

She's defending me? After how I've treated her? Well, shit, I don't deserve her kindness.

Delilah rolls her eyes. "Seriously? He dishes it out twice as bad. Trey knows the score. Pretty positive he can stand up for himself." She looks back at me. "Did you try a Dirty Mechanic yet?"

I smirk and hold up two fingers. D raises her brow and nods. "That's what I thought. So, why are you still standing here? Aren't you more of the eat-and-run type?"

"Oh, those cupcakes were just a teaser. I'm here for more than dessert." I'm responding to Delilah but looking at Raven. A blush paints her cheeks, and I fight the urge to touch the heated skin. My pulse pounds in my temple as Raven nibbles her lip. "There's a group of guys heading to the raceway tonight. A few pro drivers are dueling it out for some charity event. Was thinking you might wanna join us."

Delilah gasps. "Holy shit. Are you asking her on a—"

I cut her off and continue addressing Raven. "It's not a date. It'd be a bunch of people hanging out. That's it." I haven't taken a girl out with my friends in years. Probably since high school. But this is casual, no big deal.

Yeah, fucking right.

Raven gawks at me. "Wait a minute. You want to willingly spend time with me?"

Heat creeps up my neck as both girls watch me. My defenses flare, ready to lash out, but I hold off. "Not if you're gonna make a huge deal about it," I rasp. Sweat trickles down my spine as I wait for her decision.

"Can D and Addy come?" Raven asks, all sugar and no spice.

I clench my teeth, but agree with a sharp nod. Raven is the only one I'm willing to entertain so her friends better stay out of the way. I won't get anywhere near her real goodies with them hounding me.

Delilah squints at me, like she can't figure it out.

"What?" I snap.

"Are you feeling well? Or what's your motive here? This smells worse than horse shit." She waves the apparent stench away. And that's about all I can handle for one afternoon.

"Know what? Forget it," I spit and push away from the stand. I stalk off without a backward glance as humiliation boils in my blood. My feet feel off balance as I shove through clusters of people, pure instinct propelling me forward. It's been a month of this turmoil, and sanity is slowly slipping away. I need to lick my wounds in private before taking out my fury at the gym.

Screw this shit.

The shaded alley calls to me as the noise of The Graze is left behind. Just as I'm stepping into the narrow space, someone yanks me back. I glare over my shoulder. It's *her*. I don't want her anywhere near me.

"Didn't get the hint, Princess? Leave me the fuck alone," I seethe.

Her grip moves down until she's clutching my forearm. "Don't push me away, Trey. Before Delilah came back, you were different. For a second, you let me in so don't let this ruin it."

I scoff, venom dripping from my tongue. "What do you want from me, Raven? Want me to pour out my feelings and cry on your shoulder?"

"No," she whispers. "You brought up the past, not me. I don't expect anything. Except maybe your friendship?" she suggests with a wince.

My chest rises and falls rapidly. "You really wanna get into this again? I'm a lost fucking cause. Go waste time on some other poor sap."

She shakes her head. "Stop saying shit like that. I don't believe you."

I stretch my arms out wide, my brown eyes blazing into her blues. "This is me, Princess. Flaws and all. I've warned you off enough, and time is up. Accept me as is or get fucking lost."

Her breathing falters, making her tone hoarse. "I want it all, Trey."

Malice echoes through me. "Yeah?"

"Yeah . . ."

"Remember you asked for it," I say. Then, I push her against the brick wall.

ELEVEN

KISS

RAVEN

TREY'S WORDS SOUND LIKE A threat, but all I hear is a promise. There's no resistance as he shoves me against the brick. He cradles my head, making sure I don't smash into the unforgiving surface. But that's where his gentleness ends.

Trey roughly grabs my hips, hoisting me up, and I wrap my legs around him. He presses between my thighs and smashes my ass against the wall. Being pinned has never felt so delicious. I grab his shoulders and pull him closer, wanting his force everywhere. No way is he going anywhere. Screw the consequences. He's probably going to ruin certain parts of me, but Trey won't break my heart. I won't let him.

His coffee irises gleam with mischief, urging me to play. I lift my chin, baiting him, ready to beg for it at this point.

"I'm beginning to think you like being caught up like this. Third time's a charm, right?" Trey's voice is dripping with seduction.

"I definitely don't hate it," I say with a tilt of my pelvis.

"You drive me wild," he grates while rocking forward, letting me feel his arousal.

My fingers claw at his shirt, dragging him into me. "Kiss me," I murmur. Trey holds back. When I pull harder, he arches away. "But I want you." I prod further.

He squeezes my waist. "You like being teased?"

"Doubt it."

"Hmm, let's find out."

My protest dies off as Trey slowly inches forward. My lashes flutter as I wait for his touch, but it doesn't come. At least not where I was expecting.

He brushes his lips against my jaw before sweeping down. His mouth latches onto my collarbone, applying barely-there pressure with his teeth. Goosebumps rise in his tongue's path as he sucks along my sensitive flesh. I stretch to give him better access, and Trey takes advantage. His palms drift up my sides, settling on my back, and I'm being held captive. My head lolls to the side while I get lost in his torturous treatment.

This is foreplay . . . to a kiss.

Jesus, I can't imagine how sex with him would be. Once the thought sprouts, it grows beyond reach. My desire expands, and I can't stop imagining us together.

As Trey nibbles up my neck, I picture smooth skin and sculpted muscles. I envision him hovering over me, straining with effort. I see our bodies sliding together, hard into soft.

By the time he reaches my earlobe, I'm ready to scream. "Please," I whimper. "Stop tormenting me."

"But you taste so good," he growls. "Better than you smell, and I wasn't sure that was possible."

I'm not really listening as my body takes control and inhibitions fall away. This position restricts my movement, but wiggling is always possible. He sucks in sharply before shifting impossibly closer.

"You're a little witch, Princess."

"Stop messing around. You're getting me all riled up in broad daylight." My voice is a breathy rasp.

"Are you really complaining?" he asks.

I manage to shake my head.

"That's what I thought."

The time for talking is over when Trey's mouth crashes down on mine. My gasp grants him instant entrance, and he doesn't waste it. His palm cups my cheek, tilting my face just right. Then, he dives in with sure strokes, caressing my tongue with an erotic glide. He tastes like a Dirty Mechanic—the tang of black licorice makes my heart flutter.

My fingers spear into Trey's hair, yanking at the roots. He groans into me, and I answer with a moan of my own. Our hips roll together. The friction is electric, pants be damned. Trey hauls me closer, and our lips form a tighter seal. As our mouths are locked in a heated embrace, his hands roam and explore. My nails scratch his scalp as he palms my ass. My belly flips when he rubs me against his rigid length.

"Damn, you're sexy," he mutters before plunging back in. An explosion of color bursts behind my lids when he tugs my bottom lips between his teeth. Intense lust spills from his mouth and pours into me. All I can do is hum in response as desire for this man surges through me.

He pulls away slightly. "Is this what you wanted?"

"Yes," I whisper. My hunger is in control as I swipe along his lips, savoring each pass. I dip inside, getting drunk off his flavor, and crush him against me. Feverish heat spreads up my body, and it isn't from the humidity. Trey lets me lead for another beat before stealing the power, attacking me full throttle.

Faraway laughter drags us off the edge, and our mouths break apart. We're both panting, arousal straining through our limbs. Trey's forehead rests against mine as pent-up passion surges between us. His lips are shiny and wet, inviting me in for another round.

"You're dangerous," he murmurs.

"I could say the same about you."

Trey chuckles, the melody a dark taunt. "We're gonna have so much fun together." He grinds into me, and I shudder.

"O-okay," I exhale softly.

His nose traces a silky path up my jaw. "I'm gonna blow your mind. Over and over again."

"Now?" I breathe while my insides turn to jelly.

"Nah, you've got work to do. I can't steal you away from The Graze. Don't wanna be a bad influence." His tone says he'd love nothing more.

"Too late."

"You're right, but we're not taking it any further for now." He leans in, a soft brush of lips over my mouth, before pulling away. "This was just a preview, Princess." Trey releases me and I slide down slowly, enjoying every inch of the descent.

He curses and backs away. "Wicked girl."

I offer a saucy smirk. "Thank you for noticing. Can I still come to the raceway?"

"You wanna come with me?"

I roll my eyes. "You make everything sound dirty."

"You're welcome." His tone is coated in gravel when he says, "I'll meet you there. Delilah and Addy will know where to find us."

I tilt my head. "Not gonna pick me up at the door?"

Trey rubs down the straight slope of his nose. "This isn't a date, Princess. Don't get your hopes up."

A laugh bubbles from me, snapping the tension around us. "I'm messing with you. Pretty sure I know what's happening here," I say. Lava pools in my lower belly and the heat feels so damn good.

"Where I'm concerned, it's best to leave expectations outta the equation."

"Noted."

He scans my expression before his gaze travels lower in a lazy perusal. Every millimeter of skin burns with awareness, like he's touching rather than looking.

"Damn," he mutters.

With that parting word, he spins on his heel and walks off. I press along my abused mouth, watching Trey strut away. His gait can't be considered anything less. He walks with a confident swagger, the strides long but unhurried. My eyes linger on his ass, the glorious shape outlined in faded jeans. I bite my bottom lip and keep staring, lost in a trance.

I'm in so much trouble.

When Trey is out of sight, I wipe across my forehead. Talk about a heatwave. My stomach tightens as the haze fades. While I was making out with Trey, Delilah has been working alone. Hopefully the stand isn't too busy. My shoes pound the pavement as I rush into the event.

When Delilah sees me approaching, a grimace mars her features. "Thanks for ditching me."

I wince. "Sorry, D. Ton of people?" Glancing around, I notice the crowd is thinning out. "It's a bit calmer, right?"

"You're such a hussy," she says.

"Me? Why? Because I went after him?"

Delilah throws a hand on her hip and taps her chin. "Oh, let's see. Where to start? Your lips are so puffy they look pumped full of collagen. Your face is flushed and glowing like a neon sign. Also, there's a giddy grin desperate to break free that you can hardly contain. My dear friend. You're a walking advertisement for bad decisions."

"Aww." I give her my best puppy-dog face. "Are you disappointed in me?"

"No. I mean, maybe a little bit for chasing Trey after he took off on a tantrum. I get it though. You like him, and blah, blah, blah. I clearly interrupted a moment earlier. Feel free to fill me in on the details now, 'kay?"

"Oh, um," I stammer. My pulse pounds as I try to decide what to share.

She makes a rolling motion to speed me along. "Tell me all the things."

"We kissed a little bit," I murmur the biggest understatement of the century.

"And?" Delilah prods, unimpressed.

"What do you mean? That's all we did. Not sure what kind of girl you think I am, but alley sex is not on my bucket list."

"Don't be ridiculous. Fooling around with Trey isn't exciting. I want to know what you talked about. The good stuff."

Indecision creeps in as I wade through a jumble of benign topics. I don't want to lie but protecting the tidbit about Trey's mother and the licorice seems necessary. It feels like a secret I should cherish.

"Well, we discussed The Graze and the weather. He asked about Jitters," I hedge.

Delilah gives me a flat look. "You're a brat."

"What? There isn't much to tell. I was suspicious about his intentions, and we bickered. Then Trey wanted to know about my baking. He ate a few cupcakes. And as you know, he asked me out."

"But you two were civil?"

"Uh, huh."

"Interesting," she drawls.

"Is it?" I honestly can't tell with how Delilah is acting.

"Sure. That's what you wanted. Plus, you played tonsil hockey. Win-win. Now what?"

Before I can respond, Marlene and Betty stroll up to the booth.

In the last few weeks, I've met all the nosy old ladies of Garden Grove. These two are definitely the worst gossips of the group. My ears prickle like a keen alert system, giving me a gut feeling they've wandered over here for a reason. I plaster a Cheshire grin on my face and wave brightly.

"Hello, there. Long time, no see," I joke because this pair is always visible around town, constantly popping up at the shop too, ready to spread the latest rumor.

"Well, hello. How are you doing this afternoon, Raven?" Betty asks.

"Very good, thank you. Enjoying my first Garden Graze experience."

Marlene murmurs to Betty from the side of her mouth, "She sure is." Both ladies erupt in what I assume is supposed to be an under-the-radar fit of giggles.

Betty smooths her features and swings her gaze to my friend. "And you, Delilah?"

D rests an arm around my shoulder and pulls me close. "Stupendous. We've been selling Raven's goodies like hot cakes." She peers at me. "Huh, that's actually really funny."

The older women whisper under their breath but look right at us. Are they for real? I suppress an eyeroll while Delilah asks, "What can we do for you today?"

Marlene pipes up. "Sounds like Raven is offering up more than cookies. We heard she accepted a date with Trey Sollens."

"It's not a date," I blurt before realizing my mistake. Their eyes widen as I feed the gossip flames.

Crap, crap, shit.

"I mean, he invited me out with a group of people. Not even sure I'm going," I lie.

Delilah cuts in. "Marlene, you know Trey doesn't date. It's an innocent evening with a bunch of people. No reason to blow this out of proportion."

The nosy lady squints at me. "So, you turn down my offer to meet some nice gentlemen, but going out with that hoodlum is acceptable? I'm beginning to understand what type of girl you are, Raven."

My cheeks heat from her judgement. I look away, blinking rapidly. This is the type of verbal slap my mom is victim of, only her behavior tends to ask for it. I'm sure Marlene is over here just trying to stir the pot. Her curious approach isn't fooling me. I won't give her more ingredients to add, but the words sting regardless.

Delilah pinches me and mutters, "Don't listen to her." She raises her voice and tells them, "Raven is the most honest and caring person I know. You two should get the facts before prancing around causing drama. You're no better than teenagers."

Betty and Marlene gasp with hands to their mouths. Pretty sure this situation is about to spiral south real quick. I speak up and try diffusing this completely unnecessary conflict.

Kill them with kindness.

"I meant no offense by turning down your kind offer, Marlene. Trey is just a friend, maybe not even that. We're definitely not dating, okay? How about you two take a few desserts?" My smile wobbles as I wave over the assortment of pastries.

They grumble but eventually choose a few fruit tarts that satisfy them. For now. Betty and Marlene saunter off. They throw us a few parting glances before moving to the next stand.

"Jeez, that was painful. Don't they ever get tired of gossiping?" I ask.

Delilah shakes her head. "Are you kidding? They live for this stuff. You and Trey are the talk of Garden Grove. It's only going to get worse, especially now that things are actually happening."

I groan. "That's great. I'll have to keep defending myself until the next new girl lands in town."

"I dunno. You keep it real interesting for them. Trey hasn't asked anyone out, even in a group setting, for years. I can't even remember the last time. You're like a freaking unicorn crossed with a leprechaun. Mythical creature," she specifies. "Always knew you were special."

"Ugh, stop being strange."

"It's the truth. Look in the mirror, Rave. You're a knockout. That's why Marlene wants to hook you up with all her grandsons. Spread those genes."

"Gross. I'll pass."

"Good life choice. They're nothing to write home about." Delilah laughs, her green eyes sparkling in the sun. "Now, back to more important business. What's the plan with Trey?"

I smile and clasp my hands. "Wanna go to the raceway tonight? I'll ask Addy too."

"Oh, Lawd. You're really doing this, huh?" Delilah chuckles again. "Obviously we'll go with you. Someone has to make sure you don't dive headfirst into his lap."

A loud snort escapes me. "Jeez, thanks for the vote of confidence. Pretty sure I wouldn't dive."

She quirks a brow. "Trey is wrapping you around his finger but don't worry, I'll keep you safe." My forehead crinkles in confusion. "Condoms," she clarifies. "I'll bring extras. Who knows what those guys are planning at this fuckfest."

All I can do is gawk while she cackles.

What have I gotten myself into?

TWELVE

RACE

TREY

I TAKE ANOTHER SWIG OF cold beer while my eyes scan the bleachers. *Again.* My search for Raven is beginning to feel desperate. I left her hot and bothered, wanting more, in hopes she'd seek me out. But who knows if she'll even show up.

My fingers slide around the cool bottle, and I imagine Raven against me. Those sinful lips sliding along mine while I press into her. The curve of her ass fitting perfectly in my palm like she's meant to be there. Her quiet moans and subtle movements asking for more. My pants grow uncomfortably tight so I shift slightly, trying to alleviate the ache.

Damn, she better be here.

Engines rev from the pit as the teams prepare for start time. A couple of cars ease around the track for test runs, and I do my best to pay attention. I usually enjoy watching the pre-race rituals while everyone scrambles with last minute adjustments, but my mind is focused elsewhere tonight.

With a scowl, I turn away from the action, and my gaze stops on a blonde. My heart pounds louder than the warning signal blaring through the speakers as I try getting a better look. But when she turns and the sun glints off her too-light hair, my gut plummets along with my mood. Not Raven.

Fuck, I'm losing it. She took something from me this afternoon, but not in a bad way. Raven grabbed a piece of my baggage and offered to carry it. The honesty in her sapphire eyes said she wants to help ease the burden. All I have to do is let her. I scrub down my face, feeling foolish for even considering this shit. Raven is just another girl, one I was hellbent on chasing away. Now I want her close? I'm seriously screwed.

A slap on my shoulder jolts me back to reality. "Have you heard from them?" Shane asks for what seems like the thousandth time.

"No," I bark. "Not sure they're even coming. Already told you that."

"But, dude," he complains, "we've been here almost an hour. It's almost match time. I was looking forward to hanging out with some girls."

"If you wanted a sure thing, should've taken care of it yourself."

Shane laughs. "What's eating you?"

"Nothing."

"Maybe that's the problem," he mumbles.

I'm about to tell him off when Mitch plops down next to me.

"The fuck?" I ask him.

Mitch gives me a blank stare. "What? No one's sitting here."

"Not yet, she isn't." I point with my bottle and say, "Go over there." I don't tell them who the spot next to me is reserved for. I won't be denying Raven a seat again.

Before either guy can comment, golden hair appears in the crowd. This time the shade is exactly right. Shane notices the girls and calls out. When Raven's blue eyes clash with mine, I lift a brow and smirk, playing it cool as if my pulse isn't thundering.

Delilah leads as they climb the few steps to our section. She huffs when she catches sight of the empty space beside me. She still pushes Raven forward, and I pat the metal bench.

"Hey, Princess," I say once she's settled in.

"Hi," she replies before glancing around. "These are really great seats."

I nod. "Jack has the hookup. He does repairs for some of the pit crew and gets this row in return."

"That's awesome. I bet you love this stuff, right?"

"Hell yes. This shit's in my blood. I've spent so many summer nights at this place. Growing up, Jack would let me tag along whenever he had business. When I got older, it became our hangout. Doesn't get much better for me."

"Oh, wow. I've never been to a car race before."

"First time for everything."

A slight blush dances up her neck. "There sure is." Raven bites her lip, making my dick twitch. I glance away before my reaction gets worse. An announcer gives the five-minute countdown and a roar of applause booms from the audience. Addy passes her a beer, and Delilah hands over a pink koozie.

I snort. "You're such a fucking princess."

Raven pokes me in the ribs with an elbow. "Don't be an ass. I thought we're trying to get along?"

"What gave you that impression?" Messing with her calms the tension in my stomach.

"Oh, I don't know. The fact you invited me here?"

"That was just a ploy to get Delilah on my good side."

D scoffs and narrows her eyes at me. "In your dreams, Trey."

Raven giggles. "Pretty sure you'd have better luck with any-one else."

"Good thing it's you I want," I say and brush a finger down her flushed face.

She tucks her chin, peeking up through lowered lashes. "You're so forward."

"I'm done denying the inevitable."

"So, you wanna be friends?" She winks.

"With benefits," I add.

"We'll see."

When I lean in, her floral scent spins around me. I whisper in her ear, "Should I find a wall to pin you against? That seems to work in my favor." She chokes on her sip of beer and coughs. I pat her back lightly and say, "See? Gets you all riled up."

Raven glares. "You aren't playing fair."

"Who says? We never established any rules."

A few blonde strands tickle my cheek, the slight sensation feeling more like a jolt.

"Good to know." She places a palm on my thigh and slowly slides toward the promised land. I curse while my dick responds instantly. Raven slinks closer and coos, "You like this?"

"Too much," I grit and pluck her hand off me.

Victory laces her voice when she says, "That's what I thought."

"I like your style, Princess. Never back down." I veer onto a safer topic. "How did The Graze end up?"

Raven smiles, but her lips are tight. "Oh, fine. Had a chat with Marlene and Betty, which was thrilling. They struck a nerve, but pretty sure that was intended."

"What do you mean?"

"Eh, it's whatever. I'm sure you don't wanna know." I do, yet I don't. My jaw tics while I work through my indecision. Raven saves me when she touches my forearm and says, "I won't drag you into the drama. Mostly they were sniffing around for dirt and spreading nonsense." She rolls her eyes. Knowing those two, they gave Raven a tale about someone's booth being overrun by aliens.

"All right, I'll bite. Tell me the latest word on the street."

She glances at me before her eyes dart away.

"They found out about this." Raven gestures around us.

"Delilah and I set them straight, but Marlene is peeved. She's upset that I'll come here with you but won't go out with her *gentlemen suitors*." She says the last words with a snooty accent.

A stab of jealousy hits when I think of Raven going out with someone else. Fuck that. "Marlene is a crazy old bird. And the guys she wants to set you up with are lame. Guaranteed."

She waves dismissively. "D already warned me. Not that I would have agreed anyway."

"Oh, yeah? Why not? Pining for someone else?"

"Shamelessly digging, are we? The truth is simple. I'm not ready to rush into anything serious. Marlene seems to be match-making for committed relationships. I prefer spontaneous meet-and-greets." She offers a barely-there smirk.

"Such as meeting a handsome stranger in the bar your first night in town?"

Raven bumps her shoulder into mine. "Sounds like a fairytale waiting to happen."

"Ah, good one," I chuckle. "More like an epic disaster."

"Meh, could be worse." Her hair whips in the wind, sending flowers and citrus into the air. My fingers itch to tuck the strands behind her ear, but she beats me to it.

I scratch my temple, ready to change the subject. "So . . . did you sell all the Dirty Mechanics?"

"Nah, I saved the rest. There's new flavors for tomorrow."

Something deep inside me warms at hearing that. Maybe she wants me to have them. Or I'm being an idiot. Yeah, probably the latter.

"So, there's a chance I could have another?"

"I'd say so. You're the inspiration, after all. No one else got the significance."

"They didn't figure out I was the grease monkey you were referring to?"

"Nope. Everyone else thought it was a weird flavor and didn't even give it a chance. But they don't know the real meaning."

A tremor rolls through me as I process Raven's words. My gaze sears into her for a reason beyond the baking skills and flawless features. As I dig underneath those surface layers, real beauty stares back at me. Raven's blue eyes gleam with sincerity, like an open book, and I want to read every page.

But I won't.

"Their loss and my gain," I say while patting my stomach.

Raven watches me as though she sees the truth buried within me. She doesn't call me out on it. After that, our conversation dies off, but random chatter passes between us. Watching the race takes most of our concentration, but I'm very aware of her next to me. The metal shakes beneath us each time the cars zoom past for another lap. As the temperature drops with the setting sun, Raven slides closer and closer. I fight the urge to wrap my arm around her. This isn't a date and giving mixed signals will only cause trouble. I already screwed up earlier by acting like a sentimental weirdo. I've got to lock this shit down and be done, black licorice cupcakes be damned.

While Raven is busy chatting with Delilah and Addy, Shane nudges me. "You're the worst wingman ever," he grumbles.

"Huh?" I question, shaking off the fog in my brain.

"You're like a massive roadblock in the middle of us. Mitch and I couldn't talk to the girls if we tried. It's like we're not even here."

"Oh, chill. The night is young. And if you really want her, go sit down next to her."

Shane sighs. "The race is almost over so it'd be odd if I switched seats now."

And he wonders why she hasn't noticed him? "Dude, stop being a pansy and make it happen."

"Easy for you to say," he complains.

"Uh, huh. Sure is," I tell him and roll my eyes.

"It's true. You barely have to try. Me? I'm not sure Addy knows my name."

I rub my forehead, feeling a headache approaching. "Don't worry about it. You'll talk to her later."

"But we're leaving soon."

"And you don't think we're heading somewhere after this?"

Shane just blinks at me.

"With them," I clarify while hooking my thumb at the girls. There's no way I'm ready to say goodnight to Raven. I've got plans to keep.

"Oh. Oh!" His expression brightens. "Awesome. Where should we take them?"

I groan. "Seriously. Is this your first time?"

"Don't be a dick. I don't want to screw it up, okay? You know what to do so help me out, man."

Fuck, he's right. I'm off-kilter and taking shit out on him. "All right, whatever. Let's go to Boomers. Girls love to dance, especially those girls." I hook my thumb toward them.

Shane's head bobbles so fast I'm worried his neck will snap. "Great idea. Yeah, let's do that. Are you going to ask Raven?"

"Ask me what?" she questions, leaning forward.

"We were thinking about going to the bar after this. Would you all wanna come with?" Shane responds.

Raven glances at me before turning to her friends. They murmur quietly, Delilah's harsh tone most audible. She doesn't sound super happy about the idea, no fucking surprise. She's had a vendetta against me since I pulled her pigtails in first grade. It's about damn time to get over it. After a few moments, Raven twists toward us again.

"Addy says there's a club nearby with a live band and a huge dancefloor. That's where we're going," she tells us with no room for discussion. "Wanna come along?"

"It's Cyclone," Addison says, looking directly at Shane.

I elbow him and mutter, "See? She knows you exist."

He hisses under his breath, "Be cool, dude. Don't blow it."

"You're a moron."

Shane grumbles at me before glancing at Addy. She's already staring, at him and it's one of those serendipitous moments from the movies. Cue the cheesy music.

Raven taps my shoulder before murmuring, "I hope you'll join us."

I peek at her from the corner of my eye. Her blue gaze sparkles in the stadium floodlights. When did my mouth go dry? Not sure I could deny her anything.

My head bobs casually, playing it cool. "Yeah, Princess. I'll be there."

THIRTEEN

BACKSEAT

RAVEN

FLASHING STROBE LIGHTS BLIND ME as we enter Cyclone, causing me to stumble forward into Delilah. I blink and keep walking, trying to clear the splotches from my vision. The party is already in full swing with people crammed in wall to wall. Pretty sure the room is beyond maximum capacity, but those rules never seem to apply in a scene like this. The band hasn't started playing, but the booming of heavy bass is vibrating through the floor, making my legs tremble. This is the type of scene Addy described, which had me sold on the place.

When a popular hip-hop song begins blasting through the speakers, my hips shimmy automatically. It's one of those melodies I can't help moving to, but my parched throat is screaming for relief. When Delilah tugs me toward the dance floor, I pull away. She whips around with a questioning look, knowing I love this beat. I make the motion for a drink. She pouts, but nods in understanding.

Trey whistles at her and shouts, "Go ahead. I'll stay with

Raven."

Delilah's gaze bounces between us before finding whatever permission she's looking for. She uses two fingers to point from her to Trey, signaling that she's watching him. I laugh and shake my head. So ridiculous.

Addy and Delilah disappear into the gyrating throng as we make our way to the bar. Trey's hand rests at the small of my back, guiding me without being pushy. Easily enough, I wiggle my way between two occupied stools to reach the counter.

I gesture for him to come closer too so he can hear me. "What would you like?"

"You," he replies instantly.

I roll my eyes. "Be serious."

His hands go to my hips before dragging me toward him. "I am, Princess. But for now, I'll settle for a beer. Whatever's on tap." Heat ripples along my nape with his words.

We get our drinks, and I take a hearty gulp. The cool liquid is instantly absorbed into my system. I eagerly swallow more.

"Damn," Trey coughs. "Never thought I'd be jealous of a straw."

I peek up at him while finishing my cocktail, making sure to suck down every drop. "So delicious," I say before licking my lips.

"Fuck, Raven. You're so sexy," he breathes along my neck.

Trey's fingers dig into my waist, and I squirm as sparklers crackle along every inch of me. He rolls forward, and his hardness presses against my ass. I push back, wanting more.

"You're teasing me, Princess," he groans.

I look at him over my shoulder. "Only fair after that alley kiss."

He smirks. "Oh, you wanna play?"

My lower belly flips as I imagine what that involves. "Game on, Trey."

"Let's dance."

A sliver of disappointment takes root that we're not sneaking off to the bathroom, or somewhere equally illicit. Then again, there's plenty of time for dirty shenanigans later. Trey tugs on my belt loop and steers me ahead of him, seemingly happy to have me lead the way. I glance around, trying to spot Delilah or Addy, but it's impossible to find anyone in a crowd this size. I stop in a pocket of space near a pillar and turn to face Trey. With an arched brow, I silently ask him to choose what happens next.

He doesn't disappoint.

Trey whips me around and draws me back so we're aligned from shoulder to hip. He doesn't hesitate before grinding slowly, matching the music's rhythm perfectly. His arms wrap around me as he controls our movements, and I get lost in his guidance. Trey's fingers slide under the hem of my shirt, seeking the smooth skin underneath. I shudder while his touch lights me on fire, the flames rising in my veins. I lean against Trey's broad chest and my palms slide down his outer thighs. His erotic energy soaks into me with every pass, and intoxicated flutters go wild in my stomach. We press closer as his thumbs play along my ribs, exploring each groove with care.

When Trey rocks into me, it becomes *very* obvious how wrong I was to doubt this being the best idea ever. What we're doing is more seductive than anything I've experienced, and this is just the warm-up. The unsatisfying fumbles I've had in the sack are a weak comparison, but pretty sure this would be hard to top regardless.

"How're you feeling, Princess?" Trey murmurs against my temple.

"Mhmmm," I mumble.

"Did you know I watched you dancing at Boomers after our little chat?"

"What? Why?" I ask, suppressing the lust weighing down my limbs.

"Isn't it obvious?" He punctuates his question with a slow thrust.

Trey is giving me a fairly impressive hint and I can't deny the thrill shooting through me. His actions might be questionable to some, but I'm well aware of the score between us. I've never had a one-night-stand or fuck buddy, but am beginning to understand the benefits. Specifically, Trey's intentions. I deserve at least one exceptional encounter to reflect on later in life, meaningless or not. When Trey nibbles up my neck, I give myself permission to let go.

"Still looking for that truce?" he whispers before sucking on my earlobe.

I arch to give him more room and say, "Uh, huh."

Trey kisses along the sensitive skin of my nape. "I want more of your goodies."

A giggle bursts from me. "You make everything filthy."

"Just wait. You have no idea how dirty it can get. Ready to find out?"

The last tendrils of hesitation fall away as I straighten against him. "Yeah, let's go." The attempt to hide my eagerness is an epic fail. Trey doesn't call me out on it. With a hand on my arm, he silently directs me from the havoc of Cyclone. I greedily gulp in fresh air once we leave the building. It's still balmy outside, even though it's almost midnight. That's one nice thing about summer humidity—never worrying about being cold. We're rushing through the parking lot. I'm glad he's in a hurry too.

My voice is overly breathy when I ask, "Where are we going?"

"My truck." Trey presses his key fob, and lights flash from a secluded corner. I smile while figuring he planned this. He opens the rear passenger door and hoists me up without effort. The bite of new leather and spicy aftershave flood my nostrils. The combination is frigging yummy. But the scent fades after I take in the rest of the vehicle.

"Holy shit," I curse. "Your backseat is huge. This is bigger than my couch."

He chuckles from behind me. "Fit for a princess."

"Don't be a jackhole."

"A what?"

I settle into the seat and glare at him. "You know what I mean. It's just a random term I came up with. You're staring like I'm Christmas dinner so my thoughts are a little jumbled."

"Hmm," Trey purrs, and his brown eyes spark with desire. He moves toward me, crowding my space, until our lips almost touch. "I'm gonna eat you up."

A hitch catches in my throat before he seals the gap. In a flurry, we become a tangle of wandering hands and gliding tongues. My mouth opens, accepting more of him, while my palms settle on his biceps. Trey flexes, and I moan as the muscles bunch under my touch. He lifts me against his chest, arms banding around my back until I'm straddling him. Our faces tilt just right as we search for a deeper connection. He licks across my bottom lip before sucking me in, breaking away with a gasp. The heat in his gaze sets fire to my skin, and all I want is to feel him against me.

Trey urges me down on the center console and my back lowers to the hard leather. I blink up at the sunroof and wiggle around, trying to balance without slipping off the edge. This position gives him prime access to my lower half that's not resting on the short surface. My ass settles directly into his grip, which works fine with me. He reaches for the button of my jeans, not wasting time. The sound of the zipper lowering causes goosebumps to awaken on my flesh. When I shift slightly, Trey takes advantage, stripping me of the denim and cotton barriers. I feel my legs twitch as his fingers dance along them, slowly moving back up. He kisses my calf and knee before working toward my inner thigh. His gentle touch has electricity buzzing straight to my core. I squirm eagerly.

"Your skin is like velvet," Trey says through another soft peck. "Thought I'd be racing through this part but you feel too good." My lids slide shut as his lazy exploration continues.

"Keep going," I urge. "Please."

He nears my mound and says, "I intend to enjoy every drop of you."

His hands clamp around my hips and pull up, delivering me to him on a platter. He jerks me closer, diving in without warning, and a startled gasp escapes me. My eyes fly open as his tongue traces my center in a languid drag. Stars explode on the edge of my vision when he begins circling my clit, the pressure exactly what I need. My body twitches as he goes faster, and the climb to release feels like warp speed.

Between swirls, Trey hums, "You're so fucking responsive. That does something to me, Princess. I love how you tremble."

I moan quietly and shift against him, seeking more.

"What do you need, Raven? Tell me."

Vocalizing my pleasure has never been a strength of mine, but I groan softly to appease him. Trey shakes his head. "Not good enough. Doesn't this feel good, baby?" The tip of his tongue zigzags up my slit before he flicks my bundle of nerves.

I nod and arch my back. "Uh, huh. So good."

"So, say it. I wanna hear you."

I squeeze my eyes shut and bury the apprehension. It helps that he can't see me. "I've never felt anything like this. You're making me so wet," tumbles from my lips.

"Hell yeah, I am. You're dripping on my chin," he growls.

"That sounds . . . messy," I pant.

"Uh, huh. But I like getting dirty, Princess. This tells me how much you're loving my mouth." He licks me especially slow for emphasis. "Doesn't hurt that you taste better than a cupcake."

I do? That seems—

My musing is interrupted when Trey proves his words. His tongue attacks in swift strikes as he *really* starts eating me out. Each hit is a zap to my system, shocking me from top to bottom. He grips my ass and lifts me higher, leaving only my shoulder blades on the console. Trey's mouth latches onto my cleft, and I clench *everywhere* from the suction. I'm completely at his mercy as my climax nears.

"Oh, oh, wow. Holy shit. Yes, *that*. More, please more," I beg. My hands flail in frantic circles, desperate to reach him, but not able to. I settle for scratching along my scalp, heightening the full-body sensations further.

"That's better, Princess. Your words turn me on," he says roughly. Trey dips closer until his broad shoulders spread my legs wide. The noises he's making are filthy, considering his current position. Trey sounds like this is the best meal of his life, but I'm too far gone to be embarrassed. When his finger suddenly enters the equation, it's game over. As the tip rounds my opening and presses in, the pressure I'd been holding bursts free.

Spasms jolt through me as tingles race from my core. The intensity of this orgasm makes my eyes water as I quake help-lessly in his hold. Trey doesn't let up, riding the waves with me, and forces every ounce of pleasure out. I've been reduced to a trembling mass of Jell-O, and I've never felt better.

My heavy breathing fills the truck as I drift back to reality. I'm snapped from the lull as cotton slips up my legs. I sit up on my elbows and watch while Trey tugs my panties in place.

"Wh-what are you doing?" I clear the gravel from my throat. "Aren't we going to . . ." I let my sentence trail off, the implica-tion hanging.

Trey shakes his head. "Nah. I've got another idea."

I pause for a second, wariness slinking in. But then, I consider the fact he's getting me dressed and what the hell could be so bad about that?

"Okay . . . ?" Hesitation laces my voice.

"Don't look so scared, Princess. I'm not into anything *that* kinky." Trey's intense expression makes me squirm all over again.

He sprawls out along the seat with his back propped against

the door. His legs are stretched out wide and he pats the space between them, like a cutout made for me. I scoot off the console and maneuver into the place he's designated.

Trey places my hands on his thighs. "Just touch me," he says while dragging them higher.

My startled gaze snaps to his face. He's totally at ease. His move seems out of character, though, and has suspicion churning in my gut. Trey's default setting is vulgar so I'd be prepared for bold suggestions. It's just that this isn't one.

He's passing up sex for a hand job?

I choose not to question him and release the air trapped in my lungs. Trey guides me closer to the impressive bulge tenting his pants, my pulse rising with every deliberate inch.

Trey breaks the tense silence. "You nervous?"

"No, why?"

"You're shaking."

I take another deep breath, pushing away the residual doubt. "I wasn't expecting . . . this. I'm not sure what you're planning."

A rumble rolls through him. "That's the fun. I like keeping you guessing."

My movements slam to a halt. "You're still messing with me?"

Trey pulls against my resistance, but I'm not budging. "Easy, Princess. Didn't mean it like that. I just want your hands on me for now. There's no harm in that, right?"

I shake off his hold as my confidence pushes forward, ready to take over. He relaxes into the seat and rests his head against the window. My fingers work on undoing his jeans, and Trey shifts, allowing me to lower them under his ass. My nails trail up his briefs before I grip his covered shaft.

He jerks into my touch. "Fuck, yes. Take me out, Princess."

In the next beat, I have him free and pulsing in my palm. There's a bead of arousal at his tip, and he hisses when I spread the moisture around. I begin gentle strokes, up and down, testing his preferences. Trey has no patience for my teasing and wraps his hand around mine.

"I've waited too damn long for slow. Like this," he says while setting the pace. He's showing me how to pleasure him with quick twists and short jerks. Trey squeezes around the crown and growls in his throat. I watch our hands work in sync, studying the technique until the moves feel natural. I buck his assistance off while keeping the rhythm.

"Use some spit," he says.

I still at his unexpected words. "What?"

"Need some lube. A little saliva goes a long way, Princess. Don't be afraid to get creative.

Without overthinking, I lick my palm, making sure to gather plenty. When I touch him again, the strokes are much easier. His length slides within my grip, the movements slippery.

"Fuck, yes. Now you can really work me," he grunts.

As I grasp him harder and really take charge, the power of being in control thrums through me. He's at my mercy, and that's a heady sensation.

"Dammit, that's so fucking hot. Love you jerking me. Feels so good, baby," he pants while thrusting into my grip.

I'm discovering that Trey is a talker, and that's seriously sexy. With each filthy word, he's encouraging me to make this even better for him.

"Fuck, fuuuuuuck. You're sinful, Princess. Love getting your hands full of me." His voice is half-strangled.

My fingers tighten around his length as I jack him faster. I push him further while listening to his verbal encouragements, getting high off the expletives.

"I'm gonna come, Princess. Fuck, you're gonna make me bust so hard."

What does that mean? All over the ceiling?

My gaze darts around, searching for something he can finish

in. His truck is impeccably clean so my pants are the only thing lying around. Those won't work.

When he warns me again, I make an impulsive decision. As Trey's body locks up, I seal my lips over him. I capture his pleasure, shivering as the salty flavor hits my tongue, before swallowing several times. Unintelligible nonsense spills from his mouth as he continues to jerk against me. I keep up with the gentle suction until his muscles relax.

My cheeks burn as I sit up, uncertainty clinging like a second skin. As discreetly as possible, I wipe my mouth and ease out of his lap. I fidget and wait for Trey to say something, but he stays slouched with his eyes closed. I fidget while considering my next move. Maybe I should make the choice easy for us and head out. Trey probably wants to leave, most likely alone.

But tonight, he's full of surprises.

"Come here." He lifts his arm and beckons for me. I willingly fold against his chest. He kisses my forehead like a lover, but I'm not stupid enough to believe that's what's happening. He's just floating on his release and taking another moment to enjoy the rush. My heart pitter-patters regardless, and I sigh, trying to silence the giddy bliss taking over me.

I knew getting involved with Trey was trouble, but this is another level of screwed.

FOURTEEN

CLAIM

TREY

I STRETCH WITH A YAWN, attempting to remove the cobwebs from my brain. The coffee pot gurgles on the counter, and I track the slow drip like a lifeline. Damn, I slept real well. I smirk while thinking of the reason.

Raven has a spontaneous side I didn't see coming—pun very much intended. She took things to another level with that unexpected—yet deliberate—twist. It'll be fun discovering what else she's willing to do while testing her boundaries. Last night was the beginning, an appetizer before the feast, and I'm ready for a second serving.

I could have pushed and gone further, taken Raven all the way. Hell, that'd been the plan as we were gunning to my truck. But in the end, that didn't seem right. I fought against my body's demands, preferring to extend our time together and make this last a bit longer. I'm not in a hurry to fuck Raven and forget. She's different, meant to be enjoyed and savored.

A pit forms in my stomach when considering the lines I'm

blurring. After Raven sucked me off, I held her while the high wore off. In that moment, it'd felt impossible to shove her away. But that didn't mean I had to cuddle her. Probably didn't help the confusion either when I drove Raven home, asked for her number, and left with a smile.

Shit, I'm crossing wires left and right. Why am I acting this way?

I lick my lips and find the answer waiting. Raven's flavor lingers, just a hint, but it's there. Makes me wonder if she's still tasting me. I glance at the clock and figure she's probably at The Graze, selling cookies and cakes for Sunday brunch.

How would Raven react if I stopped by? Would she smile and be happy to see me? Would her eyes twinkle with desire? Would her fingers curl with craving? Would her lashes flutter as she remembered where my mouth was not even ten hours ago? Would she bite her lip and crave more?

I want to see her blush and squirm.

I glance at my phone at its spot on the ledge. A text is harmless. She won't read further into that than what I send. I reach for my cell, scrolling through the contacts until landing on Raven. What should I say? Thanks for the blowjob? Wanna meet up later?

With a huff, I toss the device away before typing a single word. This debate is stupid. Why am I worrying about fluffy shit? This madness can't be one-sided. At least I fucking hope not.

Suddenly I'm wide awake, and caffeine is no longer necessary. Restless energy floods my veins, and I need to take the edge off it. Kicking my ass in the gym will do the trick. I'll visit Raven after cleansing my system of this confusion. I shake the tension from my limbs before throwing on some dry-fit gear.

A convenient thing about this town is having everything within reasonable distance. Ten minutes later, I'm warming up on the treadmill while planning today's workout circuit. Dank sweat and musk hang in the air as I breathe deeply. Chicks never step foot in this place and I'm not surprised. Suits me fine not having any tits around to distract from the true purpose. Burning a few hours here will reset my mind to normal functioning. I've transitioned to weights when an unpleasant interruption shatters my concentration.

Dylan Porter saunters into my line of sight with a stupid grin on his face. "Trey, my man. How's it hanging?" I give him a chin lift before resuming my reps. Dylan doesn't take the hint. "Gonna pump some serious iron. Gotta bulk up for the ladies." He puffs out his chest before flexing, and I roll my eyes.

What a douche canoe.

"Good for you," I grit out, lowering the dumbbell. With my back to him, I start the next set.

Dylan rambles on. "Haven't seen you around Dagos lately. Heard you were at Cyclone last night. Great spot to pick up chicks."

I just keep lifting, offering nothing but an occasional grunt. Not sure what his point is, but I'm not feeding into it. If he's hoping for an invite next time, it won't come from me.

I'm switching to bicep curls when Dylan says, "Going to The Graze today. Lots of visiting hotties are looking for private tours, if you know what I mean."

Apparently, all he talks about is women. If he's trying to form a bond through our mutual appreciation for them, it's not working.

"I don't come here to socialize, Dylan. Got a point to make?"

"Not really." He shrugs. "Just being friendly."

My gaze flings to the stained ceiling as I sigh with extra emphasis. "Not the time or place, buddy. Kinda in the middle of something."

Just when I think Dylan has finally caught my drift, he tosses me a zinger. "Have you seen the new honey in town? Damn she's fine. I wanna hit that in all the right places."

What the actual fuck?

There's no way he's talking about Raven. I've never liked the guy, but he typically stays out of my way so there's never been a serious issue. Until now. My movements pause as I wait for him to elaborate.

"I'd like to pull that long hair while staring into her dark blue eyes. She's a dime, dude." Dylan continues running his mouth. I swear I can feel steam billowing from my ears.

Before knocking him out and causing a scene, I clarify. "The girl who works at Delilah's cafe?"

He claps and points at me. "Hell yes! I know you've checked her out."

That's all it takes for the impending storm to crash down. In the next moment, Dylan is smashed against the mirror with my forearm locked on his throat.

My voice is low and full of threat. "Had to be her, huh?"

His face turns red, but I don't let up.

"You'd be wise to never mention her again. Especially the way you're talking about her." Dylan struggles and gasps, clawing at my skin, but his efforts are useless.

"Her name doesn't enter your disgusting mouth. Understand?" I roar.

He chokes and sputters but doesn't give me an answer. I crush down on his windpipe until the veins in his neck are sure to pop.

"What in the hell is going on over here?"

My gaze jerks to Ben, the weekend manager, as he quickly approaches.

"None of your business," I growl.

He's smart to keep his distance. "Not sure what you're fighting about, but it doesn't belong in my gym. You know better, Trey."

I look back at Dylan while replying to Ben. "Well, this dipshit doesn't. Needs to learn a lesson or two about respect."

Ben snorts. "Give me a break. Never seen you like this so consider this a warning. Knock it off or get your ass out." With that, he turns and walks off.

I still don't release the dumbass in my grip. When I'm sure Dylan is on the verge of passing out, he slaps my arm and nods. I drop him immediately. He crumples to the floor, sucking in desperate gulps. Dylan coughs while rising on his hands and knees. I give him a few moments to recover and prepare for his backlash, weak as it might be.

Dylan doesn't disappoint.

He glares at me through watery slits. "You're a crazy motherfucker," he spits.

I quirk a bored brow. "Thanks for noticing. Stay away from Raven and we won't need to revisit this little dispute."

"She your girl?" His hoarse tone gives me vindication.

"Something like that," I say nonchalantly. She isn't my anything, but this moron doesn't need to know that.

"The way you tore at me, I'd say it's love." My expression drops as I take a menacing step toward him. Dylan throws up his palms. "Fuck, leave me alone. Do whatever you want with her."

"Damn straight and don't forget it," I tell him with a sneer.

"Didn't take you for the protective type," he mutters.

"Proves you don't know shit about me."

He rocks back on his heels. "Figured you'd be cool to swap stories with."

Fiery heat licks up my neck as I motion between us. "We're not the same. I have zero interest in whatever trash you're doing. Stay outta my business and we'll be golden."

"Gladly, dude. You're psycho."

"Yet you're still talking to me," I say. "And I'll be the one to walk away."

I do just that with aggression chasing me, desperate for an outlet. Dylan mumbles under his breath, and when I glance back, he's clicking around on his phone. Well, this will give everyone something new to talk about. Not sure I've ever lost my cool over a girl.

Totally worth it.

Most people expect this type of crap from me already. Guess I'm providing a helping hand by making it true. I can't control the shit coming out of Dylan's mouth, but hopefully he thinks twice next time.

I aim for the punching bag, picturing Dylan's smarmy face as the intended target. Thanks to him, my state is worse than when I arrived here. My focus is wrecked, and all I see is him approaching Raven. My hands curl into fists as fury pumps through my veins.

I pound the bag until my muscles are useless. Then, I push harder, making sure to drain them of every last ounce of toxicity. I collapse on the mat, wheezing as fire scorches my lungs. Once sitting up is possible, I spend far too long stretching life back into my limbs.

I'm one hundred percent spent and definitely need a shower to recharge my system. Thankfully the locker room is empty when I shuffle in so no one is around to bother me. I take plenty of time under the water, resting my forehead on the cool tile. The warm steam soaks into me while I breathe around the boulder on my chest. As I relax, my mind wanders to Raven and what she's doing. My dick stirs as I imagine her flushed skin as she bends over the hot stove. My palm trails down, but I'm too tired to answer the need trickling through me. I'll deal with it later. Better yet, I'll have Raven help.

When I'm dried off and dressed, a semblance of normal filters in. My cell beeps with a few notifications, and I check them with a barely-there glance. This time when I tap on Raven's number, I follow through with sending her a message.

ME: WHERE ARE YOU, PRINCESS?

The three dots appear immediately, and my skin tingles in anticipation of her response.

RAVEN: JUST GOT BACK TO JITTERS. WHY?

ME: NEED TO SEE YOU.

RAVEN: OKAY . . .

ME: YOU ALONE?

RAVEN: FOR NOW.

ME: KEEP IT THAT WAY.

There's a lull and I stare at the screen, ready for more. Our chat has me feeling plugged into a high-voltage outlet, and I'm waiting for the switch to flip.

RAVEN: IS IT WEIRD GETTING EXCITED BY THIS EXCHANGE?

ME: IT'D BE WEIRD IF YOU WEREN'T.

RAVEN: WANNA KNOW WHAT ELSE GETS ME GOING?

ME: TELL ME WHEN I GET THERE.

RAVEN: WHERE ARE YOU?

ME: ON MY WAY.

RAVEN: SHOULD I BE CONCERNED FOR MY LADY BITS?

ME: PROBABLY.

Lust travels straight to my dick as I pack up and rush out of the gym. Holding off on sex was the worst idea ever, but I'm about to rectify that. When I reach my truck, a shit-eating grin covers my face.

Ready or not, Princess, here I come.

FIFTEEN

BOOM

TREY

WHEN I PULL UP, THE cafe is dark and the sign says they're closed. After parking along the curb, I walk around to the back entrance, assuming that's where Raven will be. The door is propped open a crack so I kick away the stopper before stepping inside.

Low music plays from the kitchen, alerting me to her location. I watch from the hallway as she dances, unaware of my presence. She's swinging her hips while pouring something into a bowl. Raven's long hair is flowing down in a golden cascade. Her ass wiggles as she sways back and forth, hypnotizing me with the tantalizing tempo. She's wearing tight black leggings that are sprinkled with flour. Sweat dots her forehead and a radiant flush lights up her skin.

Fuck, she's gorgeous.

She startles when I knock on the wall, but the shock is quickly replaced with a smile.

"Hi, you," Raven says with a little wave.

I move into the room. "Hey, Princess. Still working?"

She nods. "Yup. Getting started on some items for tomorrow."

Raven takes a slow, and extremely obvious, perusal of my body. I prowl forward like a hunter with my prey in direct sight. Her sapphires gleam as she catches my want, reflecting her own back at me. Raven doesn't shy away. She boldly shows her longing for me.

The questions that haunted me this morning settle on the tip of my tongue. They fire out of me in rapid succession as I stalk closer.

"You happy to see me?"

"Uh, huh. I'm glad you're here," she says without pause.

My heart pounds faster. "You been thinking about me?"

Raven's lashes flutter. "Yes."

I point to her succulent mouth. "You still feeling me?"

A darker blush blooms on her cheeks as she whispers, "Yes."

"You embarrassed about what happened last night?"

"No," she says while biting her lip.

"You craving more?"

"So much," she admits while her feet shuffle in place.

Raven's sultry signals tell me everything else I need to know. While her thighs clench, the juncture between is calling to me. Her blue eyes are torches, lighting a path to the need buried inside.

I stride closer, studying the way her restless fingers tap the counter. "Finish telling me what else gets you horny, Princess."

She shoots me a saucy grin. "Stirring batter."

"Isn't that a huge part of your job?" I ask while gesturing to her discarded work in progress. My muddled brain finally catches up. "Wait a hot fucking minute. You're telling me—"

"I'm constantly turned on. Wanna see?"

"That's a question you've never gotta ask," I manage to choke out while creeping into her personal space. "Need a helping hand?"

Raven shakes her head and takes a step back. She shimmies out of her pants, exposing a pair of hot pink panties. I groan at the sight of the tiny thong, imagining the material between my teeth. Raven's shirt goes next, leaving her almost naked before me. I've never seen a hotter sight, and she's mine tonight.

She purrs like a sex kitten, "What do you think?"

"Damn, baby. You're not messing around." I'm getting dizzy while my dick turns to stone.

"I've been very busy stirring, and it's time for a break," Raven says while her fingers dance along her collarbone.

I scrub a hand over my mouth and take in the glorious view. It's more obvious than ever that yesterday was just a tease, a tiny taste to tide me over before the main event. She's been hiding all these luscious curves, but the bright dome lights are highlighting every seductive line. Raven's tits are high and perky, concealed by pink satin. Her slender waist leads to flared hips that connect to toned legs, which I want latched around me.

I bite my fist while picturing her ass. "Turn around," rumbles from my chest. She does, and those ripe globes might be my undoing. When she bends forward slightly, I curse the string of material blocking my show. "Fuck, Raven. Not sure I've seen anything sexier."

"We'll see about that." She faces me and unclasps her lacy bra.

I quickly glance over my shoulder. "Aren't you worried Delilah will show up?"

"Nope. I told her we had plans. She's out with Addy."

"That's good enough for me."

I kick out of my boots while unbuckling my jeans. In a mad flurry, I've got my pants down and tee whipped off. I stumble in my haste, and Raven laughs. My briefs are tenting big time as I stroke up her torso. When she bites her lip and drops her bra, I get a glimpse into heaven. I almost swallow my tongue, but decide on a better purpose for it.

As I lift her against me, our mouths crash together in a tidal wave. Raven wraps her legs around my waist, climbing higher, searching for a deeper connection. Our naked chests press together and static sizzles between us. She smells like sugar and flowers, making me itch for a hit of my addiction. Raven's scent is the strongest fucking drug, and I'm a willing addict. She moans into me when I grip her hips, grinding her against my cock.

I break away, and my gaze darts around, searching for a spot to nail Raven against. The gleaming surface next to us should do the trick. I set her sexy ass on the table and she practically leaps back into my arms.

"Holy fuck, that's freezing," she sputters.

I chuckle. "Hmm, I'll warm you up real quick. Lay back, Princess."

Raven allows me to press her down on the metal, and goose-bumps break out along her skin. Her nipples pebble into pointy peaks, and my tongue wags at the temptation. I gather the only scrap of fabric still covering her. With a jerk and tear, the panties fall away. She doesn't seem to care that they're ruined and swivels her core toward me.

"I want you," Raven moans while edging closer. Her yearning echoes in my ears before traveling south.

"Oh, yeah? Let's see," I say with lust coating my tone.

My fingers swipe through her wet slit, finding proof that stirring is a wicked form of foreplay. She's already primed and ready to go, which is the biggest fucking turn-on. I've barely touched Raven, but she's already squirming, her thighs trembling in my palms. My cock jolts with need, desperate for a turn, and ready to go off like a rocket.

She reaches for my briefs and snaps the elastic. "Take these off."

I gladly shove the confining material down, studying Raven's alluring features. Taking a deep breath, I try to stave off the demand already tightening in my balls. Everywhere I look appears coated in desire, which only makes shit worse.

Fuck it.

With a crinkle of foil and snap of rubber, I'm sheathed and ready. In the next beat, I'm lining up and pushing in. Her mouth hangs open on a soundless scream as I punch forward a few inches.

"Christ, you're tight. Squeezing me like a fist, Princess," I mumble. My thumb seeks out her clit and circles quickly, hoping to relax the stranglehold she's got on my cock.

Raven pants, "It's, uh, been a while. Oh, my, yes . . . far too long."

My eyes cross as she clenches tighter around me. I yank her to the end of the counter so she needs me to keep her steady. Having that control over her makes me hungry for more.

"You like being dirty, Princess? Getting fucked at work?"

"*Yessss,*" she says on an exhale.

"Someone might catch me sliding deep into your pussy. You like that?"

Raven arches into me. "I do. I really do."

After a few shallow pumps, I'm able to drive in all the way. Even through the condom, her slick heat blazes into me. Her tits bounce in rhythm with my thrusts, captivating me with each upward swing. I lean forward and suck a nipple into my mouth, biting down gently. The new sensation seems to add another level to Raven's pleasure.

Her fingers spear into my hair as she begs. "Oh, ohhhhh, more. *Please,* Trey." While slamming forward forcefully, I pull more of her silky flesh between my lips. I hit a special spot inside her, and she squeals. "You're so big, it almost hurts."

I'm being brutal, unable to hold back, as my body slams into hers. Raven doesn't seem to mind. I nibble and lick across her chest before latching onto the other taut tip. Her nails dig into my triceps, and the sting feels electrifying. I decide she's being too quiet.

I release Raven's tender skin with a pop before catching her feverish gaze. "Give me your words, baby. I want to hear all your pleasure."

A beautiful red hue paints her neck as she bows into my clutches. "It's never, ah, felt like this. Oh, my Lord, this is incredible. I feel you *everywhere*. Please keep going. Don't stop. Ever," she pleads on a gasp.

"I won't, Princess. My dick is gonna be stamped here forever. You'll be feeling me for months," I say through gritted teeth.

"I better be."

"You doubting me?"

"Not sure you're that powerful." Raven's taunt zaps straight to my balls, as if she's teasing them with her mouth.

"Better be careful what you're asking for," I growl against her throat.

"Make me," she replies on a groan.

Challenge accepted.

Pressure floods my groin as I hammer into her. I shove in before dragging out, again and again. Raven's pussy cinches around me and I almost shout from the pinching pleasure. Her muscles clamp tighter as we barrel toward climax. Tingles prickle my scalp as I plunge in and pull out in a rapid beat. My pelvis rolls into hers and Raven pushes back, creating electric friction.

I toss her leg over my arm to spread her even wider. This position allows me to reach that special place hidden deep within her. She tells me when I hit it.

Raven claws at my chest. "Wh-what are you doing to me? Oh, oh, fuck. I'm gonna come, yeah, almost there," she says.

"Give me what I want, Princess. Let me see you explode."

I'm pounding her into the table, threatening to topple the entire thing over. Pots clatter, and one crashes to the floor. The contents splatter over my foot but I hardly notice. Fire licks up my spine as our skin slaps together with my punishing thrusts.

"Co-coming," she wheezes. "Yes, yes, yes! Ohh, yes!" Her

core muscles spasm and quake, triggering my orgasm. My release shoots forward, blasting out like a shotgun. I'm jolting into her as nonsense expletives fall from my mouth. Any ache I've ever felt pours out of me as raw satisfaction floods in.

I fold on top of Raven, panting like a marathon runner. "Jesus, that was something." I can't seem to catch my breath as ecstasy thrashes within me.

The rapid rise and fall of her chest rocks my body. "I can't even . . . I mean, wow," she stutters while combing through my hair. "There isn't a definition for *that*."

My pride swells with her comment. "Couldn't agree more." And that's the truth. I'm committing this fuck to memory under *Best Yet*.

Peeling away from Raven's sugary skin feels like a crime, but I'm sweaty as fuck. When I pull out, she whines and tightens her legs around mine. Starting at her stomach, I kiss my way up until reaching her sinful lips.

"Don't worry. I'm not going anywhere," I murmur against her pout.

Raven's hands roam along my sides. "Good because I'm not ready to leave yet. Plus, you've gotta help with this mess."

I glance around, assessing the damage, and there's definite cleaning up to do. Utensils and pans are scattered everywhere, but that's not what catches my eye. A batch of something gooey managed to survive the assault and looks damn appetizing.

I dip a finger in the mixture before popping it into my mouth. Chocolate bursts on my tongue, and I moan. This goodness would taste even better served off Raven's tits.

Hmm. That's not a bad idea.

I glance at her and notice she's watching my movements. I gather more batter and bring it to her lips. She sucks my coated finger into her mouth, swirling around like a tornado. I choke when my dick hardens so fast it's got to be some sort of record.

Raven's gaze gleams with suggestion as she says, "I'm not called the master baker for nothing."

I smear frosting over her nipple before voicing the obvious. "How 'bout another round, Princess?"

SIXTEEN

DEAL

RAVEN

NOT SURE I COULD MOVE, even if someone paid me a million bucks. Aftershocks from my last orgasm twitch through me as I recover on the thick floor pad. This squishy rubber makes a great mattress in a moment of need. I crane my neck to glance at Trey lounging next to me, wearing nothing but a satisfied smirk.

I clear my scratchy throat. "Well, that was . . ."

"Fan-fucking-tastic," he finishes.

"You've got serious skills. Not sure I'll ever be the same," I confess.

"Fuck, yeah. My ears are still ringing from all your screaming." He mimics my breathy voice when saying, "More, Trey. Please, harder."

"Don't be a cocky dick," I laugh.

"What's that? You want more?" He nudges against me. We're naked and he's still . . .

"How are you hard?" I question with a gasp.

He looks at me like the answer is clearly written on his penis.

"I'm always horny. Plus, you're smokin' hot."

My cheeks heat at his compliment. "Thanks, I think. You're not so bad either." My gaze trails from Trey's dark hair to his scruffy jaw, down all those mouth-watering slabs of muscles lining his abdomen, and ending on that enormous—

"See something you like?"

My eyes snap up to his. "I'm totally busted, huh?"

He wags his brow. "Big time. I don't mind though. Take your fill," he says while humping the air.

My face bursts into flames, but I don't back down. "Oh, I definitely am."

"Don't be afraid to admit it. What's between us is combustible."

My lips purse. "For tonight."

Trey shakes his head. "Oh, no. I'll need a few more times, *at least*. We're just getting started, Princess."

A knot forms in my chest as I contemplate that concept. How long can I do this without getting attached? Maybe we should make this a one-and-done deal. A strange prickle rolls up my arms as I consider ending this so quickly. I'm not sure what's best.

He smooths the crease on my forehead. "You're thinking way too much. This is uncomplicated fun. Nothing to worry about."

Easy for him to say. Isn't this type of arrangement always more difficult for women? I think of my mother, and nausea attacks my stomach. She's had an endless list of flings while attempting to find the right man. I don't want to be like that. What if this wrecks me for the long haul? I swallow heavily while trying not to curl into a protective ball.

I decide to follow his lead and force my muscles to relax. "Guess fooling around a bit longer won't hurt," I say softly.

"Exactly. I need to know what else this naughty princess has up her sleeve," Trey muses while plucking my nipple.

I giggle and shuffle away, the tension disappearing as he shifts the mood. "Gah, no more. Pretty sure my body is in shock from all the pleasure."

I blindly reach for my clothes and find his shirt instead. As I toss the fabric over my head and inhale his delicious woodsy cologne, another round seems like a great idea. I pull the material to my nose and breathe deeply, getting dragged into the earthy scent. When I look over, Trey is pulling up his briefs and snaps me out of the crazy hazy. Or so I thought.

As vulnerability cloaks around me again, I blurt a truth. "I've never, ah, done anything like this before."

His complexion goes a little pale. "Please don't tell me you were a—"

I hold up my palm. "No, I wasn't a virgin, thank you very much. But I'm not very experienced. I've never had a random hookup and banging on the kitchen table is a tad out of my wheelhouse."

Trey snorts. "I'd hardly consider this random. We've been crossing paths since you arrived. This was bound to happen."

"And once we're done, it'll be hella awkward," I mumble.

"Only if we let it be," he says with a shrug. "When was the last time you had sex? No wait. A good, hard fuck."

I cough at his abrupt change in topic. "Um, that's none of your business."

"Don't be a prude, Princess. I'm just curious. Your dirty secrets won't end up in the tabloids."

I huff and shove his shoulder. "Don't be a jerk."

Trey chuckles. "I like that you call me out without being a bitch. It's nice. But seriously, just tell me."

I squint and tap my chin. "Well, there's not much to share. The last time was months ago, maybe almost a year." He looks shocked by that so I say, "Sex has never been that important to me. I've never understood why some people go so crazy for it. For me, it's more about the emotional connection, the deeper feelings. Sex is purely physical without any intimacy attached. A few pumps, grunts, wham, bam, and it's over. Love is more special."

Trey blinks slowly before scrubbing a hand over his mouth. "Wow, that's the saddest shit I've ever heard. The lazy saps you've fucked deserve a swift kick to the nuts. Good sex is everything, Princess. Yes, it's a physical act, but chemistry and passion give the motions life. It's a full body experience. You been doing it wrong, but I'm gonna change that."

"Excuse me?" I sputter.

"You heard me. If you think sex isn't important, there's something missing. The limp dicks you've fucked haven't done it right." Trey tickles up my arm before cursing. "Jesus, I can't believe the horrible injustice you've been subjected to. Someone needs to take care of you and put an end to this blasphemy."

"Oh, and this is the part where you volunteer?"

"Damn straight."

I cover my face and groan. "You're so ridiculous."

Trey shifts closer. "Why? Because I want to show you the light? What happened today was the tip of the iceberg. Pretty sure you said I've got mad skills. Let me show you all of them."

My pulse goes berserk thinking about all the orgasms I could have with him. "I'm honestly not sure how to respond."

"Just say yes. Let me be your sexpert."

"My what?"

"Your sex expert," he clarifies. "I'll teach you all the good stuff. I know positions that will keep you coming constantly." My thighs clench just thinking about that. Trey notices and smirks. "Uh huh, you like the sound of that? I'll expand your mind while exploring your body. We've already experimented with food, but there's plenty more where that came from. There's toys and games to push your boundaries . . ."

I'm getting concerned that my lady bits will spontaneously combust. "Okay, stop right there. This seems like a weird thing to plan. Can't we just have sex and see what happens? Like normal?"

Trey circles my elbow, making the slight touch erotic. I shiver and my nipples turn into pointed peaks, poking through his shirt. I have to stop myself from moaning when he leans forward and presses soft kisses up my neck.

"Your body thinks this is a great idea," he whispers in my ear. Trey isn't wrong. I'm ready to offer him whatever he wants when his fingers skim up my leg.

I manage to ask, "And what do you get out of this?"

He pulls away and stares at me with a blank expression. "Is that a serious question? I get to have sex with you."

"With no feeling," I mumble.

"Don't get stuck on the fluffy shit. You'll be feeling plenty."

"That's not my problem. I'm worried about getting too invested."

Trey clucks his tongue. "Falling for me? Nah, that won't happen. I'm an asshole, remember? No one can love me," he says in a tone that leaves no room for argument. "But if you start heading down that path, we'll stop. This won't be anything serious, okay? We'll have fantastic sex for a bit until you're ready to move on." He practically spits the last part out. I study his expression and find a sliver of frustration. Trey's jaw tics as his nostrils flare. When he catches me looking, his features flatten like the aggravation was never there.

I decide to let his reaction go, for now, and bring up another concern with the sexpert thing. "Planning for sex seems odd. This entire situation makes me a tad queasy. Maybe it's too much," I mumble, resting on my knee.

"So, it'd be better if we spontaneously hook up when the mood strikes? Because I'm totally fine with that."

I laugh. "You always know what to say. That does sound more natural. We've already discussed my satisfaction with your skills so far. And we've agreed to a few repeat performances. Pretty sure this topic is covered."

"I'm glad you agree," Trey hums.

I nod in response and silence settles in. Glancing around, I take stock of the epic disaster this place has become. Batter is dripping off the table, pots and pans are scattered on the floor, a bag of flour is ripped open, and the rest of our clothes are strewn about. It's a hot damn mess. Pretty positive I'm not much better. Reaching up to smooth my hair, I attempt to get the madness in order. I peek over at Trey to find him watching me. My eyes focus on the ink coloring his right side. This is the first chance I've had to actually study it.

"Will you tell me about your tattoos?"

Trey's posture visibly stiffens when my words register. He sucks in sharply. "Well, there's a bullshit explanation I usually share." His coffee eyes sear into me. "But maybe you'll get the truth outta me, Princess." He scrubs along his head and a rumble rises from him.

I touch his shoulder lightly. "You don't have to tell me if it bothers you."

He blows out a loud exhale. "It's fine. I just . . . don't talk about this shit. There's something about you, Princess. Feels like I can talk to you." His Adam's apple bobs with a slow swallow. "This one," Trey taps his pec, "is a combination of birthdates. The outer ring is my dad, my mom is second, and my sister is the center."

I edge forward to get a better look as he describes it. The design is a bunch of Roman numerals forming three circles within one another. I reach out but stop before my fingers touch his skin. Trey grips me, halting my retreat, and places my palm over the tattoo.

"It's okay," he mumbles. "I'm not fucking fragile."

"I never said you were," I murmur.

He searches my face before saying, "The one down my ribs are tire tracks." Trey moves my hand there. "My dad's car was a piece of shit and always breaking down. He'd never sell it though, called that Mustang his first love. The accident was fatal because the brake line was broken. My dad couldn't stop and smashed head first into a semi-truck. They all died on impact. These," he brushes my fingers down his waist, "are a replica of the marks left on the road." I gasp and press closer, needing to feel more of him. Trey rests his palm over mine before telling me more. "Jack went to the scene and took pictures. Didn't show me for a few years, which was smart. He went with me on my eighteenth birthday to get the ink done."

While gulping down emotion, words tumble out. "Wow, I'm not sure what to say. That's so special and thoughtful. What an incredible way to honor them, Trey. If you ever want to talk about them, I'd love to hear more. It means a lot that you told me." I want to smack my forehead for sounding desperate. "Just, thank you for trusting me with the truth."

Trey smirks and brushes hair off my cheeks. "Flustered looks good on you, Princess. But it's no big deal, I'm still sitting here. This is my life, and I'm used to it. Been dealing with this alone, other than Jack, but didn't wanna bullshit you."

I blink quickly, trying not to cry. Something tells me Trey wouldn't appreciate my tears. I stare at the black tracks permanently etched into his skin and reflect on the significance. My mind swirls as I think about his family. Then, I think about my dad. Now seems like my chance to tell him—who knows if I'll get another.

After clearing my throat, I go for it. "I'm really sorry for bringing them up that way at Jacked Up. I hadn't apologized yet. I shouldn't have mentioned them while we were fighting. My timing was rotten. I'm usually far more sensitive considering, um, well . . . I know how it is. I've experienced a horrific loss too." I lick my lips and take a deep breath, unsure why there are nerves bubbling all about. Trey waits silently while I struggle, until finding comfort in his brown stare. "My dad was killed in a car accident. Drunk driver to be exact."

"Fuck," Trey curses. "I'm damn sorry, Princess. Do you, uh, wanna talk about it?" His gaze darts away before coming back to mine. "I'm really bad with this shit. Clearly."

I cup his jaw, feeling a potent dose of intimacy in this moment. Invisible binds loop around us, the ends twisting together, and tying an indestructible knot. Maybe we won't always get along, or even talk, but this type of bond is forever. I feel it down into my marrow.

My nails scratch against his coarse stubble, soaking in this strange sensation a bit longer. "I don't have too much to tell about him. He died when I was five so even my memories are cloudy. But it was harder without him around, not having his presence and influence. Thinking about his death is terrible, but everything he's missed makes me the most upset. All those what-ifs. Does that make sense?"

He nods into my palm. "It does, and I totally get it. This explains that understanding I see in you."

Suddenly that glimmer I witnessed in Trey spreads wide open and the possibilities sparkle bright.

"Yeah, exactly. You don't have to be alone, Trey. There are supportive people who care about what's happened. It doesn't have to be a solitary suffering," I whisper.

He frowns, his brow falling low. "Don't push it, Princess. I'm not interested in lasting relationships or companionship. Swapping sob stories is bad enough."

My heart hurts hearing him say stuff like this. "Why do you feel that way?"

Trey scoffs, and his walls slam down. "Let's not go there, all right? You caught me in a weak moment, but I'm not pouring out my soul."

I watch his expressive features morph into an impassive mask.

The thickness in the air threatens to strangle me, and it might be too late to protect my heart against this man. I break our connection by pulling my hands away and scooting back. The time for being close is over, especially when Trey is all but shoving me away. He doesn't comment about my withdrawal, which isn't surprising. But his words stop my fidgeting fingers from reaching for my clothes.

"How's your mom? Are you guys close?"

I glance at him before focusing on a pile of flour on the floor. "Uh, she's fine, I think. We don't talk much."

"Why not?" he prods.

I'm not sure why he's asking, especially after shutting down my last question. My mother is a sore subject and difficult to talk about. But if knowing my story can help him, I'll spill my guts. I take a moment to steel my resolve against the negativity that surrounds her.

Tilting my chin to the ceiling, I blow out a lungful of bad energy. "My mom never got over my dad's passing. I lost a huge piece of her when he died. She became a hollow shell, shallow and plastic. Her attitude and personality changed dramatically, along with her life goals. She decided finding love was the answer but went about it the wrong way. With every new guy, she'd adapt to what he wanted. It was extremely upsetting to watch over and over. I learned pretty early that her priorities were out of whack, but she wouldn't listen to me. It created a huge divide between us and now, the gap is bigger than an ocean. Literally," I grumble.

"Damn, that sucks. I was hoping she made up for his absence and you lived happily ever after," Trey says.

"Hardly. Maybe that's why I've been more cautious and uninterested in sex. I've seen my mom use her body as a tool, and it makes me so sad. She puts out in hopes the guy will care about her. I don't ever want to be like that," I tell him honestly.

He groans. "Shit, you're making me feel like a schmuck for

sleeping with you."

A humorless laugh tumbles out of me. "Don't, seriously. I've come to terms with my mom and her type of dysfunction long ago. What we're doing is different. Plus, this isn't a habit for me, and I don't plan to make it one."

"Good, good. Not sure many could handle your claws," he says while pointing to marks on his arm.

My jaw drops. "Holy shit. I did that?"

"You see any other wild women in this kitchen?"

I press over my scorching cheeks. "I'm so sorry. Wow, those are pretty deep." My fingers trace a few of the scratches.

Trey shrugs. "I like it. Shows you were out of control. Also, makes me feel like I accomplished something else you haven't done."

"You're a special case, all right."

"As your sexpert and post-coital chat buddy," he clarifies.

I flick his bicep, attempting to dissolve the remaining strain inside of me. "Yes, you jerk. Don't worry, I won't fall in love with you. I have no expectations of more from you."

He wipes fake sweat off his forehead. "Glad that's taken care of. I think this calls for a drink. You got anything good hiding around here?"

I make a show of scanning the room. "Uh, that's a negative."

"Didn't think so. Let's clean this up and I'll buy you a beer."

I relax, realizing this will work out. "That sounds just right."

SEVENTEEN

SURPRISE

TREY

THE LOW BUZZ ECHOES OFF the concrete walls as the Camaro rises before me. When the hydraulic lift jolts to a stop, the garage is silent again. I like this quiet solitude, especially today. My mood is already piss poor and the sun is barely visible over the horizon. It's a welcome reprieve that no one is here yet. I don't need more reminders of what used to be.

Flashes of wrapped presents and cheerful singing threaten to crack my concentration, but I force them back. Those memories belong in the past, as in ancient history. Grabbing a wrench and a ratchet, my focus locks on the job.

Just as I'm loosening the drainage plug, Jack strolls in and ruins all my intentions.

"Hey, birthday boy. What the hell are you doing?"

I roll my eyes. "What does it look like?"

"You're not supposed to be working. I told you to do something fun to celebrate," he says while stepping under the car with me.

"I'm having a blast. Can't you tell?"

"Always a smartass."

"That's what you love most about me."

"Well, hurry up with that oil change. I'm taking you to break-fast."

I rub my forehead, feeling grease smear all over. "Thanks for the offer, but I'm not going. There's plenty to do here."

Jack tosses me a rag. "Not taking no for an answer. You can spare an hour or two. I'll even let you pick the place." He's more stubborn than me so arguing is worthless. Doesn't stop me from trying.

"Wow, thanks. Still gonna pass."

"Too damn bad. Your grumpy ass is getting fed."

"You're so damn kind," I gripe sarcastically.

"Only a few times a year, kid. Don't waste it."

I turn back to my tools and get going on completing the job. "Fine. We can go to Mel's after this is done."

Jack claps. "That's the spirit. I appreciate your enthusiasm."

"Your sarcasm sucks."

He rubs his nose with his middle finger. "Meet me outside. I'll be your personal chauffeur for the morning. Consider it part of your birthday gift."

I laugh at that. "You never buy me anything. Don't bother pretending."

"If you weren't such a shit about it, I'd get you all sorts of stuff."

"What a crock," I mumble.

"Aww, don't be a spoilsport. I've been extra creative this year. You'll be thanking me later, guaranteed." Jacks wags his brows.

My gut clenches when I think of the horrible possibilities. "Please don't tell me you planned a party or something stupid like that."

"Ha, I know you better than that. This is something you'll

actually enjoy."

I scratch my head absently. "It makes me nervous when you're secretive."

Jack backs away, giving me a thumbs-up. "That's the entire point. Now get your ass moving. I'm hungry."

It doesn't take long for me to finish the Camaro and clean myself up enough to be considered presentable. I stride out to Jack's truck and get situated in the passenger seat without a word. He pulls out of the lot with a shit-eating grin, which increases my suspicion about this entire outing. I stare out the window in an attempt to remove the boulder off my chest. It doesn't work, at all.

"What the hell do you have planned?" I ask after several minutes of silence.

He gives me a few side-eye glances before saying, "Not sure why you've always gotta ruin my fun."

"How is this fun for you?"

"Watching you squirm? It's one of my favorite hobbies."

I slouch deeper into the leather. "Not gonna tell me, are you?"

Jack purses his lips. "Not a chance, so stop obsessing about it."

"I do not have the patience for this," I say while glaring at the ceiling.

"What's got your balls in a twist?"

"Everything. It's just a bad day."

He reaches over to rub my shoulder. "They'd love to be here for you. Birthdays were always special at your house."

Fuck, how does he know me so well? I scrub down my face and curse loudly.

Jack sighs and says, "You can always talk to me, kid. I'm here for you, especially for these occasions."

I nod, a bit of the tension easing away. "Thanks, man. I appreciate it."

There's no way I'm telling him the extent of what's mixing me up. I've been thinking about my family more than usual since

Raven told me about her dad. The shit with her mom is screwed up too. After she shared all that with me, I wasn't sure how to act. I sure as shit didn't handle the situation well, playing it off like we should just fuck again. It's been almost a week, and we haven't talked. I'm not sure what the hell to do . . . about anything.

Jack continues reading my mind when he suddenly asks, "How's your girlfriend?"

I cough into my fist until the shock wears off. "Excuse me?" I croak.

He chuckles. "Can't fool me, kid. You've been seeing that pretty blonde baker a lot."

"Don't know what you're talking about." I would hardly classify my time spent with Raven as *a lot*.

We're pulling up to the diner as he says, "Heard Dylan Porter was showing interest in her but you slammed the brakes on that."

"Ah, hell. Seriously? Where'd you hear that crap?" I question, true as it might be.

Jack shrugs before getting out of the truck. When I get around the hood, he simply tells me, "There's some buzz in town about you two."

I snort. "Are you a permanent member of the gossip gals now? That's cute."

"Jealous?" he retorts. "They're a great group of ladies. If Marlene was thirty years younger, I'd be all over it."

Bile rushes up my throat. "You're gross. She's like a pesky grandma."

Jack's torso shakes with a hearty cackle. "Oh, kid. Your face is priceless."

"Such a dick," I say.

"Gotta keep your ass in line."

"The hell you barking about?"

"You need to lighten up. All gloom and doom. Pay attention

to what's happening around Garden Grove. It'll improve your mood."

"Fuck that noise. I have no desire to get involved. Plus, you're doing a fine job filling me in for whatever dumb reason."

"Ah, touché."

He slaps my back as the hostess shows us to a table. After we're seated, Jack leans back and smiles. "Does blondie know it's your birthday?"

I open the menu while muttering, "No. And I prefer to keep it that way."

He hums, rubbing his chin. "Interesting."

"Why is that? I don't like making a big deal about it."

"What?" He laughs. "You don't want a little something extra from her? Girls love an excuse to party."

"It's all good. I haven't spoken to her in nearly a week. Not sure Raven cares about celebrating with me."

"Couldn't be further from the truth," Jack mumbles under his breath while looking away.

I lean closer. "What was that?"

He faces me with a smirk as the server comes over. "Nothing. Never mind me. Whatcha getting to eat?"

After ordering, we spend the rest of our meal talking about nothing of importance. The space between us is filled with nonsense banter like usual. It's comforting and relaxing and makes me glad we did this. I tell him as much on the drive back to Jacked Up.

"Happy to force you out. Everyone needs a good breakfast on their birthday," he responds with a wink. "Cake too, but that's not my department."

It's Raven's, but I don't say that. Instead I tell him, "An omelet was plenty. I don't need anything else." Especially when the only dessert I crave is served off a sexy princess.

A warm sensation creeps up my neck as we pass Jitters. My

thoughts venture to the beautiful blonde baker, and I wonder what she's doing. Maybe I'll text her later.

"Any plans tonight?" Jack asks when we arrive at the garage.

I shake my head. "Nah. I'll see if anyone wants to grab a few beers."

He parks in front of the lobby but leaves the truck idling.

"Aren't you coming in?" I ask.

"Negative. Got some, uh, errands to run," he says while peering out the window, very obviously avoiding eye contact.

I scowl at him. "Don't you have a full day of repairs?"

"Meh, I'll get it done later."

"You're meeting up with a woman, aren't you?"

Jack hoots and smacks his palms together. "Yes! That's exactly what I'm doing."

I stare at him silently, assessing his behavior, but decide to brush it off. "All right. Whatever, man. Guess I'll see you whenever."

"Yup. Shouldn't take more than a few hours. You won't miss me."

I roll my eyes, done with this strange conversation. "Uh huh, sure." When I hop out of the cab, dense moisture from the humidity soaks into my arms. The temperature is already out of control, and it's not even noon. I salute Jack as he drives away before heading inside. I find the shop is empty, which really doesn't make any sense. Shane and Marcus should definitely be here by now. Fucking slackers.

Whatever. I'm not their boss. Jack is off fucking around so maybe they're on the same page.

Suits me fine.

I'm starting on the next car in my lineup when the entrance bell chimes. About damn time someone else shows up for work. I don't step away from the engine, not planning to pay them much mind.

"Well, hello there."

I whip around so quickly, my head almost slams into the hood. My eyes bulge when landing on Raven. "Jesus, Princess. You trying to kill me?"

She struts into the shop like a sex goddess. "Why would I want to do that?" Her voice is a seductive purr.

"I'm not sure, but you're a damn fine sight." And I'm not lying. Raven clearly came here with the intention of getting filthy.

I eat her up, savoring every piece like a buffet of delicacies. Raven's long hair is piled up in a messy bun, like a sassy golden halo. Those sinful lips are coated with bright red lipstick that's begging to be smeared off. She smiles sweetly when my eyes linger on her mouth, and I hold back a moan. Her taut stomach is exposed thanks to a tiny crop-top. And Lord have mercy, she's wearing cut-offs so short they should be illegal. Thinking about guys catching a glimpse of her ass has my blood boiling.

"You like?" she asks while spinning in a slow circle.

"So much," I tell her honestly.

"Mission accomplished."

"I'm impressed, Princess. This is the best surprise I've ever received," I say.

My visual foreplay ends at Raven's feet. Her murder-provoking outfit ends with a shiny pair of black high-heels. My cock twitches while picturing the spikes digging into me while I'm pounding into her.

Talk about walking temptation.

I'm so hard, my dick could jack up this vehicle. All brain functioning is focusing on bare skin so I barely notice what she's balancing on her hand. By sheer force, I bring my eyes to hers. Raven's expression is straight sex shooting into me.

"Whatcha got there?" I manage to choke out while gesturing to the pink box.

"Your birthday cake." Her tongue peeks out, and I groan.

"You baked for me?"

Raven nods. "Sure did. Jack made the order earlier this week. Told me to bring it by today."

"Sneaky bastard," I mutter while moving closer to her. "I'll need to send him a thank-you card."

"You definitely owe him. I don't do deliveries for just anyone."

"Glad you made an exception," I say while creeping into her personal space. "Haven't heard from you, Princess. Figured you were done with me."

Raven shrugs. "My phone stayed silent too. Goes both ways, Trey."

"I'll make up for staying away too long. Way, way too long."

She sets the cake down before running her palms up my chest. "I'm here now."

"You certainly are." My fingers dig into her hips before roaming down.

Raven tugs on my shirt, drawing me in. "You might be my favorite thing about Garden Grove," she whispers against my lips.

I chuckle, the sound turning into a dry rasp as she presses against me. "Princess, that means you haven't seen enough of this town. I'll show you more when we're done here."

"Oooh, a private tour?"

"*Very* private," I say before kissing up her throat. Raven's intoxicating perfume calls to me, like always. The sweet flowers permeate the oil and grease, mixing together in harmony.

She bows into my touch and murmurs, "Ready for your gift?"

I grind against her. "Never been more excited in my life."

In the next breath, I've got Raven hoisted up on the car's trunk. I wedge between her spread thighs, my hands skating up the smooth skin. Grease smears with every stroke of my palms. I never thought motor oil could be sexy, but Raven makes anything possible.

"You're filthy," I murmur against her parted lips.

Her tongue peeks out, almost licking me. "You've made me this way."

She breaks away, only to devour me with her hungry eyes. Her fingers reach for the zipper of my coveralls, pulling it down painfully slow. Raven leans in and whispers across my jaw, "Happy birthday."

EIGHTEEN

FLIRTING

RAVEN

I SWITCH THE WINDOW SIGN to closed before turning off the foyer lights. Thankfully no one is loitering at the tables so we'll be able to leave quickly. That works perfectly with my plans for the night.

Tingles dance up my spine as I think about Trey and our mid-morning fun at Jacked Up.

Planning the surprise for him was simple. Following through wasn't as easy. I'm not skilled in the art of seduction and wobbled in my heels more than once. Somehow, I collected the courage and managed to pull it off, which is so unlike me.

The shock on Trey's face was worth every nervous flutter in my belly. Being wild and reckless for a few weeks is giving me a huge confidence boost. Stepping out of my comfort zone of va-nilla sex and predictable partners is definitely accomplishing that.

I'm practically skipping my way back behind the counter when Delilah catches me.

"You're still smiling hours later. Must have been one helluva orgasm," she muses.

I shoot her a wide-eye stare. "Will you keep your voice down?"

Delilah glances around the empty cafe. "Because I'll offend all the customers?"

"Whatever, brat. Don't be jealous."

"Oh, I'm bright green with envy."

"What?" I sputter, my brow furrowing.

Her palms fly up. "Oh gosh, not about Trey. About the extreme fucking. You're playing out so many wild fantasies. If you ever decide to write a book, he's giving you great material." A soft giggle escapes me because I only gave her a very glossed-over version. Delilah doesn't pick up on my reaction before asking, "Where's he taking you for this date?"

I shake my head. "Not a date."

"Do you want it to be one?" She joins me near the bakery display case.

"No, no. I'm totally okay with our arrangement. We're having a little summer fling with no strings."

She tucks her chin and pierces me with a knowing look. "Whatever you say. Don't go falling for a guy like him."

I cross my arms. "Yeah, I know. He's emotionally unavailable. You're beating a tired horse." Even though I say the words with conviction, my stomach takes a dip. I circle back to her other question to distract myself. "I have no idea where we're going. He told me I need to see more of Garden Grove."

"What does that mean? I've taken you around."

"Well, yeah. But I guess he has other ideas."

"All right, whatever. When will he be here? I'm pretty impressed he's picking you up for this non-date."

I tap my phone on the counter to check the time. "In about fifteen minutes. What else needs to be done?" I scour the pristine interior of Jitters, searching for anything to tidy up.

Delilah shoos me away. "Nothing. Go upstairs and freshen up.

I'll finish counting the drawer and take inventory."

My heart warms at her thoughtfulness. I loop my arms around her for a quick hug. "You're the bestest. Thanks for everything."

"Uh, huh. You're welcome. When I'm getting all the good sex and you're going through a drought, remember this moment." Her heavy sigh puffs against my hair.

I pull back and give her a pout. "Do you wanna come with us? I'll tell Trey to bring a friend."

Delilah bends over, laughing hysterically. When it's all out of her system, she straightens and wrinkles her nose. "Um, you're hilarious. Thanks, but no thanks. I know all his friends and not happening. The only one I'd maybe consider is Shane, and he's got it bad for Addy. Don't worry about me, babe. I'll catch some swoony man meat soon enough."

I shimmy my shoulders and aim for the hallway. "Suit yourself. Maybe we can meet up later?"

"I can always assemble a squad for drinks and dancing. Text me when you're done with lover boy."

"Very funny," I call out before climbing the stairs to our loft.

I dig through my closet and settle on a blue strapless dress. The sweetheart neckline is killer for my boobs so hopefully Trey takes notice. I scoff at myself for that. If he didn't, I should be seriously concerned. That man gives off erotic vibes constantly.

When all my bits are covered by the silky material, I go into the bathroom to take care of the rest. I loosen the band holding up my hair and the blonde locks tumble down. Thankfully the topknot added a natural wave so I only add a few loose curls. A few dabs of rose perfume go on my neck. I smooth floral-scented lotion over my arms. I add another light layer of makeup. Anything more will immediately melt off in this heat.

After a final appraisal in the mirror, I grab my purse and check my cell. Trey has sent a message letting me know he's outside. A quiver of anticipation zips through me as I hustle to the street.

Trey's truck is idling in front of the shop, and I eagerly hop in.

"Hey, you," I greet him. My raspy tone is cringeworthy, but no one's here to blame me.

He's so effing handsome that a raging inferno is igniting in my lower belly. Trey's short hair is in careless disarray, like he's been running his fingers through it. The stark contrast between his dark features and white tee is shamefully delicious. I take a deep breath and inhale woodsy pine, which makes my mouth water.

Damn, I'm so screwed.

Trey's thumb swipes along my flushed face. "You look gorgeous, Princess. Might have to throw a few punches to keep other guys off you. That dress is . . . something else," he says while staring at my cleavage. His coffee eyes shine with hunger, and I shiver.

I try playing off the giddiness inside me by saying, "Better stop giving me compliments. I'll start to think you actually like me."

He pulls out onto the road before glancing over. "You're definitely growing on me. More to some parts of me than others." Trey points to his lap, and I roll my eyes.

"Always so dirty," I mumble.

"Don't pretend to hate it. You were all about my filthy hands earlier."

My cheeks suddenly blaze so I crank up the air conditioning. "Damn, it just got really hot in here."

"Did you do a lot of baking this afternoon? Were you stirring up a storm?"

I squirm in my seat as the temperature continues rising. "Maybe."

"Should I check?" Trey asks while his fingers skim up my thigh.

"Gah, stop. You're driving me crazy."

"With desire," he adds.

I nod. "Yes, obviously. You're turning me into a nympho."

He hums. "I really appreciate your honesty. You deserve a

reward. Maybe we should pull over."

"Or we can let it simmer so later will be more explosive."

"Damn, Princess. I've created a sexy spitfire."

I bite my lip and peek up at him. "You sure have."

"You're so fucking tempting," Trey groans. He adjusts his pants, but can't hide the enormous bulge tenting the zipper. He clears his throat and says, "Wish I hadn't picked a spot so far away."

"Where are we going?"

"There's this bistro brewery combo by the lake a few towns over. Takes about thirty minutes to drive there, but damn worth it. Hops isn't technically part of Garden Grove, but this is one of my favorite spots around these parts. It's definitely something for you to see. The view alone is incredible."

"Sounds pretty romantic," I find myself saying. My hopeless heart races at the implication. I silently berate the overly emotional organ.

He shrugs. "It's my birthday. I deserve to be spoiled."

"Speaking of, did you try the cake?"

Trey's hand is still on my leg, and he squeezes slightly. "So damn good, I almost ate the entire thing. The guys had to pry the fork from me so they could get a piece."

His praise makes me smile. "Good. I'm glad. I never know how the new recipes will turn out, but so far, there haven't been many complaints."

"You're really talented, Raven. Did you take classes? Or are you self-taught?"

I tip my hand back and forth. "Mostly watching a lot of You-Tube and cooking shows. I took an evening course in college, but it was mostly for fun. Baking has always been a hobby of mine. Guess it's paying off."

Trey bobs his head. "Hell yeah. Delilah is lucky to have you."

I laugh and glance out the window as we turn onto a gravel lane. "I'll make sure to tell her you said that." My eyes scan the expansive fields stretching in every direction. "Where the heck are you taking me? There's nothing around here."

"You'll be eating those words soon enough," he says while we travel over the rough terrain. "This place is a hidden gem. It's off the beaten path down this bumpy road, but we're almost there."

Trey wasn't lying. A few minutes later, we're parked by a stunning building that looks like a fancy log cabin. There are strings of lights lining the roof, windows, and doors that give the structure an iridescent glow. Even before going in, I can tell this place has a magical quality.

"It's something to remember," he murmurs. I turn away from the glorious sight to face him, sucking in sharply at the flames in his brown eyes. I nod mutely, not sure words can escape my throat.

"The restaurant isn't bad either," Trey adds.

Fire spreads in my chest as we stare, silently devouring each other. He leans forward, his fingers wrapping around my nape. I edge toward him, and Trey tugs me in the rest of the way. Our mouths meet in a soft press. When his tongue drags across my bottom lip, I gasp, and he dips inside. My palm cups his jaw, tilting just right, and we explore further. Sparks flare from my core when he sucks me deeper into him.

Trey breaks away, panting heavily. "Shit, Princess. You're too much. I can barely control the urge to toss you into the backseat and have my way with you."

"You won't hear me putting up a fuss."

He dives back in, but only for a moment. This kiss is brief, but no less tantalizing. The slow glide of his mouth against mine is a promise of more. "Waiting will make later even better, right?"

Trey makes me regret saying that earlier. I force myself to put necessary space between us, reaching for the door.

"You're right," I say and hop out. "Let's go. I wanna see inside."

He shakes his head. "Oh, no. We're sitting on the patio. That's the best part. It overlooks the water."

When we meet at the front of his truck, I reach for his hand.

"What the fuck are you doing?" he asks, jerking away.

"What does it look like? Holding your hand," I say and try again.

Trey lifts his arms up, far above me. "I don't do that fluffy shit."

I raise a brow. "So, you'll sleep with me but won't hold my hand?"

"Glad you're comprehending."

"Seriously?"

"Absolutely. I don't need another line blurred. Holding hands is too intimate."

I blink at him slowly. "That's such a pile of crap. If you hold my hand, that doesn't mean I'll fall head over heels."

Trey shrugs. "Not a chance I wanna take."

"You're no fun," I pout.

"Not happening, Princess. Not now, or ever. Now, get your ass moving. Ladies first." He gestures to the stone walkway. "We'll sit at the bar out here."

I grumble, just for fun. "Some gentleman you are."

Trey snorts. "Nope, don't even start with that. Made it perfectly clear the day we met I'm no Prince Charming."

"That's super true," I sigh.

He nudges me. "Don't be disappointed. I'll make up for it in other ways."

I lace my fingers together and mutter, "It's fine. I still don't understand all the guidelines for this no-strings fling thing. But I'll play by your rules. No worries." Tingles streak along my skin, and not the good kind. I gulp down pebbles of doubt and follow the path to the outdoor seating area.

Trey strokes up my back. "Just don't overthink it and go with the flow. There are certain things, like holding hands, I don't do because it muddies the water."

"Got it," I say. "Just sex, no mushy crap." I grin, but I feel my expression go brittle.

We're getting settled on a pair of stools when he replies, "You're making me feel like a dick for not holding your hand."

"What? I'm not doing anything. I didn't think it was a big deal. Let's move on."

"Okay," he says but doesn't sound convinced.

The bartender glides over, wearing a mini tube top that shows off her impressive rack. I check out the goodies while she bends toward Trey.

"Hi, handsome. Haven't seen you in a while."

In a snap, Trey turns on some swagger. I watch their exchange in fascination as an idea forms. He leans forward on the counter and smiles wide at her. "Hey, babe. Nice to see you. How've you been?"

"Oh, real good. Can't complain about spending summer hours out here. How's Jack?" she asks in a throaty tone I'm instantly jealous of.

Trey chuckles, the sound smoother than sex on the beach. "Yeah, I miss being out here. The garage has been so damn busy. And Jack is enjoying the bigger paychecks for sure."

She hums, licking her lips. "That's real nice. What'll you have to drink?" The hidden meaning is he can have *her* to eat.

"I'll have the new IPA you're brewing," he says and turns to me. "Vodka soda with lime?" A warm sensation floods me when he remembers my drink of choice.

"Yep, thanks," I tell him, purposely avoiding the chesty bartender.

After a few more blatantly obvious advances on Trey, she sashays off to get our drinks. I stare at him silently for a few beats, my gaze surveying his ridiculously sexy face. His usual smirk replaces the fake-ass smile he used with her.

I swallow the hurt down, fighting against my gut to keep this going. Trey is practically spelling out the shallow definition to our arrangement. My heart needs to stay the hell out of it. If I was smart, this would be our final night together. Not sure I can pull the trigger on walking away yet.

"What's up? You've got a strange look in your eye," he says, shifting closer to me.

I squint. "Maybe I should be offended by all that, but it was fun to see. You're suave as hell."

His forehead creases. "Not sure what you mean. That"—he motions between himself and her—"is harmless. We go way back."

"Yeah, sure. That girl is begging to hop in your lap," I say.

"Nah, she's an old friend. Nothing more."

"I don't really care what you consider her. What I'm upset about is missing out on the Don Juan goodness. When we met, it was instant enemy battle. I never got the nice Trey performance." His blank expression is priceless. "See? That's all I get. A bland look. I want you to reel me in."

Trey rubs his chin. "Let me get this straight. I'm supposed to flirt with you like we don't know each other?"

"Yeah, hit on me. It'll be fun."

"For who? I already know we're leaving together."

"Don't be a party pooper. Do it for me since you wouldn't hold my hand."

His lips flap with a heavy exhale. "This is the weirdest request, but all right. Wanna couple lines to make you blush?"

I shake my head. "No. I want it all. The full Cadillac experience. Really sell me, okay?" Trey rolls his shoulders like he's preparing for battle, and I crack up.

"Don't overthink this. Just go with the flow, right?" I repeat his bullshit from earlier.

"Yeah, yeah, very funny. Okay, look away. Pretend I don't exist to you."

I do what he says, turning toward the rippling lake. My gaze settles on the serenity of it, and for a moment, I almost get lost in it. My chest deflates with a sigh, and I relax into the seat. I feel a slight touch on my forearm and peek down at the source.

Trey clears his throat. "Hey, babe."

I raise my eyes to his and lift a brow.

"Yeah, you."

I look around, playing into his setup.

"Stop looking over your shoulder. And don't bother avoiding me."

I turn to face him, narrowing my eyes with false suspicion. "Do I know you?"

He bites his lip, and tendrils of lust unfurl in my veins.

"I've been watching you check me out. There's no denying it."

"Are you sure? I don't remember looking at you," I say.

"Oh, yes. You're still staring."

He's right. I am.

"Keep looking. It turns me on."

Wow, Trey is cranking up the heat, and I'm starting to feel the burn. "You're very forward. Has anyone ever told you that?"

He nods slowly, his coffee gaze making a lazy scan of my body. "And you're new around here, right? You must be. I'd never pass by a beauty like you."

My heart flutters—he's definitely getting to me. The pull is strong, and I already want to give in. "I've never been to this place before."

"How does it feel? Having all this attention solely on you? Pretty great, huh?"

I laugh as a very real blush rises on my cheeks. "Yes, it does." Oh, man. My voice is breathy, from fake flirting.

Trey's finger trails up and down my arm, goosebumps breaking out in his path. "Well, I can make it even better. Are you interested?"

I get captured by the desire pooling in his unwavering stare.

My throat bobs with a hefty gulp while I nod rapidly.

"Only for tonight," he adds, and I sigh. I've heard this part before. My lips purse as I wait for what's next. He chuckles, reading me well. "No promises. No romance. No tomorrow. But I'll guarantee one thing—pure, raw pleasure. The toe-curling, scream-so-loud-you'll-be-hoarse kind. Sound good?"

"Who would say no to that?" I ask in awe. He's selling me on this deal, all over again.

"Yeah, I thought so. Just don't go expecting more, all right? You'll only be disappointed," he says, and I guess this means all the ladies get the same spiel. I look away briefly, my gut churning with a mixture of lust and disgust.

Busty Bartender drops off our drinks, slamming my glass down rather aggressively. Vodka and soda sloshes over the side. I purse my lips and quirk a brow. She glares and huffs off. Seems someone is jealous. Trey picks up where we left off, bringing my focus back to him with ease.

"This is all I have to offer," he murmurs. "Can you handle that?"

"Sure," I mutter while contemplating the decision I made by playing this game.

He keeps going, his touch shifting to my bare thigh. I tremble in spite of the conflict waging within me.

"I bet you can, babe. Don't worry. I can be gentle . . . at first. You'll be begging for more in no time." I stay silent so he fills the gap. "You're not used to this, huh? Well, I take what I want. And honey, I want you real bad. I don't mind being forward and obvious about it. Why waste time, right?"

I glance at him, my jaw going slack at the raw passion reflected at me. "Yeah, might as well take what we want."

Trey hums. "Let me take care of you. I've got exactly what you need to soothe that ache." His hand drifts up my leg. My muscles jump beneath his palm, and he squeezes slightly.

"I like your hands on me," I say and shift against him.

"Now we're getting somewhere. I like hearing those words. Tell me more," he urges.

Trey loves the dirty talk. I circle his wrist, dragging him higher, until his fingertips brush my panties. I erase the distance between us, whispering in his ear, "You feel that? I'm so wet for you."

He coughs into his fist. "Damn, girl. You're asking for trouble, saying shit like that. Better save that sass for when you're under me. Then we'll see who's the cocky one."

I'm done messing around, ready to turn the tables. "Oh, yeah? Maybe I wanna be on top. Could you handle that?"

Trey wags his brow. "Fuck, yes. Does right now work for you?"

"I'll let you decide. It's your birthday and all," I say with a wink.

"Good choice, Princess. I'm about to show you the greatest night of your life," he murmurs against my neck. "You smell so fucking good."

I bow into him, stretching to give him more of me. "Was that all fake?" I moan quietly when he bites down gently.

Trey breaks away, his coffee browns searing into mine. "Nah, Princess. That was all original, just for you."

Damn, this man. He just reeled me all the way in.

NINETEEN

BET

TREY

SWEAT DRIPS OFF MY CHIN as I reach deeper into the engine. The ratchet clicks twice, signaling the bolt is set. I straighten from under the hood before wiping my face. It's hotter than hell in the garage with the air conditioner busted. The small space is boiling. It makes completing a job nearly unbearable.

I'm expelling a lungful of pure fire when my phone dings. I clean off my hands and check the message.

RAVEN: HEY, DIRTY. PLANS TONIGHT?

I grin at the nickname. She's been using it nonstop since my birthday. When I flirted with her at Hops, it was the real deal. She wanted the charm, so I gave it to her. Of course I made it dirty for her. I made sure Raven knew those words were just for her while she was screaming my name after dinner. I showed her just how filthy my mouth can be.

I shuffle my feet in front of the industrial fan while typing out a response.

ME: YOU? BECAUSE THAT'D BE AWESOME.

RAVEN: THAT'S WHAT I WAS THINKING.

We've only met up once since last weekend and that's not nearly enough. I'm teaching Raven the art of sexting though. We've been experimenting with that plenty. Her skills are a work in progress and I'll gladly make this a learning opportunity. Practice makes perfect, right?

ME: WHATCHA WEARING, PRINCESS.

RAVEN: AN APRON.

ME: AND?

RAVEN: THAT'S IT.

My eyes widen.

ME: LITTLE LIAR. YOU'RE AT WORK.

RAVEN: I'M IN THE LOFT. ALONE.

ME: WHY'S THAT?

RAVEN: JITTERS GOT TOO HOT WITH ALL MY STIRRING.

Damn, She's a quick study. And I'm hard.

Shit. Think about clowns and spiders and—

I'm glancing down at myself when my cell alerts me to another text. Any attempt at diffusing the situation in my pants is blown to smithereens when I tap on the picture. The screen *fills* with her cleavage, and it's surrounded by pink fabric. The image isn't pornographic. It's barely indecent. What I'm drooling over isn't anything more than a glimpse down her shirt, but it's the hottest fucking tease.

Yeah, it's official—Raven is trying to ruin me, and it's working. All I can do is stare while my dick pitches a serious tent. Good thing I'm already facing the wall.

A new notification yanks my focus off her tits.

RAVEN: STUNNED SPEECHLESS?

ME: KINDA BUSY TRYING TO CONCEAL A LOADED WEAPON AT WORK. WANNA HELP?

RAVEN: NOPE. ALREADY GOT MY HANDS FULL. GOOD LUCK WITH THAT.

RAVEN: BUT LATER, IT'S TOTALLY ON.

I don't reply, allowing her suggestion to hang in the air between us. Raven can squirm while wondering if I'll meet up with her. I glare at my dick, knowing there's no doubt about it, but a little guessing game won't hurt.

After getting my insatiable appetite under control in the bathroom, I get back to work. Focusing is a challenge, though. My thoughts continuously drift to blonde waves and sparkling sapphires. Lust isn't the only thing thrumming through my veins when it comes to her. Denying Raven's influence over the rest of me is no longer possible. The impact is a slow drip into my system, entering undetected until the potency builds.

I've kept myself numb so these feelings are unfamiliar, but not unpleasant. A calming sensation has been soothing my bitterness whenever she's near. That flood of peace is the greatest drug. Raven is dangerous and lethal, which makes her too fucking good to quit. There's no way in hell I'm ready to stop.

I'm ignoring the shifts in our connection, which makes me a coward more than anything. This shit is sure to explode in my face because I'm treading into dangerous territory. If I was a better man, Raven would be free of me already. But I'm a selfish prick and want to bask in these good vibes a bit longer.

The stifling heat gets worse at the peak of the afternoon, threatening to suffocate me. I've guzzled about two gallons of water, but my mouth still feels like a desert. Quitting time can't come soon enough.

I'm finishing up my last repair for the day when Shane saunters up to me. "Wanna go to happy hour?" he asks, leaning against the car's bumper.

Mirroring his pose, I say, "Sure. Where you thinking?"

He glances at me from the corner of an eye. "Heard from your girl? Maybe we could meet up with her."

"And Addy?" I add, not bothering to correct his label for Raven.

Avoiding my stare, Shane finds sudden interest in the ceiling.

"Uh, sure. That'd be cool."

"She mentioned hanging out but didn't say where. Wanna hit up Dagos? I can text her," I say.

"What about Boomers? We could play pool or something."

I scratch my chin. "Sure. It'll give us something to do. Is there a band tonight?"

"Doubt it. They're saving up for Garden Daze in a few weeks. I heard there's a rooftop party this year," he whoops.

"Right. Well, in this weather, I'll stay inside."

"Yeah, right. You've gotta give Raven the full experience."

That reminds me. I've got to plan a few more outings for her. She hasn't seen nearly enough of this town, and being the one to show her gives me a strange sense of pleasure.

"Whatever. Not the time to worry about that. Get cleaned up and we'll head out. I'll let her know where to meet us," I say before heading to the sink.

I scrub my hands until the skin burns. There're still grease stains. I'm fucking dirty, just like Raven calls me. I scoff at myself while grabbing my phone.

ME: WE'RE GOING TO BOOMERS FOR HH. YOU IN?

RAVEN: WE? AND WHAT'S HH?

ME: WE AS IN SHANE AND I. HH IS HAPPY HOUR.

She sends me the forehead-smacking emoji, and I laugh. Guess I'm teaching her new shit on the daily.

RAVEN: WHAT TIME? D JUST WENT UPSTAIRS TO GET READY. WE CAN LEAVE IN THIRTY.

ME: SEE YOU THEN.

Glancing at the clock, I do a quick calculation and kick my ass in gear.

"Hey," I call to Shane. He turns. "Going home to shower. The girls are meeting us there in half an hour. Hustle up."

He waves as I jog out to my truck. I peel off like an asshole on a mission, getting half-hard picturing Raven's outfit. She loves shocking me so I wonder if that pink apron is involved.

A few moments later, I'm pulling up to my place, not wasting time before racing inside. It doesn't take much for me to get ready so I'm back out the door in less than fifteen.

The parking lot is half-empty when I arrive, a decent sign we'll get a pool table. Boomers at daytime is a mellow scene so I easily spot the girls at a high-top table. I stop at the bar and see Shane huddling with Addy by the digital jukebox. Based on their matching grins, he's making a move. After ordering a beer, my feet automatically carry me to the empty seat next to Raven. She smiles at me while I sit down. To my disappointment, there's no apron in sight.

"Hey, Princess," I whisper.

Delilah makes a gagging sound. "That's still happening? What's the deal? Raven doesn't act like a princess."

I roll my eyes. "And this involves you how?"

"I think it's cute," Raven says. "At first, it was meant to be a dig. But I like it now. You wanna be a princess too, D?"

"No," Delilah replies quickly. "I don't want a silly nickname."

Raven holds a hand up to her mouth, stage-whispering to her friend. "Don't worry, your secret is safe with me. No one else needs to know what we called you in college."

Delilah's eyes widen, and she gasps. "No way, Rave. Keep your trap shut."

My gaze bounces between them, not sure I want to be involved in this. Until I see Raven's shirt and bust out laughing.

"Are you one?" I ask while point to her chest.

She glances down, tugging on the hem to get a better look. "What?"

"A badass."

Raven chuckles. "Um, duh. Haven't you noticed by now? D bought these for us as a symbol of our awesomeness. It's even better when we're both wearing them. I think the donkey is cute too."

I snort and shake my head. "Princess, I wanna record the things you say and collect them for a rainy day."

"Aww, that's kinda sweet. Your own Raven soundtrack. Will you play it when you're lonely?"

Prickles attack my neck, and for a second, I contemplate a fast getaway. If this uncomfortable conversion is any indicator, I'm in for a long fucking night. Raven is practically beaming at me while Delilah raises a bored brow, and I want off this loopy ride. My mind searches for anything else to talk about.

Raven pats my shoulder. "I'm totally messing with you, Dirty. Don't leave, okay?"

Before I can say anything, Delilah chimes in. "Oh, Lawd. There's too much sugar in the atmosphere for me. I'm going to the bar," she complains. "Have fun, lovebirds."

Once D saunters off, the pressure in my chest loosens. I reach for my beer and chug it, assuming rehydrating with booze is the best answer.

"How's Jacked Up?" Raven asks before taking a sip of her drink.

I comb through my hair and sigh, slouching deeper into the chair. "Hot as hell. The air condition busted yesterday so it's been a real treat."

Her nose wrinkles. "Ew, gross. I can't imagine. Sounds like you need a vacation while it's getting fixed."

"Nah, that stuff is overrated."

"Air conditioning?" she gasps.

I chuckle at her stunned expression. "No way, that's a necessity. I meant taking time off. If I need a break from reality, there's plenty of time after work. And I've got Sundays off."

Raven's lashes flutter as she takes in my words. "What? You've never had vacation time?" I shake my head.

"What about going away on a trip?"

"Everything I need is here," I say.

She tilts her face, appraising me. "Have you always lived in Garden Grove?"

"Yup. Born and raised."

"Always plan to stay?"

"Absolutely. No reason to leave. Next year I'll be twenty-five and Jack plans to make me co-owner of the garage." A curve lifts the corner of my lip. "Why you ask? Planning on moving on already?" My voice sounds gruffer than I thought it would. Her answer means more than it should.

Raven waves me off. "No, not at all. Just curious about you. So, no recent trips, but what about growing up? Where did you go on spring break and stuff?"

"Here," I say simply.

"Haven't you been outta state? What about going fishing in Canada or something?"

I rub my temple. "Nah. There's plenty of local lakes for that. I'm not much for travel, Princess. But tell me about your jet-setting and I'll pretend to care."

She shoves my arm. "Don't be like that. We're having a civil conversation. Your snark isn't warranted."

"Always calling me on my shit," I say.

"You'd be bored without me."

Instead of falling into that trap, I scan the game area, finding a few open options. "Wanna play something?" I ask, jutting my chin toward the corner.

Raven glances over and nods. "Sure, that'd be fun."

"We can make it more interesting," I suggest.

She turns back to me. "Such as?"

"A bet. There are three games so we can make this an arcade trifecta event. Winner takes all."

"What are the terms?" Raven is smart to question me.

I look around while considering the options and new territory to explore. I snap my fingers when an idea hits me. "If I win, we screw in the bathroom." I hitch my thumb in that general direction.

Raven sucks in sharply. "Here?"

I trace along the blush covering her from neck to cheek. "It'll be so hot, Princess."

She swallows, and her focus skitters down the dark hallway. "What if people hear us?"

"You'll have to be quiet."

Her lips purse. "You're always telling me to be louder."

"That will only be an issue if I win. Better make sure that doesn't happen," I taunt.

Raven rolls her shoulders back. "Right, okay. When *I win*, you have to tell me a secret. Something really juicy that no one else knows."

My gut clenches. "Good luck with that," I grit. No way she's getting anything significant out of me.

She pokes my bicep. "If I agree to bathroom sex, you can handle spilling a secret."

"Fine. Let's shake on it," I say, flipping my palm up.

Her hand slips into mine, and some sort of vibration passes between us.

"Deal", she agrees.

I order another round of drinks from a passing server. Then, I guide Raven to the dartboard. "Ever play before?" I gather two sets for us while waiting for her answer.

"Pffft, duh. Hasn't everyone?" Her confidence turns me on. Like everything she does, really.

I pass her three darts. "Ladies first."

Raven throws the first one wide, as in almost hitting an innocent bystander. She winces and apologizes to them.

"I'm a bit rusty." She peeks up at me and shrugs.

"Uh, huh. I bet that's all it is, Princess. You're making me feel pretty good about my chances," I say with a smirk.

Raven sticks her tongue out at me. "You're going down, Dirty."

"We'll see about that," I chuckle.

She proves fairly quickly this game is mine. I hit 301 before she understands what's happening. I offer Raven a high-five, which she begrudgingly accepts.

"Solid effort," I commend. "You almost got a bullseye."

Raven crosses her arms. "I lost count how many you got."

"Hey, we can't all be winners."

"So humble," she mutters.

I grin at her adorable pout. "Another?" I ask, pointing to her empty glass.

"Trying to get me drunk? Last time I was here, you had to drive me home. Not sure you want a repeat performance."

I tuck a loose lock behind her ear. Raven's blue eyes glow in the overhead lights, drawing me in. "I didn't mind, Princess. Couldn't take my eyes off you all night. You were tempting me something fierce with those dance moves," I murmur along her jaw. She leans into me as I press gentle kisses along her skin.

"But you were with another girl." She stretches her neck saying it.

"A poor attempt at distraction. I wanted you."

"Lucky me," she says and pinches my ass. "What's next?"

"In a hurry to lose, Princess?"

"Hardly. I'm ready to beat your butt."

Our drinks arrive, and we shift over to Big Buck Hunter.

"How's your aim?" I ask while handing over the orange rifle.

"Guess we'll see," she says.

We choose a safari theme and hold up our weapons. Before I can react, Raven is on the hunt. She's pumping the handle so fast, I can hardly see her hand. My dick jerks with jealousy, and all I can do is watch. It's safe to say she's won this round.

"Damn, Princess. I'm impressed. How'd you learn these mad skills?"

Raven blows on her nails before dusting them off. "I played a lot in college. The local dive bar had one, and we'd have tournaments for Thirsty Thursday."

I snort. "Wow, that's payed off. You kicked my ass. But"—I crack my knuckles—"there's one game left. This determines the winner."

"Bring it on. I'm ready," she says, bouncing on her toes.

With an arm around her waist, I steer us to the open pool table.

"Tie-breaker round," I whisper in her ear.

Raven shivers and twists slightly. I press my lips against her forehead.

"Full disclosure—I've never been very good at getting the balls in," she says.

I smile against her skin. "I'll help you, Princess."

She giggles. "I'm sure you will. Straight to the bathroom."

"Wanna rack?"

"Is that a new position we're gonna try?"

I feel my chest shake with laughter. "You're too much. Rack the balls," I say while gesturing to the triangle on the table. "Then you'll break."

"Um, maybe that should be your job. Pretty sure I'll screw it up," she mumbles.

"I don't mind."

"Of course not. The sooner you win . . ." She lets her words trail off.

"That's right." I set up the rack. "Grab a cue and come here."

She does as I tell her without hesitation. It fills my mind with filthy ideas. "Now, lean over and slide that wood between your fingers. Crack those balls hard," I rumble.

Raven chokes on a laugh. "Oh, my. I'm not sure we need to

bother. Let's skip right ahead—"

"No, this will be fun," I assure her.

She huffs but gets into position. I step behind her, real close, to guide her moves. My hand rests on hers, gliding along the smooth pool cue. My other palm drifts up her thigh before landing on the table, eliminating any space between us.

As her breathing picks up, I provide some inspiration. "Think about me guiding you to the sink. Your fingers will grip the cool porcelain while I unzip my pants. I'll yank those sexy leggings down before bending you over, and our eyes will clash in the mirror. When I enter you, we'll see the pleasure unfold there. I'll have to cover your mouth because it'll feel too good. I always wanna hear you. But this time, it has to be quiet. You'll whimper into my palm as I go faster. I'll get to watch you fall apart, Princess. How does that sound?"

Raven is putty in my grip and nods eagerly. "G-great. Now?"

"You don't wanna play first?"

"I forfeit," she croaks. "There's only so much I can take."

I chuckle, nipping along her shoulder. "You're in so much trouble, Princess. I'm gonna make sure you'll never forget me."

She shakes her head and mutters softly, "Too late."

TWENTY

MORE

RAVEN

THE RED FABRIC STRETCHES BETWEEN my hands as I hold up the swimsuit to get Delilah's opinion.

"What about this one?"

She fans her face. "Ooh, la la. Talk about a teeny-weenie bikini. Trey will love it."

I smirk at her. "Because you care what he thinks."

Delilah lifts a shoulder. "Meh, I'm working on it. Slowly. You're really good for him. That's become very obvious. I've never seen him so relaxed and . . . I don't know. Happy? When you two were messing around in the arcade at Boomers, it looked like a lot of fun. I sort of think he needs you in his life."

Her words hit me like a punch to the stomach. What's happening with Trey is purely physical. I know this, even if it seems like more to me. I can't fool myself into believing otherwise. Regardless of blurred lines and mixed signals, I'm aware of his rules. Or lack thereof. But going with the flow has never been this difficult.

I blow out a breath and glance out the boutique's window, watching leisurely traffic pass by. No one out there is in a hurry, so I shouldn't be either.

I can be patient and see where this road leads me. If we hit a dead end, so be it. Either way, I'm enjoying my time with Trey, in any capacity.

Delilah resumes her diligent search of the clearance section, and I stare at the suit in my grasp. I smile, considering what Trey has planned for us today. He didn't reveal much aside from we'd be getting wet, as in swimming. He made sure to clarify that I'd be plenty soaked by other means afterwards. My lower belly flutters once those thoughts take over. Sex with Trey is unconventional and exhilarating, and I love every minute of it.

Who needs commitment, right? I pinch the bridge of my nose as frustration builds. How long will I bobble back and forth? Until Trey breaks things off? I decide to take a chance and discuss the mess in my brain with Delilah.

"Hey, D."

Her head pops up over a clothing rack.

"Trey and I aren't dating or in a relationship . . . or anything with substance. Am I being stupid?"

Her forehead scrunches. "Still? It's been over a month. I figured if it was just sex, you'd be over it by now."

"But we don't see each other much at all, a few times a week, tops."

"What does that matter? Chemistry is instant, but your connection continues to grow. If this was only a fuckfest, Trey wouldn't have wasted time showing you around town. Trust me, he's never been like this before. Pretty sure you're together as more than *just friends*," she says with air quotes.

I rub my temples. "I seriously doubt he feels that way."

Delilah crosses her arms. "How do you know? Have you talked about it?"

"Not super recently, but there have been random occurrences. Trey has been very firm—*sex only*." I slash through the air, mimicking a judge's gavel.

She scoffs. "Survey says that's bullshit. I see how he looks at you. Ever since the beginning, you've been different for him. I bet if you gave him an ultimatum—"

"Are you serious? No way," I interrupt. "Not that I have personal experience with this, but backing him into a corner is a terrible idea. He should want to be with me on his own, not because I force him."

"Okay, that's true. What about a gentle nudge in the right direction?"

"Not sure that would go over well either."

"You'll never know without trying. If you want to be more than fuck buddies, make it happen," she states confidently.

"Yeah, I'm not so sure." This internal conflict is making me nauseous.

Delilah sighs. "Listen, Rave. I'm being a pushy bitch because you clearly care about him. If this keeps going, you're gonna fall in love." She curses when I dart my eyes away. "You're already at that point? Dammit, Raven."

I try digging myself out of this hole. "I'm not in love with Trey . . . yet. But I see it going somewhere."

"You two need to talk. Like today."

"I'll think about it," I say.

Delilah quirks a brow.

"What? I don't want to topple the house of cards," I admit.

"Where is he taking you?"

I grin. "His favorite place for swimming. That's pretty much all he told me."

She rolls her eyes. "He's so into you. Talk about romance with a side of cheese. Maybe he'll provide an opening to discuss your future together."

A snort bursts out of me. "Doubt it."

"You'll know when it's right. Just don't wait too long. It'll end up driving you crazy."

I tilt my head and study her expression. "Sounds like you're talking from experience."

She bites her nail. "What makes you say that?"

"Your words. And that expression," I say and motion to her face. "You have a secret, D?"

A rare blush paints her cheeks. "Um, well . . . there might be some truth to that."

I slap her arm. "You hussy! I've never heard about any guy who's twisted you up."

"That's because I prefer not to think about him," Delilah grumbles.

"Holy balls, I can't believe this." I clap excitedly. "Hard as nails Pookie-Pie has a weakness."

She glares at me for using her horrible nickname.

"You have a soft spot! What's his name? I want to know everything. It will take my mind off this Trey disaster for a bit."

She huffs. "I'd rather not discuss him, especially sober."

I give her the best puppy-dog eyes imaginable. "Pretty, pretty please?"

"Fine," she relents rather easily. "Pay for your sex suit and we'll get a drink at Dagos. If Addy is working, I'm not saying shit."

"Why?"

"Because she went to school with us and knows all about him. We made a pact never to speak of him again. Sound familiar? I'd hate to go back on my word," she says haughtily.

I giggle. "Pretty sure you do that constantly."

"That was the joke," she deadpans.

"Hardy, har, har. So hilarious."

"Promises are meant to be broken, right?"

"Not always, but okay. We'll dissect this in a second. I'll be right back," I tell her before heading to the register.

"Meet me outside," she calls from behind me. "I need some air."

I send her a thumbs-up as the stress within me releases. Delilah's secret is distracting me from my own. I'm not ready to face the truth and basking in hers is a great alternative.

The young cashier takes my card before swiping it. "You're really pretty," she blurts and looks away.

I'd been lost in thought so her comment surprises me. "Me? No way. But you must drive all the boys crazy at school," I tell her. Her youthful features are flawless.

She smiles and shakes her head. "I'm too shy for them. They don't notice me."

"Well, that's their loss."

"Same goes for you." She beams with bright blue eyes. "I hope you're getting treated like a princess."

I laugh at her choice of words. If only she knew. "Thanks, sweetie. That's really nice of you. You deserve to be spoiled like a queen. Wait for the guy who does, okay?"

She nods and hands over my goodies. "I will. No kissing frogs for this girl."

"Exactly. You've made my day and given me a needed boost. I really appreciate it."

"You're most welcome," she chirps. "See you around town!"

With a wave of goodbye, I walk to the door with a spring in my step.

"Dude, what took you so long?" Delilah complains when I get outside. "It's hot and I'm thirsty."

"You're just grumpy because I'm gonna find out about the one who got away."

She swats at me. "Shut up. I've been over him for years." Her stilted stride says otherwise.

When we step into the bar, I glance around for an available

spot. There are a few stools open, and the regular bartender, Greyson, is working. Before I can move that way, Delilah snags my hand and hauls me to a dark booth in the corner.

I bump into the edge and curse under my breath. "Seriously, D? I can hardly see across the table. Who's this space usually reserved for?"

"Dark and dirty discussions only. They're making a sign," she says.

Myla, a server who always seems to be here, drops off drinks we didn't order yet. "Wow, awesome. Just what I needed," Delilah tells her while taking a sip. "You're a lifesaver, My. Can you bring a couple more?"

"Uh, huh," Myla agrees before turning to me. "Want another right away?"

"That'd be super," I reply. "Thank you."

When Myla walks away, Delilah grabs my cocktail and chugs it down. I watch in fascination until only ice cubes remain. "You're starting to freak me out, D. I've never witnessed this side of you. What's the deal?"

She gnaws on her lip. "Just thinking about . . . *him* makes me antsy. Bleh, I'm pissed at myself for being like this. It's been too long." Delilah slouches into her seat. "I'll tell you everything now so we never have to discuss him again, okay?"

"Yeah, of course," I agree.

Her face tilts toward the ceiling as she blows out slowly. "Zeke was my neighbor growing up, he lived in the house right next to mine. The day he moved in is one I'll never forget. Shit, he was so dreamy, even at thirteen," Delilah sighs.

"Zee was a missing piece in this town and changed everything for me. Each time he walked into a room, my pulse went wild. It was so stupid, but I was young. My heart never stood a chance," she explains with a flourish. "Our bedroom windows were across from each other, and we'd sneak out at night, that whole cliché.

We were dumb kids with big dreams that mostly involved each other. Of course life isn't that easy, and shit went south. Zee's dad was a real asshole, he oozed cruelty. I'm surprised Zeke lasted that long living with him."

"What do you mean?" I ask, expecting the worst, a knot forming in my stomach.

Delilah has a faraway look in her eyes, like she's trapped in the past with him. "I heard him leaving after they'd had an especially bad fight. I'd always listen when the yelling started just in case the cops needed to be called. They often did. Zee said he'd come for me after I graduated but never did. He just got in his truck and left without a backward glance."

I lean forward, my elbows on the table. "Would you have gone with him?"

She shrugs and empties a third glass. "I wanted to, which says a lot. Garden Grove has always been my forever home, and I never planned to move away. I would have for Zee. Turns out our relationship was a sham, though. He didn't really want me, but I loved him something fierce, Rave," Delilah whispers with a bite.

"Shit, that's really sad. I had no idea there was a tragic romance in your past," I say softly.

She scoffs loudly. "Puh-lease, it was nothing but a teenage fling. Any true feelings were completely one-sided as it turned out, which is why your situation with Trey reminds me of Zee and me. I don't want you to get buried that deep without knowing. There's a familiar sparkle in your eye, Rave. Don't settle for the scraps he's offering when you want the entire meal, all right?"

I exhale a breath as I soak in her words. "Don't worry. I'll stop this thing with Trey before it gets to that point. I'm still safe, okay? I'm not completely sunk yet."

"Are you sure?"

"Yes, but I'm still processing this . . . unexpected revelation from you. Is Zeke the reason you're never interested in dating anyone seriously?"

Delilah waves me off. "Not on purpose, no. I don't know . . . maybe on some stupid subconscious level? I've gotten over him. Mostly, I mean. There are moments that make me weak and he comes back for an unwanted visit.

"It's water under the bridge and all that, though. He's long gone. I guess the moral of this story is 'Don't waste your love. Take what you want and don't be afraid to get what's deserved.' It's worth the risk, you know?"

Nerves bubble in my veins as I think about broaching this subject with Trey. "It can wait a few more weeks, right?" I ask her, my voice holds a gravelly plea.

She laughs and points at my face. "You're in control and know what's best. Follow that beautiful spirit of yours, Rave." Delilah looks off into the distance. Her gaze comes back to me when she asks, "Don't you need to meet him soon?"

I check the time and realize she's right. "But what about you? I can cancel so we can hang out. I'm not sure you're done venting . . . or coping," I motion to the row of drinks in front of her.

Delilah picks one up and takes a swig. "Pffft, no way. I'll call Addy and finish getting drunk. Go have fun on your next sightseeing adventure. You don't need my type of negativity right now."

"But D—"

She cuts me off. "Nope, don't start with the pity voice. I just need more vodka to cleanse my system. I'll have Zeke blocked out again in a few hours. Just don't let him break your heart and I'll be happy."

"Yeah, that makes two of us," I mumble quietly.

TWENTY-ONE

SECRET

RAVEN

ANOTHER WEEK HAS PASSED, AND I haven't found the guts to bring up the status of our relationship with Trey. Some might consider me a coward, but they're not enjoying the benefits of Trey's attention. My body is constantly buzzing with arousal, and it's a peak I'm not ready to fall from.

The words burn on my tongue each time he's around, which has been a lot over the last few days. Trey is keeping me occupied by showing off the best parts of this town, at least according to him.

I glance over at him while he drives, calm and relaxed behind the wheel. Today we're visiting Grove Park, and from his description, this could be the romantic spot I've been waiting for. The other locations haven't felt right for having a serious discussion. My cheeks heat as I recall a few . . . steamier highlights.

Trey appreciated my bikini choice when we visited his favorite camping spot by the river. I press against the leather seat and a delicious burn settles in my back. There are tender spots from where the tree's bark dug into me. I smile at the reminder.

"What's that look for, Princess?" Trey asks, catching my grin.

I bite my lip. "Just thinking about the secluded clearing you showed me after swimming."

He chuckles, and the deep rumble causes my thighs to clench. "Oh yeah. That was fucking hot. But what about before we went fishing? That alcove under the dock?"

"Oh, and after brunch at Mel's," I add. His favorite diner is delicious, for many reasons.

"We can't leave out the quickie behind Dagos."

I sigh happily at the memory. "Damn, we've got a lot of great moments."

Trey's hand settles on my knee. "And there's plenty more to come."

My eyes snap to his face when he provides me with the perfect opening. "Funny you say that," I start, but stop when we pull into a driveway.

I look up and around through the windshield, confusion filtering in. "Where are we? Whose house is this?" I ask as Trey puts the truck in park.

He's quiet for a moment, and I watch a crease form between his brows. "This is mine. Well, it is now. This was my house growing up."

I gasp as my gaze flies back to the structure in front of us, now holding much more meaning. Bright blue shutters pop against the white siding of the two-story home. There's an adorable wraparound porch with two empty chairs waiting for guests. My pulse pounds while I stare at the scene before me, allowing the significance to sink in.

My attention flickers back to Trey, finding him already looking at me. "What do you think, Princess?"

"Uh, I thought we were going to Grove Park?" I want to smack myself once the sentence tumbles out.

Trey coughs out a laugh. "Not happy with this spot? It was a last-minute decision. I've been feeling pretty bad about rigging our bet at Boomers. Seeing as you never stood a chance . . ."

I scoff at that but he keeps talking.

"I wanted to make it fair. So, this place has some secrets not many know about."

"W-why? I mean, what made you wanna show me? This is a big deal, Trey," I point out like an idiot.

He shrugs and slings an arm over the steering wheel. His coffee eyes peer at the house, *his family home*, before coming back to me. "Fuck if I know. I've given up trying to understand the madness you cause. I find myself doing all sorts of shit that never would have crossed my mind before."

His words spread warmth through me. They're like sweet honey in my veins. 'Wow, I'm speechless."

"Really? No more questions? You've always got something to say."

I pinch his bicep. "Fine, maybe one. Do we get to go inside?"

Trey swallows heavily and glances away. "Nah, Princess. I never go that far. We can check out the backyard though. There are a few things to see there. Better than nothing, right?"

"Don't be silly. Just bringing me here at all is something I'd never expect."

"Good," he hums. "That's what I was going for."

Trey steps out of the truck and I follow suit, meeting him on the cobbled path. We walk silently around the house before reaching a tall wood fence. He opens the gate, letting me go first. My eyes bounce around the lush expanse. Everything is green and alive, filling the space with color. The lawn is perfectly manicured without a single weed. Flowered plants line the sides and far edge. But a large oak tree in the right corner is what steals the show. There's a swing hanging from a thick branch, and Trey leads me over to it.

"Here, sit down and I'll push you. I've got some stuff to tell you."

I do what he says without hesitation, my skin prickling as a breeze floats through the air. This moment vibrates with importance, like something monumental is about to happen. I scoot to the edge of the seat, eager to hear anything he's willing to share. Glancing up over my shoulder, I wait for Trey's next move. His fingers wrap around the knotted ropes before drawing me back and letting go. I sway forward gently before moving back, Trey keeping me going with a press to my shoulders. The slow rhythm lulls me into a sense of peace.

Trey clears his throat, and my ears perk up. "The house belongs to me, but I never go in. It's too big, too haunted. My parents left it to me in their will for when I turned eighteen. Jack had been taking care of it prior to that. I contemplated selling it, but even my cold heart couldn't do it. There's just something about this place that calls to me. Always has." He lets out a deep sigh. "It's bare now, a clean slate, ready for a fresh start. Guess it's a symbol of my life. Just waiting for . . . something right to fill the blank walls and empty space. Shit, that's depressing as hell," he mutters.

My hands circle his wrists, a tremble passing from him into me. "It's not, Trey. This is life and you've suffered a horrific tragedy. I think your words are inspirational."

He snorts, threatening to slam a barrier down between us.

I have to tread lightly. "Keep going, please."

After a minute of silence, he does. "I'm not ignorant enough to believe no one else understands loss. People deal with death on the daily. That's the harsh truth. But for a kid, losing his parents and sister, it's totally obliterating. What's left, you know?"

The question is rhetorical, but I nod regardless, encouraging him to continue.

"I've never been an emotional guy, even as a little tyke, but after the accident, I really shut down. When people smothered me with attention, it got worse. Everyone was a target for the anger inside of me, and I released it whenever they tried comforting me. I pushed them away until they finally left me alone. There was nothing I gave a fuck about, so what was stopping me? Eventually the shitty attitude became habit, taking root and growing beyond reason. I felt better staying closed off and detached than allowing grief to rule me. I didn't know how to balance it. I still don't, clearly.," he says honestly.

"You're doing a good job now," I tell him, unable to control the wobble in my voice.

Trey grumbles, "Yeah, because of you. First person to come along that saw me and wanted different for me. Not sure why with how I was treating you. Damn lucky you didn't give up on me. That cupcake pushed me over the edge, though. You've made me realize life doesn't have to be the pitfall of isolation I've created. It's not bad to rely on others and let them offer support. And I'd never admit that to anyone else." He shrugs.

Trey's words are a balm on my ragged nerves. I've been waiting to hear this from him, and it gives me hope that we're becoming more than a quick fling. This must be a huge step for him. He's peeling away the damaged layers, exposing the tenderness beneath. I'm sure Trey doesn't let many people see this side of him and it means everything that he's choosing to show me. I don't need to ask where we're headed—the gears are already in motion.

Suddenly the confining pressure around my ribs gives out and I can breathe freely for what seems like the first time. I gasp while emotion stings my eyes. I blink quickly to ease the burn, thankful Trey can't see me. I swallow past the lump in my throat, but still can't speak. When my silence stretches on, Trey notices.

"You okay?"

Nodding quickly and sniffling gives me away so I stand before creating some space between us. My skin is on fire from my reaction, and I don't want to freak Trey out. He'll think I'm a basket case and take it all back.

Dammit, I'm a mess.

He misinterprets the reason for my tears and follows me. "You don't gotta cry over my shit, Raven. It's in the past."

I let him believe that's what has me choked up. "You're an amazing man." My feet carry me to him automatically, like a pulley system wheeling me in.

"Nah, Princess. I've blinded you with too many orgasms."

"That might be true," I titter against his chest.

His humor rumbles through him, in some places more than others. "Want a few more? We can go in the treehouse. I've never had a girl up there. It'd be nice to christen this place. It's sturdy and safe, I promise."

I shiver before peeking at him from under lowered lids. "How could I refuse an offer like that?"

"Easy—you don't," he whispers in my ear.

With a palm on my lower back, he guides me up the ladder. Trey pinches my ass a few times, and I giggle uncontrollably. It's like I've taken a shot of bliss. Heck, I might be riding a rainbow straight to Utopia. All because of the man behind me. I crawl onto the floor and take in the small space. There isn't much to the room except unfinished wood and a stack of blankets laid out in the corner.

Who needs a bed, right? Not us . . . *ever.*

Trey explains, "I come up here sometimes. As an escape. No one knows that either. Guess you're getting all my secrets tonight."

My stomach flutters with his confession, and I turn to face him. His brown eyes are flaring with heat, but something else is flickering there too. "Hey, you," I say, simply.

"Hi, Princess. C'mere," Trey replies with a curl of his pointer finger.

I shuffle closer, and he tugs me in. He lifts my chin and stares into me, straight down to the very essence of my soul.

"You're so beautiful." The words scratch from his throat like they hurt.

My belly takes a little dip. "Why does that sound like a bad thing?"

His nose brushes mine, barely-there strokes that I feel everywhere. "It's not, but you're turning me upside down. I'm not sure what do with myself anymore." I wait for Trey to say more but he doesn't. Instead his lips press to mine, the touch gentle and soothing.

Talking isn't necessary as we lazily strip out of our clothes. Each newly uncovered piece is meant to tease as our hands explore further. I can already tell this time is different, the typical hurry between us absent. When we're completely bared to one another, Trey lays me down on the soft fleece. I arch against him, and he presses into me, we join in a new way.

As our bodies mold together as one, a stronger bond forms. If there are any lines still separating us, this will obliterate them. Each slide is slow and smooth, the glide a silky caress to be savored. It's like he's cherishing every moment like this time together is precious.

Trey showers every part of me with delicate kisses, making sure to cover every inch. My hands dance along his sculpted forearms, following the veins like a map to his heart. Hushed whispers are exchanged in the sliver of space between our parted lips. He doesn't encourage me to talk dirty or tell him how filthy I feel. Those words don't belong right now.

His palms drift over mine before our fingers lock, the connection sealing between our heated skin. In one second, a single breath, so much can change. It's a moment in the span of a lifetime. Who notices such a small detail? I do. And right now, I'm aware of many things. My eyes water at our intimacy and I don't stand a chance. Not against this.

We ease over the edge in languid ecstasy, the fall steep but expected. I gasp into Trey's mouth, and he captures my moan with another kiss. We're clutching onto each other like a lifeforce, and I never want this moment to be over.

Unfortunately, it ends all too soon. I notice the moment Trey realizes what's been shared between us. His entire body goes rigid before he rises above me. His wild gaze searches mine, mirroring the frantic desperation of my own. The difference is I'm pulling closer and he's pushing away. We stare silently, saying so much without uttering a single syllable.

When Trey rolls away, his movements are stiff and jerky. "Fuck. Dammit. Why did we do that?" He gives his dark hair an absent tug. Pain slices into my abdomen as he keeps going. "This was a mistake, Raven."

"W-why do you say that?" I ask, reaching for the covers.

He still isn't looking at me. "It should never have happened like . . . *that*," he spits the last word out like a curse.

After all that sweetness, he yanks me back to harsh reality. His rejection hits harder than any physical blow. I remain mute, unable to form a coherent thought in my jumbled brain. I need to tell him the feelings building inside me, love dueling with hurt. It will only get worse the longer I wait. But I can't force anything past my strangled throat. I choke on a garbled sob, and Trey twists around. His coffee eyes have never been so distant.

"Don't make this a big issue, Raven. It didn't mean anything." His flat tone makes me wince.

Blowing out evenly, I face the cut-out window and beg my eyes to stop leaking. When my emotions are collected enough, I work on the next hurdle. I wrap the top blanket around me before scooting off the pile, heading for my clothes. Trey gets up too, picking up his briefs and slipping them up his legs. As I'm stepping into my jeans, Trey fills the silence.

"Don't freeze up on me, all right? I've never done this

before—*ever*. I'm all fucked up after talking about my family. And being here, at this house . . . it's too much," he says, but I'm not listening. I don't want to hear his excuses, especially when my chest feels like it's caving in.

When we're fully dressed, Trey gestures to the ladder. "Ladies first."

"Such a fucking gentleman," I mutter.

He chuckles as I descend. "Never claimed to be one, remember?"

I curse all the way down because he's right. I was foolish enough to fall hard when he never really promised anything.

The blame rests heavy on my shoulders and I've got a decision to make. I can't keep going on like this so maybe it's better to just walk away. The thought stabs into me like a like a hot stake. But what other choice do I have?

Trey hops off the last rung and lands in front of me. "Listen, we're a bit raw and exposed at the moment. Let's get out of here and get a drink. We'll cool off and figure out what the actual fuck went down up there," he says, pointing to the treehouse.

"Whatever," I mumble and turn for the gate.

"We'll be laughing about this in no time," Trey murmurs.

Highly effing doubtful, but I don't have the strength to argue.

TWENTY-TWO

BURN

TREY

GREYSON BRINGS OVER ANOTHER ROUND, setting a beer in front of me. He wags his brows, gesturing to Raven, and I scowl. There's nothing to be happy about. Regret churns fast in my stomach, and I chug half the bottle in one swallow. As I recall the last few hours, moments blur into a heap of terrible decisions. What the hell happens now?

Raven is perched on the stool next to me, yet she seems miles away. I'm ignoring the enormous elephant in the very crowded room. It's nearly impossible. My instincts are blaring like a foghorn, telling me to get out before this gets worse. I've never been very good at listening though.

"You gonna talk to me?" I ask her.

She shrugs before sipping on her cocktail.

"What's wrong, Princess?"

Her spine snaps straight as the nickname leaves my mouth. I'm expecting a tidal wave of expletives, but all she says is, "Nothing."

My intuition with women tends to be narrowly focused on

certain aspects, but I can tell when they're upset. And Raven definitely is.

Giving her a solid onceover, I take inventory before pressing the issue. Tangles knot the ends of her blonde hair, makeup is smudged around her eyes, and her naturally pouty lips are extra plump. Raven looks well fucked, but that isn't what happened tonight. She's going to make assumptions and have higher expectations, and I want no part of that. Raven got a big fucking hint when I slammed on the brakes after . . . whatever that was in the treehouse.

I gave away too much, pouring my pent-up grief all over her. Raven accepted the burden with open arms, and without thinking twice, I gave her even more of me. With each piece, the space between us gradually erased until nothing remained. I practically collapsed into her welcoming embrace, and Raven clutched me tighter. I didn't read the signals or pay attention to her reactions. Once we were naked, I was too far gone to realize the epic disaster looming around us, waiting for the ideal moment to strike.

I rub my temples while I try to figure out how to fix this. I've really screwed this shit up and am not sure how to get us back on even ground. Before I can broach the subject, a raspy voice calls out to me.

"Hey, handsome. This is a wonderful coincidence."

I turn my head toward her, blinking rapidly. "Olive?"

Her face brightens. "Ah, great memory. Wasn't sure you'd know who I was." She takes a seat and leans closer, her perfume is a sickly-sweet cloud. I cough while she says, "I'm ready for that raincheck."

From the corner of my eye, I watch Raven peer around me. Olive doesn't notice, or if she does, is choosing to ignore her presence. Her nails dig into my shoulder. The aggressive touch feels all wrong. My teeth clench shut, the strain adding tension throughout me. I twist toward her, hoping to block Raven's prying stare.

"Ah, thanks for the offer, babe." I pluck her hand off me. "I've already got plans." I gesture to Raven.

Olive shifts to see who I'm referring to, and I wait to see how this will play out. My gaze bounces between them as I contemplate the outcomes. Raven is focusing on the way Olive's fingers gouge into my skin. The threat in her expression is crystal clear, yet she doesn't say anything. Raven's sapphires are sparking with fury, but the hurt behind them pummels me.

Fuck, this shit storm is brewing fast, and Olive isn't helping.

"It was great seeing you again," I lie straight through pinched lips.

Olive doesn't give up easily. "Give me a call when you're done with her," she murmurs in my ear. Disgust snakes up my spine as she slides something into my pocket. In the next breath, she's strutting across the bar and out of sight.

I take a deep breath before facing Raven, preparing for the worst. She attempts to cover her watery eyes with a yawn, but I see her reaction for what it is. Before I can try repairing the damage, a voice like nails on a chalkboard interrupts.

"Well, if it isn't the happy couple. Everyone in town will be so relieved you two have finally made it official," Gossip-Queen Marlene chirps like an annoying canary.

Can I catch a fucking break?

My fists tremble under the counter. "Not sure what you're talking about, ma'am." I try to remain calm, but my blood pressure is rising through the roof.

Marlene clucks her tongue and looks between us. "You're being very obvious. Anyone with decent vision can see the love connection."

I choke on my sip of beer. "Just friends out for a drink, Marlene. Stop creating gossip, yeah?"

Raven sucks in sharply before swiveling on her stool. When

I glance at her, she's packing up her purse, getting ready to flee. "Where the hell you going?"

"Away," is all she says.

Of course Marlene can't stay quiet. "Oh, my. Did I cause a squabble?"

Raven smiles at her quickly, but the expression is fake. "Not at all. Friends bicker all the time." She looks at me. "It's nothing serious."

A hollow pang echoes off my chest. I rub at the ache. "Uh, yeah. What she said," I tell Marlene as Raven wanders off.

"I was just offering my congratulations. What's going on? Is there anything I can do?" The words are meant to sound genuine, but her jovial tone exposes the truth of her intrusion.

"Bug off, Marlene. You've done enough," I growl and slide off my seat.

"Well, good luck. Looks like you'll need it," she calls behind me.

My middle finger itches to lift at her, but I hold back. I've got a much bigger problem currently dashing out the door. Raven is hauling ass along the sidewalk when I catch up.

I grip her arm and steer us into the nearby alley. "Where's the fucking fire? We heading someplace else?"

Her head is shaking so fast, all I see is a blonde whirlwind. "I'm going home," she says with a tremor in her voice.

My jaw tics. "The fuck? Is this about what Marlene said?"

That makes Raven's blazing blues snap to mine. "No, moron. I'm upset because of you." She stabs a finger into my chest.

I scrub down my face and groan. "What'd I do to piss you off?"

"So many things, Trey. I can't begin to count them," Raven says and crosses her arms.

"Try me," I insist.

She rests against the brick wall and stares up at the sky. "Are we together, Trey? Dating? In a relationship? Anything?"

My neck jerks back. I wasn't expecting that. "I'm not your boyfriend, Raven. This is just casual fun, like we agreed on."

Her lids slam shut while she mutters, "Nothing has changed?"

"Why would it? We made it clear before anything happened, and I've reiterated it several times since. This is convenient fucking," I explain simply.

Raven gulps audibly. Then, she focuses on me. "How can you say that after everything we've done? How can you be so crude and careless?"

My pulse roars as I begin to feel cornered. "What are you expecting from me, Princess?"

"Stop calling me that," she clips.

"How much did you have to drink? Why are you acting this way?"

Apparently that was the wrong thing to say because her entire face morphs into an angry mask. Pretty sure there's steam billowing from her ears. "Me? You're the one tossing out the rules and destroying boundaries. It was your choice to take things slow up in the treehouse. You led us, and I thought it meant something," she mutters.

"Dammit, Raven. I already told you that was a mistake. It was the aftermath of an emotional outpouring that I'm not used to. I'm sorry if that was crossing the line but it was an easy way to tie everything together."

"Easy?" she sputters. "I guess that fits with your motto, right? Just go with the flow until stupid Raven assumes your actions mean something."

I hold up my palms. "All right, listen. Shit is getting a bit heated. Maybe we should sleep this off and talk about it in the morning."

"No," she says, slashing a hand through the air. "We're hashing this out now. Who was that woman, Trey? We"—she motions between us—"aren't anything significant. How many other *convenient* hookups do you have going on?"

"Not sure what that has to do with anything," I tell her as a different battle begins. She's upset and needing comfort, but I refuse to back down.

Raven pushes forward as if I hadn't said anything. "We're exclusively screwing, right?"

I scoff. "No rules, remember?"

She places a palm to her forehead. "Oh, wow. I can't believe this."

Taking a deep breath, I attempt to dilute the mayhem raging within me. "I'm a lost cause, Raven. I was never offering more than sex. I'll never be the domestic type, all right?" I point to myself. "Lost fucking cause right here."

She tilts her chin, studying me closely. "You know what? I don't believe that's true at all."

"Well, you're wrong. It's an indisputable fact." I roll my neck, trying to alleviate the pressure.

"Says who?"

Her questions never fucking stop. A tremor ripples through me, and I spit, "Me. I'm in charge of my destiny, and this is what it is."

"What are you afraid of, Trey?"

"Fucking shit, Raven. You never stop, huh? If I wanted to play twenty questions, I would have asked."

Her forehead crumples. "This is important to me," she whispers.

"Fine," I say. "You want the ugly truth? I'm not interested in losing anyone else, and this way, there's no threat. If I never care about people, it won't matter if they disappear."

Raven's eyes widen. "That's not something you can control. People walk in and out of your life daily. By closing yourself off to possibility, it's a serious injustice to what might be."

I shove my hands into my pockets. "That's a far easier risk to take."

"Trey," she murmurs. Her fingers touch my flexed arm. "I want better for you."

I glance away from her wounded stare. "That makes one of us, Princess." Raven doesn't yell at me for the nickname this time.

She chews on her lip before quietly asking, "Why can't you let me in?"

Frustration blazes through me like a wildfire. "I have, Raven. You're closer to me than anyone else. We have a great arrangement going. Isn't that good enough?"

"Keeping your bed warm every other night with no plans of commitment or monogamy? Ever?"

"What's wrong with that?"

She throws her hands up. "It's leading nowhere. If you at least promise—"

"None of that shit," I cut in.

"You're not even listening at this point."

"Because you're not hearing me. I've given you huge chunks of myself others will never know. You've heard about my family directly from me, not through the grapevine. That shit doesn't happen, Raven. It's something special I've offered to you," I say. And since I can't leave well enough alone, I add, "Plus, I've taught you how good sex can be."

She huffs but doesn't comment on the last part. "But I'll never have your heart?" Raven questions sadly.

"My heart is overrated."

"And you're a fool."

"Thanks for noticing."

Her petite figure has been full of energy, but suddenly the subtle vibrations fade. Raven's lashes flutter, and she inhales slowly. "I'm done fighting about this."

"What we have is perfect, Raven." I reach out and play with a strand of her blonde locks. She leans into me, and for a moment, it seems like we're reaching an understanding. "All those mushy feelings only complicate shit. Go with the flow, right?"

When she looks at me from under lowered lids, I see resolution in her blue eyes. "Not for me, Trey."

I shake my head, refusing to budge. Raven will accept this from me. She has to because it's all I have to give.

But she doesn't.

Raven cups my cheek as tears glitter in her sapphire eyes. "You're truly an amazing man, and one day, a very lucky girl will steal that stubborn heart."

"Why are you crying?" I ask stupidly.

"Because this isn't the ending I wanted."

"What are you talking about? Nothing has to stop. We're having a great time."

Her chin wobbles, and a few drops fall, streaking down her flawless face. "I can't stick around with no hope for a future. My mom put herself through hell trying to find love and all I could do was watch from the sidelines. I refuse to sell myself short like she did."

I'm about to interrupt but Raven holds up a hand, cutting me off.

"You don't want feelings and emotions, but it's too late for me. I've already sunk. It's my fault. I get that and take blame for my choices. I surrendered knowing full well things could go this way. But I wanted to leave my heart open." Raven knots her fingers together before delivering a final blow. "I was actually beginning to believe—"

"Don't say it," I stop her.

Raven sniffs and wipes her cheeks. "Why?"

"Because only fools fall in love."

She laughs. The sound is full of pain. "Guess this makes me the biggest one."

I reach for her, but she dodges my touch.

"Why are you doing this?" I whisper.

"I deserve the entire meal, Trey. Not just scraps."

"What the hell is that supposed to mean?"

"It's something Delilah said."

Outrage rolls off my tongue. "You told her about this?"

"Of course," she says like that should be obvious. "I had to weigh my options with someone."

"Why didn't you talk to me?"

Raven gestures frantically around us. "Are you joking? This is precisely why, Trey. I wasn't ready to face the fallout."

I'm not ready to admit defeat. Deep down, my instincts switch sides and force me to realize I'm directing anger at the wrong person. But that doesn't stop me.

"Maybe this bullshit argument could have been avoided if you'd brought it up weeks ago." Shifting my stance, I prepare for battle.

"I've already admitted fault on my part. Care to join me? Maybe for crossing some of those fluffy and mushy lines?"

"You read too far into all that," I tell her. "I never wavered in what this was." The lies taste bitter, and I swallow them down.

Raven waves and pushes away from the wall. "On that note, I'm gonna go. This has been . . . enlightening."

I squint at her. "Huh? We're going in circles and not resolving anything. Just text me tomorrow after you've slept this nonsense off."

She shakes her head. "It's so much more than that, Trey. I really hope you'll realize that eventually. Take care of yourself."

A bizarre tingling snakes through me as she pulls back, putting more distance between us with each step. This isn't right, yet I don't stop her. I silently stare as Raven grabs her purse and walks away.

A war surges within me, two sides battling for ultimate control. My heart and body fight against my brain, begging for a chance to be heard.

I'm starting to believe those sappy parts are right.

TWENTY-THREE

AWAY

RAVEN

THE DUFFLE TREMBLES IN MY grasp as I stuff more clothes in. Tears blur my vision, but none fall. It's stupid to be so upset over this. I freaking knew this was the most likely outcome with Trey. He made it clear, and I heard his message loudly. That still doesn't ease the sting.

I stumble into the bathroom to grab my toiletries and makeup. When I catch sight of my appearance, a startled gasp escapes me.

Good God, I'm a mess.

I grab an elastic and tie up the rat's nest on my head. After wetting a washcloth, I scrub over my blotchy face and remove the smeared makeup. When that tedious process is done, I look marginally better. My eyes betray me, though. Nothing can help my swollen lids at this point, but no one will see me escaping in the dark. I'll make sure to bring an extra pair of sunglasses, just in case.

Once my bag is packed, I open a new search window on my phone. Minutes drag by as I contemplate where to go. There's no plan or destination. Pure impulsivity is steering this decision. I suck air between my lips while typing *best beach resorts near me*. A slew of results filter in and I randomly choose the third name on the list.

Upon closer inspection, Sandbar Shore looks just right for this impromptu vacay I'm taking. The exterior is made up of more windows than siding. There's several floors, but not so many that it would feel crowded. Several rooms overlooking the water are available. Plus, they've included images of the adorable town with cutesy shops and diners. I'm sold.

I store the address in the map app before taking a look around the loft. A sinking feeling hits me, like I've swallowed a bag of rocks. Is this the right choice? Should I sleep off this restlessness and wait until morning?

Ugh, no.

If I don't leave tonight, there's a chance it won't happen at all. I'm due for a trip and dammit, this is the perfect reason. Delilah will be madder than a cat getting a bath when she wakes up, but I'll deal with her then. I don't want to ruin her night with my boy drama. I'll text her tomorrow while sitting in the sand with a drink in my hand.

Without further hesitation, I heft the duffle onto my shoulder and head out the door.

The car is chilly when I slide behind the wheel, but the cool air is welcome on my heated skin. Trey instantly barges into the forefront of my mind. Seems I can't even go a few moments without that jackass interrupting.

My heart sinks as I recall his outrage at the possibility of having something more with me. I was almost certain bringing up my feelings would cause conflict, but we were already waist deep in shit. When that Olive chick was digging her nails into him, she gave me fuel for clarification. So, here I am, sitting on the edge of another breakdown.

Of course, this pain is my own fault. It was only supposed to be physical between us. The end was always coming. It's just sooner than I wanted.

I wipe at the tears leaking down my cheeks. Then I pull away from the curb. It took Trey longer than he expected, but he's finally chasing me out of town.

But no, this isn't his choice. This trip is for me, because I want to. Nobody is forcing me to go anywhere.

The tires bump along the pavement as I drive toward the freeway. The pinch in my sore muscles intensifies with each additional mile, urging me to turn around. I'm not listening to that bologna, though. I'm reading the ache as a note for my head and heart to recalibrate on a consistent beat. These days will be good for me. They'll be like a reset button.

I blink rapidly while passing the farewell sign, and uncertainty makes another appearance.

You're always welcome back in Garden Grove.

Am I running away from my problems and searching for a solution in the wrong spot? Am I acting like my mom? An eerie sensation cloaks around me, and I realize similar thoughts plagued me not too long ago. I glance at the clock, and a thought strikes me. What if I went straight to the source?

I grab my cell and dial her number. It rings a few times before the call connects.

"Ravey? Is that you?" my mother asks from the other end. I roll my eyes at the nickname. In her special way, she still treats me like a child.

I clear my throat. "Hey, Mom. I hope you're not busy . . ."

"What's wrong?" Her voice sounds worried when she cuts me off.

"Nothing. Well, that's not really true, but nothing serious. I'm driving and wanted to say hello."

She sucks in a breath. "It's the middle of the night over there.

Where on Earth are you going?"

I huff, not wanting to delve into this immediately. "A few hours away for a little vacation. I want to explore the area a bit." A pang radiates through my chest while thinking of Trey showing me around. I shove those memories back and say, "I'm a bit blue. Can you give me a boost?"

"Oh, sweetie. I haven't heard those words in years. What's the matter?"

I set the cruise control and prop my foot up on the seat. "I'm lost and lonely . . . and need some guidance."

Her gasp echoes across the ocean separating us. "Wow, you never come to me for this stuff. I figured you had others to rely on."

I smile sadly. "You'll always be my mother, regardless of the distance between us."

"You're such a wonderful spirit, Raven. Always willing to forgive. Not sure I deserve such kindness, but you never quit on me. I'm always here for you, no matter what. I'm all ears. Tell me all about it."

"That means a lot," I reply before swallowing thickly. "Do you ever regret anything? Looking back on all the moving and the bad relationships, do you wish it'd been different?"

The line is silent for a moment before she responds. "Why do you ask, honey? Tell me what's on your mind."

"You didn't answer my question, Mom."

"Because you don't really want to hear that from me. You're searching for something else. What is it?"

I blow out a heavy breath. "I'm terrified of doing the wrong thing and making stupid decisions."

"And turning into me," she adds.

"Gah, stop reading my mind."

"Don't make it so easy for me."

"I'm scared of screwing up," I say. "My confidence has been

a little shaky lately."

"And why is that?"

"I don't know," mumbles from my mouth.

She laughs softly. "Raven, you're too young for this type of concern. You've got years of messing up left before buckling down and getting serious. You're allowed to make mistakes. Learning from them is half the fun."

"It's not that simple."

"Of course it is. Just go with the flow and do what comes naturally."

I bang my head against the seat. "You did not just say that."

"What's so bad about that?"

"Ugh, never mind. I'm second guessing everything. How do I stop?"

"Oh, Raven. I've done a serious disservice on your behalf. You never had the opportunity to blossom and spread those creative wings growing up. There's so much strength buried within you. Don't question yourself so much. Live your life however it's meant to be."

I rub my forehead. "That sounds like a fortune cookie."

"Good, that's my intention."

"Right, and I'm realizing this conversation is going nowhere fast."

"Okay, okay," she relents. "I'm aware that my parenting was lousy and you grew up under unstable conditions. Those were my bad choices, and you had no say in it. But you're free now. Don't let my errors hold you back. We aren't the same, Raven. You don't need to panic about becoming like me. Pretty sure your good sense will kick in long before the crazy ideas can take over," my mother explains swiftly. "More proof? I can't sit still for longer than five minutes. I've been pacing this entire time," she says, and I already pictured her doing that. "You're grounded and dedicated, meant to grow roots somewhere special. Just follow your beautiful heart."

"You sound like Delilah," I tell her.

"Ah, perfect. She's a good friend. Full of sound advice."

I snort. "Uh, huh. Sure. You two make quite the pair."

She hums. "And we balance you out."

"So, choosing a resort at random and driving there at two o'clock in the morning isn't going to turn my life upside down?"

"You don't need me to support or deny anything, sweetie. You're doing an amazing job."

A dry chuckle escapes me. "Not sure about that."

"Lucky for you, I am. And a mother always knows best." We share a laugh at that.

"Thanks, Mom." I swallow a lump of emotion. "I needed this."

"You're welcome, but I didn't do anything. The answers are always within you—I've always believed that. Your father would be so proud."

I release a shuddering exhale. "Love you, Mom."

"Love you more. Don't wait so long before calling me again. It's fun catching up. And good luck with whoever the lucky guy is."

My stomach leaps. "How did you know?"

"Raven, I'm your mother. Even with an ocean separating us, I can see exactly what's going on. There's always a boy."

"That's creepy."

"You asked."

"All right, I'm really hanging up now."

She chuckles. "Bye, sweetie."

I press end and toss the phone into my purse. She might not be the greatest role model, but my mother erases the threat of panic faster than anyone. My shoulders feel looser, and I'm ready to see what tomorrow offers.

This experience with Trey won't break me, even if it's causing a few cracks. I'll gather some glue and mend the damage. Hopefully I'll be stronger with reinforcements holding me together.

I roll down the window, allowing the cool breeze to blast in. Gulping down some fresh air, I'm ready for an adventure. I stare across the darkened freeway while the wind whips in my ears. Soon I'll be lying on some beach, soaking in the sun, and that sounds just right.

TWENTY-FOUR

REGRETS

TREY

I KNOCK ON RAVEN'S APARTMENT door and lean against the railing. I inhale the fresh morning air, savoring the lingering coolness from overnight. Tension radiates from my neck. I wince, trying to roll out the knots.

The moments tick by, so I try again. Still no answer. After checking the time, I realize she's probably already at Jitters. I stomp down the loft stairs, thinking about her baking before the crack of dawn. My eyelids feel like they've been coated in concrete. I didn't sleep for shit, and my ass is dragging to prove it.

The toxic shit I spat at Raven kept me awake, spinning on a constant loop in my mind. She's become real important to me over the last month and I didn't tell her the truth. Not even close. What I gave her was a pile of rotten garbage that she didn't deserve. Raven was right to be pissed and I've got to own my part of this fight. We'll come to an understand and move forward for the better.

The back entrance is locked, which doesn't surprise me. I'm

not sure the place is technically open yet. As I make my way around the building, visions of Raven stirring chocolate batter filter in. A noticeable twitch tightens my jeans, and I'm hoping we can solve this spat quickly.

I've got my tail tucked between my legs when I slink into Jitters. But what the fuck ever. If groveling gets me back into Raven's good graces, it'll all be worth it.

I glance around the empty cafe with coffee and sugar saturating my lungs. My filthy princess is nowhere in sight. With a sigh, I walk toward the only person in this place. There's no way she's going to help me, but I've got to try. I clench my teeth and approach the counter.

"Hey, D. I need to talk with Raven. She in back?" I ask, purposely avoiding eye contact.

She snaps her fingers at me. "Hey, jackass. If you're going to waltz in before I've had any caffeine, at least have the decency to look at me."

I do, knowing full well it's more of a glare. "Better?"

"Not at all." Her eyes are spitting green flames at me. "And no, Rave isn't here."

"Where is she?"

"I'm not her keeper, Trey. If you happen talk to Raven before I do, let her know it's still polite to leave a note on the counter."

I fake a yawn. "What are you blabbering about?"

"Need me to write it out? She left town, asshole. No thanks to you, I'm sure."

A clap of thunder booms in my chest as I process her words. My windpipe seems to be collapsing, making it hard to breathe, but I keep a straight face. "Where did she go?" I still manage to choke out.

Delilah picks at her nails. "If I knew, you wouldn't be hearing it from me."

"So, Raven just left? Without saying anything?"

"Pretty sure we've already covered that," she drawls.

"How do you know she didn't just go to the store or some shit?"

She taps her chin. "Oh, that's a great question. Maybe because her closet was all torn apart and her makeup is missing? A girl doesn't take that with her unless there's a good reason. This one most likely being she won't be back for a while."

"But she didn't take everything?"

"Looked like her duffle was gone, but that's a big bag. She could stuff a lot of clothes in there."

A growl rolls off my tongue. "What the fuck, D. How am I supposed to find her?"

"You're honestly barking up the wrong tree, hound dog."

My fist slams on the counter, rattling a few dishes and containers. Delilah just raises a slim brow.

"You're dumb," she states calmly.

I take a moment to study Delilah. She's missing that usual edge. "You okay? Something seems a little . . . off with you."

Her jaw ticks. "Oh? Pretending to care? How cute. I'm fine, just worried about my friend."

"I've fucked it all up," I mumble.

Delilah makes a sound of agreement. "I'm assuming she talked to you about wanting more?"

I nod.

"And that didn't go so well?"

"Obviously fucking not or I wouldn't be standing here talking to you."

She wrinkles her nose. "So moody. Maybe you should get laid."

"Don't be a bitch, D."

"Well, you're making it really easy for me."

I tip my face to the ceiling. "Why do you hate me so much?"

"I could ask you the same thing."

My hard stare meets hers. "I want this to work out with Raven.

You're her best friend. It'd be nice to have you in my corner."

Delilah laughs, the bitter sound making me cringe. "I've watched you sleep around for years, Trey. Girls have never been more than an easy fuck for you. Pardon me for being a tad wary when it comes to your intentions with Rave. My approval is hard to get."

I rub over my dry eyes. "She's different for me, dammit. All that other shit is over and done with."

"Prove it."

"What the hell do you think I'm doing?"

"Wasting time," she says and arches a brow.

"Why am I still bothering with you?"

"Another good question. You're on a roll."

Pressure squeezes my skull. "You're fucking impossible."

"In my own way, I was rooting for you guys, and look what happened. Thanks for screwing it up, asshole."

"This isn't all my fault," I tell her with a sneer.

"Puh-lease. She was happy here, and you ruined it. Hope you're real proud, Trey."

I squint at her. "Man, that dude fucked you up good, huh? Still haven't gotten over him, D? What was his name?"

Delilah's bored expression vanishes, and a red hue splashes up her neck. "Take your foul attitude and get outta here."

"My pleasure," I say with a bow. "Thanks for nothing."

"You're most welcome. If you ever come back, it'll be too soon."

I turn away without another word, dragging my battered pride with me. As I shove open the door, the bell clangs loudly. I hardly notice with all the static in my brain. While pacing in front of the café, I get my anger in check. Getting more pissed won't help anything. Taking a load off and trying to calm down seems like my best bet.

I settle on an empty bench to kick off my pity party. After

grabbing my phone, I send Raven a text.

ME: MORNING. D TOLD ME YOU LEFT AND WE NEED TO TALK. LET ME KNOW WHERE YOU ARE.

I press against my temples, attempting to alleviate the pounding. When this started months ago, I wanted Raven gone. Now that I've chased her away, it's becoming painfully obvious she belongs here. *With me.*

Fuck, I'm so fucking fucked. I hunch over, elbows on my knees, trying to decide when shit changed for me. It's impossible to pinpoint when all I see are stunning blue eyes and golden hair. Dammit, where is she?

I check my cell, but there's no response. My fingers type out some sweet for her.

ME: I MESSED UP, PRINCESS. GIVE ME A CHANCE TO EXPLAIN, YEAH?

Staring down at the screen, I wait for the three dots to appear, but nothing happens. The gravity of this situation seems impossible. How can I look for her if I don't know where to look? I yank at my hair, realizing it's only been ten minutes. Raven leaves for a few hours, and I immediately lose my shit. Awesome.

Brisk footsteps interrupt my self-scolding. I look up and see Jack approaching. He waves and plops down next to me.

"Hey, kid. What's the matter?"

I shoot him a half-ass smirk. "Can't I take a load off without it meaning anything serious?"

Jack chuckles while patting my back. "You can, but not without me assuming something's wrong. What's eating your ass?"

I glance at where he's pointing. "What were you doing at the Greasy Spoon? Meeting Marlene and company for a gabfest?"

"Nice diversion. Glad you still got jokes. Does this have anything to do with Blondie?"

"Her name is Raven," I grumble.

"Ah, great. So, you broke up? Or she's on the rag? Oh, shit," he says, his eyes widening. "Please don't tell me you knocked her up."

My pulse stalls before taking off at breakneck speed. "What the fuck? No. Don't even go there. Ever. And we were never dating. Guess that's part of the problem."

"Kid, that's the largest load of crap I've ever heard. Hate to break the news, but you two were in a relationship. Whether you're ready to admit that or not is another story. I watched you haul her around town, showing her all the good spots. You were smiling too, and it warmed my shriveled heart a bit," he tells me with a wink. "So, what happened? Last I saw, you guys were crazy about each other."

I blow out a long breath. "We got into a fight," I say, assuming that explains it all.

"And?"

Apparently it doesn't.

"I fucked up."

Jack nods. "That's part of our job. You'll fix it."

"Kinda hard when she's not here," I tell him.

His brow pinches. "What do you mean?"

"Delilah told me Raven left town."

"Ah, hell. That sounds real familiar."

"What do you mean?"

"Remember that girl I told you about? The great love of mine that got away?"

Pieces of his story from that day in the garage come back to me. "The one you didn't follow?"

"Yup, that's her. Your Raven flew the coop, just like Penny did. My greatest regret is not going after her. Don't make my mistakes, kid. You let her go, and that could be it. You'll never get another chance at the whole love thing."

I cough into my fist. "Yeah, that's so not what this is."

"Uh, huh. Keep lying to yourself. See how far that gets you."

I feel my shoulders deflate. "I don't even know where she is."

"She packed up all her shit and took off or something?"

I shake my head. "Nah, just a bag."

"Then she'll be back. Even if it's only for a minute, take advantage of that opportunity. Don't waste it. You only need a few words."

"But I have no clue when that'll be. In a day? A month?" I chuckle quietly.

"News travels fast in Garden Grove. You'll hear about it." Jack salutes to a car driving by. "And if you don't, I'll use my connections to get the scoop."

"No way. I don't want those nosy ladies involved more than they already are," I tell him sternly.

He nudges me. "Don't get huffy. They sense fear, kid. You give 'em any indication there's something to know, it'll blow up. Aren't you all about going with the flow?"

I scoff. "Fuck of a lotta good that's done lately."

"Just chill out, yeah?"

I glare at the silent phone in my grip. "She isn't answering my texts."

"It's still early. Give her space to cool off. In the meantime, let's have some fun. You know what works when dealing with lady trouble?"

I shrug helplessly. "What's that?"

"Get real stinkin' drunk," Jack hoots.

Laughing, I reply, "It's not even nine o'clock. Shit, there's still a chill in the air."

"And that's a problem because?"

I give him a blank stare.

He adds, "We'll have a liquid breakfast while sharing stories about beautiful women and the saps who fall for them. We can head to the lake, do a little fishing. Got nothing better to do than make this a real Sunday Funday."

"You're joining me?"

He guffaws. "It was my idea, right? I'd never pass up an

opportunity to watch you drown some sorrows."

"My misery is entertaining to you, isn't it?"

"Kid, I've been dealing with your incorrigible ass all these years. I deserve this."

"You're a real dickhead sometimes."

"Takes one to know one."

The wood creaks beneath me as I shift off the seat. "Lead the way, old-timer."

Sharp laughter booms from Jack. "Better watch it, Trey. You're gaining on me."

"Nice try, gramps. I've got plenty of time before going gray," I say while we walk toward Boomers.

He scratches his sideburns, the only area showing sign of age. "The ladies love a silver fox, and I get no complaints."

"They probably feel bad for you," I joke.

Jack smacks the back of my head, making me wince. "Respect your elders, dammit."

"What the fuck?" I rub the sore spot. "You raised me this way."

"Exactly, so I'm always right," he says and opens the metal door. "Looks like the early birds get their choice of stools. I'll let you pick." Jack gestures around the empty space.

The sour scent of stale beer wafts over me. I close my eyes, wishing for sweet flower perfume.

An elbow to my ribs knocks me out of it. "Look, they've got a power hour starting in a few hours. All you can drink, Bloody Mary or Screwdriver. Pick your poison. We'll start out slow until then."

I grunt. "Oh, yeah? Wanna take me on?"

He claps once and rubs his palms together. "Like you're reading my mind."

"Let's do this shit."

TWENTY-FIVE

BEACH

RAVEN

MY TOES DIG INTO THE cool sand while I watch the sun slowly dip below the horizon. No one else is around, but I'm totally fine with that. I'm not in the mood for company so the solitude suits me fine.

Everywhere I look is brightly colored or glowing with natural light. This beach is a little slice of heaven, the perfect escape from reality. My body thrums with a peaceful energy that's purely organic. I could lounge here for hours without getting bored.

Too bad Trey isn't here to experience this.

I shake my head and shut down those wayward thoughts. He wouldn't make this trip more special. If anything, he'd be grumbling about missing work or being too far from Garden Grove. The stunning view before me wouldn't be enough to drag him away.

The waves crash along the shore, echoing in my ears. I gaze out over the restless water, watching the rippling tides. When I talked to Delilah earlier, she mentioned Trey stopping by Jitters. I didn't pry for details, and she didn't offer much, but he was there looking for me. I've been silently obsessing over that snap judgement all afternoon. If I ask D, she'll tell me, but I'll have to listen to some serious gloating first.

I'm not that desperate.

My cell sits on the blanket, far too quiet for my liking. Trey had been blowing up my inbox all day. The last one he sent was hours ago, and the silence is mocking me. My chest tightens when considering the reasons why. Pushing the worry away, I scan through his texts again.

TREY: HEY, YOU. READY TO ANSWER ME YET?

TREY: I TAKE THAT AS A NO.

TREY: I'M THINKING ABOUT YOU, PRINCESS.

TREY: HOPEFULLY YOU'RE SAFE.

TREY: COMING BACK SOON?

TREY: JACK SAYS HI.

TREY: I DO TOO.

TREY: IT'S NOT THE SAME WITHOUT YOU.

The messages got more bold and suggestive as the day wore on. My lips and spirits lift while reading them.

TREY: WHY AREN'T YOU RESPONDING?

TREY: IGNORING PEOPLE ISN'T NICE, PRINCESS.

TREY: WHERE THE HELL ARE YOU?

TREY: JUST TELL ME.

TREY: WHAT'RE YOU WEARING?

TREY: NOTHING?

TREY: YOU STIRRING ANYTHING? IF NOT, MAYBE YOU SHOULD BE . . .

TREY: THE LETTERS ARE STARTING TO BLUR TOGETHER.

TREY: WISH YOU WERE HERE.

TREY: I MIGHT BE DRUNK.

He's left a few voicemails too. They're short and to the point, but hearing his voice is plenty. Trey's tone is raspy, bordering on hoarse. I could listen to him asking me, rather nicely, to call back over and over. The words flow over me like melted butter, but the serenity doesn't last. The fleeting sensation is representative of our . . . *fling* or whatever.

I feel my shoulders slump with a defeated sigh. I'm unsure what Trey is expecting to happen from his efforts. I should probably find out. This subject seems like something we need to handle in person, though, and I'm not ready to face him. My tears have dried up for a hot minute, and I'd prefer to keep it that way.

I tip my face to the cloudless sky and inhale the damp breeze. Staying here another night sounds like a better idea with each calm breath I take. After lying down, my eyes slide closed, and I allow the tranquil climate to create a lullaby.

As I'm beginning to doze off, my cell starts vibrating. I squint at the unknown number flashing across the screen. It's a Garden Grove area code so I take a chance and answer.

"Hello?" I question softly.

"Raven?"

I press the phone closer to my ear. "Addy? Is that you?"

"Yeah, hey," she murmurs.

"Why are you whispering?"

"Oh, I'm at work," Addy explains. "I can't talk long, but need to tell you something. Trey is in rough shape. He's been here for hours with Jack. He's been drinking all day," she says in a rush. "Anyway, Trey is blubbering on and on about you."

Flutters erupt in my stomach. "Um, all right. That's cool, I guess." I cough into my fist, trying to pull myself together. "And I needed to know this because . . . ?" My sentence trails off in hopes she'll fill in the gaps.

Her sigh crackles through the speaker. "You had a falling out, right? I'm not sure what happened, and you don't have to tell me, but crap is hitting the fan. I'm not gonna tell you what to do, but he's obviously hurting. Never thought I'd see him this way over a girl."

My tongue feels like sandpaper as I force a swallow past my

dry throat. "Uh, well, it's over between us. Not that there was ever anything to begin with."

"What?" she gasps. "No way. I saw you two together all the time. You're so good for him. And there were serious sparks flying all over town. Girl, plenty was going on."

I rub my forehead and mumble, "Yeah, I dunno about all that. Whatever we had is done now. That's why I'm here, instead of there. Needed a little time to myself, you know?"

Addy hums. "I get that, one hundred percent. Boys are dumb as hell sometimes. Especially Trey. I'd say he's paying for whatever went down, and I'm pretty positive he's sorry. You'll have to hear him out one way or another. You know what I mean? He seems pretty set on finding you," she warns. "Keeps repeating you're avoiding his messages."

"I just . . . well, it's kind of complicated," I stutter, trying to collect my scattered thoughts. "I don't know how to respond yet. Everything is a mess that I helped create. Trey hurt me badly."

Her tone is understanding when she says, "I can only imagine. It's probably good you're not here for this. That man is the definition of a sloppy mess, and it's not getting better. He's a sad sight and needs to sober up before talking to you. I think Jack took his phone away."

The clamp around my torso loosens as she gives me the explanation I've been desperate for. The lift in my voice is clear when I ask, "He's missing me?"

"Big time. I'm getting pretty annoyed with him. He's like a broken record. If Trey's drunk babbling is any indication, he's forming a plan to win you over. It's pretty cute actually."

She's tossing me crumbs, like a trail back to him, and I'm struggling to resist. I suck air between my teeth, trapping the slew of questions begging to escape. I squeeze my eyelids shut, settling on a simple one. "Is he okay?"

"I'm not sure, to be honest. I've never seen him this way. Jack is no help either. That man was screwed over by his ex, so he's pouring gasoline on the flames. At least he stopped drinking and switched to water. One of them has to be responsible. Shit," she spits out. "I spoke too soon. Jack just ordered another round for Trey."

The phone tightens in my grip. "Do you need to get help?"

"Ugh, probably. Greyson looks pissed. He'll probably make Jack take him home soon. Maybe I should give Twisted a heads up."

"I don't know that place," I say.

"For good reason. You only stumble in there at the very end of a long night. It's a tiny dive on the edge of Main and Escrow."

"You think he'll go there?"

"Not sure about him in this condition. I've never seen him so . . . vulnerable."

Nausea churns in my belly like the waves crashing in front of me. "Gah, that makes me feel horrible. What the hell should I do?" I ask, biting my lip.

"Nothing. I shouldn't have said that. I'm doing a shitty job not taking sides, sorry about that. Take care of you. I've got Trey handled," she says.

"You sure?"

"Positive."

"Good luck with that?" I offer.

Addy laughs. "Thanks, babe. You're coming back, right? Like, soon?"

"Ah, yeah. I talked to Delilah earlier. I'll probably be back tomorrow. It's too serene and pretty here. I can't leave yet."

"Oooh, where are you?" she asks, interested.

I glance around the empty beach before looking toward the resort. "Sandbar Shore."

"That little lake town up north? How'd you choose that spot?"

"A random search," I confess.

"Those are the best finds. I've never been, so take lots of pictures. Please tell me the moment you're back."

I exhale the weight of a brick. "Okay, I will."

"Don't sound so excited about it," she says sarcastically. "You'll be all right, Raven. We'll stick together."

I smile at that. "Thanks, Addy. You're a good friend."

"Heck yes. You're part of us now. No more leaving unless you take us along."

"Deal. We'll have to plan a weekend getaway sometime."

A loud crash on her end has her cursing. "Crap. Shit is going down for real. Gotta go!"

The line goes dead before I can respond. I look at the darkened screen, considering my options. I could rush back to Garden Grove or stick around for another day. Am I being overly dramatic about this? Is Trey struggling more without me there? I gradually blow out all the air trapped inside me. The safest choice is to phone a friend. I scroll through my contacts and tap Delilah's number.

She answers on the first ring. "Hey, Rave. Calling me on your drive home? That's sweet."

I lean back, resting on my elbow. "Sorry to disappoint, I'm still here."

Delilah's frown is all over her voice. "Lame. You had my hopes up. I've gotten used to having you close—I hate this a lot."

"Sounds like you're not the only one," I say softly.

"Oooh, who've you been chatting with? I didn't spill any dirt earlier."

"Addison called me. Trey is sloshed at Dagos. Guess he's been there for a few hours. Jack is with him, at least."

She puffs out a breath. "I believe it. He wasn't exactly pleased this morning. I'm sure he's taking the edge off."

I wait, biting my tongue before giving in. "Tell me what happened with him at Jitters."

"Hmm, I've been wondering how long it would take you to

crack," she says. "He came in way too early for me to consider being civil, especially when you left without a word. I hadn't heard from you yet so he got the brunt of my frustration and tried arguing with me—"

"Get to the good stuff," I interrupt.

Delilah snickers. "Yeah, yeah. Long story short, he wants you back."

I gasp and lunge upright. "Did he say that?"

"Not exactly, but he made it very obvious in his own way. Such as demanding to know where you are and having a hissy fit when I couldn't tell him. Have you talked to him?" she asks.

"No, not yet. He tried, but I didn't answer. Does that make me a chicken shit?"

"Nah, you're allowed to step away and process alone. You're not at fault."

I stretch a kink from my neck. "I'm responsible for my feelings and not bringing that up sooner."

Delilah makes a noncommittal noise. "Don't go searching for blame. You both made mistakes. The question is, now what?"

I shrug, then realize she can't see me. "I'll be home tomorrow and we'll see."

She doesn't let me off the hook. "What're you thinking, Rave?"

"I don't know. Would you give him another chance? I mean, if that's even a possibility."

"I'd hear him out," she states.

"Really?" I arch a brow.

"Does that surprise you?"

I think about it for a second. "Yeah, kinda. I figured you'd be anti-Trey all over again."

"Meh, you're too good together. It's a losing battle."

I smile. "That's nice of you to say."

"You're rubbing off on me, turning my insides all gooey. It feels weird," she mutters. "Just what I need—more sugar."

A laugh bubbles out of me. "I'll make extra special cupcakes to make the transition easier."

"Freaking yum," she says. "So, tomorrow? Promise?"

"Don't worry, I'll be there."

"Yay!" she whoops. "All right. Go to sleep and get up early. See you soon."

"Bye, D," I say and press end.

I sit out here a moment longer, enjoying the cool breeze against my chilled cheeks. Scooping up a handful of sand, I funnel it between my fingers. A shell stops the flow, its smooth texture slipping against the gritty granules. I dust it off and inspect the distinctive shape. The heart is whole without cracks or divots. My vision blurs while I rub along the edge, suddenly overwhelmed by the symbolism.

Even though my spirit is bruised, everything is going to be just right.

TWENTY-SIX

RAMBLE

TREY

THE STOOL WOBBLES UNDER MY swaying. Blinking is a chore for my sticky eyelids. Fuck, I'm drunk. When did that happen? Everything in this place is blurry and distorted, including the two people watching me.

"What's with the stare-down? Do I have something on my face?"

"Just waiting for what'll come outta your mouth next," Jack explains.

"Well, knock it off. Your leering is creeping me out."

"You're the one spitting truth bombs left and right," Addy chimes in. "I like Raven and all, but there's other subjects we can discuss. Oooh, like The Daze. The rooftop at Boomers is gonna be killer."

My chest tightens in a vice. "I was gonna take Raven there."

"Oh, Lord. Not again," Addy mutters.

"Maybe we should go," Jack suggests and pats my shoulder.

I don't have the strength to shove him away. A breath sputters from my lips, each movement feeling like a struggle. "Why is it so bright in here?" My words slur together.

Addy huffs. "Probably has something to do with all those beers you've had."

And I'm thirsty for more. "Can I have another?" I point to my empty bottle.

"No way, cowboy. You've had plenty," she replies.

I squint, closing one eye to focus better. "Addy? Since when do you have a twin?"

"Ah, intoxicated Trey has jokes. He should come out more often."

My tongue is heavy and feels swollen. I cough, trying to alleviate the dryness crawling up my throat. I shift to rest my elbow on the bar but miss, almost toppling over in the process.

"Jesus, kid. You're a mess. Pull yourself together and have some water." Jack pushes a full cup toward me.

I grip the cool glass and lift it to my lips. I'm sloppy while guzzling the liquid down, but there's no one here to impress. The only one who matters is gone. With a forced exhale, I feel my posture deflate.

"Raven isn't coming back," I say quietly.

Jack hears me. "She will because Garden Grove is her home now. Stop obsessing."

"You don't understand," I start, but he interrupts.

"The hell I don't. And we're not talking in circles again, all right? We already went over this."

"But I want more with her, and she doesn't know. How do I win her back?"

"Look," Jack says and points to the television above the bar. "The game is on. It's all tied up. Let's see who wins."

I'm not listening to him. "I need a grand gesture or something." I snap my fingers. "I'll buy her flowers and chocolate and . . . and . . . jewelry. Girls love that shit, right?" My bleary gaze lands on Addy until I get distracted by the empty space around us. "Where the hell did everyone go?"

"It's Sunday night, Trey. They cleared out hours ago," she responds. "You've been waxing poetic without a huge audience. Be happy no one else will know about this sensitive side unless you piss me off."

"Well, fuck. I better watch my back. If Marlene catches wind, I'll be ruined."

Addy laughs. "You're a dork. And for the record, your sweet words will be enough for her. That's what she wants to hear. Don't worry about the extra stuff."

"But what if I don't get a chance to tell her?"

"She'll probably be back tomorrow."

I perk up. "What? How do you know?"

Her eyes dance around, not settling on me. "Uh, I've gotta start cleaning up. You good here, Jack?"

He waves her off. "Yeah, yeah. Thanks for the help."

Addy nods at us and scurries away. Her sudden departure seems odd but what the fuck do I care. I shake my head, liquor sloshing in my brain. "Damn, I'm drunk."

"Yeah, we've established that."

I turn to Jack. "You're such a quitter, old man. I totally beat you."

He peers down his nose at me. "Wanna repeat that?"

"Getting hammered was your grand plan but I'm the only one seeing double. You've only had a handful of drinks all day. What the fuck? Just admit it—I win." I burp into my fist.

Jack slouches against the rail behind him. "Should I get you a trophy? Damn, you're a riot. I'm being smart and responsible. You've got sorrows to drown. This," he gestures between us, "is me along for the ride. I'm keeping your whiny ass outta trouble."

"Remember Charlie Brown? You sound like his teacher right now. Wah, wah, wah. You can't keep up, gramps. Plain and simple."

"Whatever you say."

"So, why are we still here?"

"Good question, kid."

"What time is it?" I search my pockets. "Where's my damn phone?"

"I took that stupid device away hours ago. All you wanna do is text Raven and bitch about her not answering. Then gush about how you care for her. It's fucked up. Rinse, wash, repeat. Give it a rest," Jack demands.

"But I've got things to tell her."

"And all those jumbled thoughts can wait until you're sober."

"Raven needs to hear me so she'll come back," I insist. "If I stop trying, she'll think it's over."

"Trey, it's been one day. Chill out. You'll get the point across," Jack assures me. "No doubt about that, considering you've been yammering on all night."

"I blame you for all this. You wanted to bond and shit." My mouth is moving but I feel numb. "Did someone give me Novocain?"

Jack chuckles. "Nope. Just a bunch of booze. But hey, I'm glad you're feeling relaxed."

I take a deep breath, the scent of popcorn and beer thick in the air. Maybe that's me. I sniff my shirt and almost gag. "I smell like garbage," I complain and swallow the threat of vomiting.

"You are so damn random when you're drinking. I can't keep up with you."

"Because you're old."

He punches my arm. "I don't speak idiot."

I almost tip off the stool, but catch myself at the last second. "Why am I such an asshole? I've done so much stupid shit, Jack.

How the hell do I fix that?"

"Runs in the family," he says. "I've already told you about my fuck ups. Your dad wasn't innocent either. His surly attitude got him into all sorts of trouble with your mom."

The buzzing in my mind screeches to a halt when he mentions my father. "Really? I don't remember him that way."

Jack scrubs a hand over his jaw. "Yeah, she whipped him into shape. I fucking idolized my older brother. He was a hellion, a lot like you. Didn't give a crap about nothing but fast cars and partying hard. Your mom loved him, though. Saw past his foul language and nasty behavior, but he didn't make it easy on her. Sound familiar?"

"Sure does. Why didn't you tell me sooner?" There's a marching band playing a crescendo in my head as I wait for him to respond.

He shrugs and takes a sip of water. "We don't talk much about this sort of thing, remember? Would you have been open to any of this if the liquor wasn't flowing?"

"Nah, probably not. Glad we are, though."

"Me too, kid. Didn't bring it up to cause pain. Only wanna make a point," he reiterates. "Your woman wants to know she matters. That she comes first. You don't gotta plan something outrageous. You already told me Raven wants your heart, so give it to her. Don't push her away."

I lean against the bar. "That isn't easy for me."

He slaps my back. "You're already taking the right steps, so don't freak out. You're not beyond repair. Think of this like the beginning of an engine overhaul."

I groan. "That's so much work."

"It doesn't have to be. One step at a time, kid. Don't get ahead of yourself. We'll talk more tomorrow when you're in better shape. Who knows if you'll even remember this in the morning," Jack jokes.

"I'm wasted, not blacked out. I'll recall all this just fine, fuck you very much. Gimme my phone back," I say and hold out my palm.

Jack raises a dark brow. "Why?"

I roll my eyes. "None of your business."

He grunts. "Never seen you this way, Trey. This girl is your real deal. I'm damn happy you found her."

"She found me," I correct. "And all I've done is treat her like a convenient hookup. Fuck," I curse and grip my hair. "Raven deserves to be worshipped. I never should have assumed otherwise."

Jack crosses his arms. "You'll make all that nonsense up to her and correct the mistakes, but now isn't the time. Try again when you wake up, after sleeping this shit off."

"All right," I grumble. Maybe he's got a point. I can almost hear my bed calling. All the drinks and fried food are catching up to me. "Can I get a lift home?"

"Your chariot awaits outside," he hoots.

I cover my ear. "Why are you so excited?"

"Because my babysitting shift is almost over. I can meet up with my honey after this," he says with a wag of his brows.

"You're such a dick." I hiccup, feeling bile swirl in my gut.

Jack snorts. "Jealous?"

"Obviously!" I shout and a pang echoes in my ears. "I want to be with Raven. Why is she acting like I don't exist?"

He pulls me off the seat and guides me to the door like a toddler. "Quit bitching. I'm sick of it. You'll be good as gold tomorrow."

I stumble over the floor mat but Jack catches me. Black dots speckle my vision as I say, "I'm not so sure about that."

TWENTY-SEVEN

TAKEN

TREY

THE RINGING DOESN'T STOP, IN my head or on the nightstand. Blindly I reach out, swatting at my phone, trying to silence the torture. To my relief, the room remains quiet. My lids slide shut as I try letting sleep take hold of me again.

No such luck.

My cell calls out from the floor, insistent and blaring like a foghorn. I almost fall off the mattress while grabbing for it.

"What?" I bark, my voice gruff.

"You're still sleeping? It's four o'clock in the afternoon," Addy scolds from the other end.

I rub my throbbing temples. "Who the hell cares?"

"Me. And you should too."

"Do you need something?" I bark.

Addison huffs, her annoyance clear. "Maybe I shouldn't be helping you after all."

I groan, the pounding in my skull almost unbearable. "Tell me what you want so I can go back to bed."

"And wallow in your stupidity some more?"

Flashes from last night flicker through my foggy brain. Addy was at the bar, serving me several drinks. Far too many based on the ceiling spinning above me. This is just great. My mouth tastes like mothballs, and I'm nauseous as fuck.

"How 'bout you spit it out?" I demand.

Addy laughs. "Aww, you have a hangover? I'm not surprised considering you practically drank a keg of beer. I stopped counting your shots. You're kind of a moron, Trey."

"Tell me something I don't know." I snort, immediately regretting it as blinding pain jabs into me.

"Yeah? All right. Raven is at Dagos," she says calmly.

That wakes me up real quick. "What?"

"You heard me."

"When the hell did she get there?"

"About thirty minutes ago."

I growl, "And you're just calling me now?"

"I've been blowing up your cell since she walked in the joint. Not my fault that you don't answer."

I check my notifications. Dammit, she's right. I toss the blankets off and sit up. "I'll be there in ten."

"Better hurry. Who knows how long she's gonna wait," Addy says.

"Keep her busy," I snap and hang up.

I rub my dry eyes and stand too fast, almost tipping over from the momentum. I stumble into the shower and wash yesterday's regrets off my skin. My limbs are sluggish. For a moment, I lean against the cool tile for support. I'm cursing Jack and his genius plan of male bonding. The jackass stopped drinking before dinner but kept rooting me on. I'm paying for dumping all that poison in my veins.

I hang my head as the water rains down, pouring life back into me. Thinking about Raven speeds up the recovery and a semblance of normal returns. I shut off the stream and grab a towel, ready to face my future.

I peer at my foggy reflection and wince. My eyes are bloodshot and weary. The scruff on my jaw is bordering beard territory. My complexion is pale, showing evidence of the weakness still brewing inside. This is who'll be greeting Raven—lucky lady she is.

It doesn't take much after that because I'm edgy and eager as hell. Delaying this further isn't possible. After tossing on jeans and a shirt, I rush out the door.

With newfound purpose and a clear mind, the drive flies quickly. I park my truck in front of Dagos like usual, but everything else is different. Today, I stare at the windows littered with neon signs and picture the girl waiting inside. The weight of these coming moments is a hefty stack pressing on my chest. My pulse roars while I consider the possible outcomes. Raven is a game changer, and I'm prepared to do whatever it takes.

Suddenly, her significance blazes through me. It's an inner strength I wouldn't possess on my own. I don't deserve forgiveness, but that doesn't stop me from wanting it. I step out onto the curb, take a fortifying breath, and prepare to face her verdict.

I glance down at my empty hands. Dammit, I should have picked up flowers or something. Too late now. Fuzzy memories from last night are trying to break through the haze but don't crack the surface. Am I forgetting something? I scratch my scalp and stop overthinking. If Raven wants more with me, and I really fucking hope she does, my words will do the trick for the time being. I'll shower her with gifts later.

My hand rests on the wood door and I bow my head. Here goes all I have.

She's all I see while walking into the dim bar. Raven is sitting alone, but not for long—or ever again—if I get my way. She doesn't see me so I take a few minutes to appreciate her stunning beauty. Loose curls cascade down her back, like a golden beacon reeling me in. Raven's slim shoulders are perfectly straight while she studies a menu. But it's what she's hiding from view that I'm most interested in. Hopefully I'll speak to her heart tonight.

I stride forward quietly, noticing the empty stool next to her. I smirk at the sight, recognizing the irony. The roles are reversed. I guess we've come full circle, and this all makes perfect sense.

My fingers itch to touch her. I still resist. After clearing my throat, I ask softly, "Is this seat taken?"

She looks over her shoulder, sapphire eyes wide and searching. Raven doesn't answer at first, just keeps watching me. Several tense beats later, she bites her lip and says, "Don't even bother."

My stomach drops, not expecting any resistance from her. "What? Can I sit down for a minute? Real quick?"

Raven shakes her head. "You're wasting time hitting on me."

I stare at her, the dots not connecting in my brain. "I'm not—"

"Listen, babe." She raises a sassy brow. "I know why you're over here. I'm not interested, okay?" She crosses her arms and I finally understand what's going on.

"Hmm, reenacting our first chat? Turnabout is fair play."

She shrugs. "Call 'em like I see 'em."

"Well, this is the only open spot in the place. I'd love the chance to know you better."

Raven makes a show of glancing around the empty room. "Oh, really?"

I take a chance and stroke down her arm, getting a thrill from her slight shiver. "You're here." The surprise in my voice is blatant, but I'm done holding back.

"Where else would I be?" she mumbles.

"You were gone. Just, up and left."

Raven squints at me. "It wasn't even two days."

"Felt a lot longer than that," I mumble.

"What's that?"

"Where did you go?" I pull out the available stool and sit

down. She doesn't protest.

"Sandbar Shore," she replies, offering a weak grin.

"Where the hell . . . ?" I pause, rubbing over my mouth. "I mean, why didn't you answer my texts? I even left a few voice-mails."

She props an elbow on the ledge, resting her cheek on a fist. "I'm really mad at you, Trey. Just needed to be alone yesterday to work through that. I planned to respond today but didn't hear from you again. Figured we'd talk . . . whenever."

I scratch the base of my neck. "I was sleeping off a hangover."

"Drinking to forget?" She purses her lips.

I grunt and roll my eyes. "Never wanna do that when it involves you. I just needed to do . . . *something* while waiting to hear from you. Damn, I didn't know what to do with myself. I blame Jack, mostly. It was his genius idea, rooting me on to keep chugging while he was sipping water. Shit got pretty blurry by midnight."

Raven nods. "I heard."

I groan loudly. "Let me guess. Marlene beat me here?"

She smiles, a little brighter this time. "Nope. Addy filled me in on all the drunken details."

"Fuck, I don't wanna know. Can't be too bad if you're still sitting with me."

Her hand seesaws. "The jury is deliberating."

"Let me take you on a date. A real, official one."

"When?" Her tone is skeptical.

I look around, checking out my options. "How about now?"

"Uh, I dunno. I'm pretty busy."

"Come on," I urge. "We can sit in that booth over there. Plop a candle in the middle, spruce up the table and add some ambiance."

Raven wrinkles her nose. "Is this where we cue the cheesy music?"

"Sure, why not."

"I might need more time. You really hurt me," she says.

Raven's words gut me and the soul-deep need to soothe her pain takes over. "Let me make this right. Please?" I'm not above begging at this point.

She blinks at me, not saying anything else.

The distance between us, both physical and emotional, is making my skin crawl. I tug on her belt loop, shifting her toward me. I lean closer and whisper, "I miss you, Princess."

She scoffs. "You miss having sex with me."

"Nah, it's far more than that."

"Post-coital chat buddy?"

"Wrong again."

"What then?"

I rest my forehead against hers, rolling back and forth. "I said a lot of really stupid shit, Raven. I need to apologize. Will you hear me out?"

Raven's minty exhale breezes along my skin, making me desperate to inhale her. "I suppose," she mumbles.

"I was aware that lines were blurring, but chose to ignore them. I'm a coward, okay? I didn't want to face my feelings. The bullshit excuses I make don't matter. All that does is letting you know how damn sorry I am," I murmur across her lips. "You're not a convenient fuck or easy lay or temporary fling or casual screw. Princess, you're so much *more* to me."

"Where is all this coming from? On Saturday you were singing a very different tune."

"In the heat of the moment, I was too damn proud to admit my feelings. That isn't the case anymore. I've had the sense knocked into me. I don't wanna lose you, Raven."

"Oh, wow. I wasn't expecting this," she says softly.

My nose brushes along hers. "Better get used to it. I've made some decisions."

Raven tenses slightly. "Oh, yeah?"

"Uh, huh. I want all the fluff and mush. With you, only and always. No one gets this from me except *you*," I whisper. "I'll never share this part of me with another person. Just you, Raven."

She sniffs and sucks in her cheek. "You better not be saying this stuff just to get laid."

I chuckle into her neck, pressing kisses there. "I don't need to make up shit for that to happen. But really, you're different for me. Always have been since the day you moved to Garden Grove. Right away, I was drawn to your golden hair and sapphire eyes. After spending so much time by myself, it was a serious shock to find someone I could tolerate. You're always questioning and pressing me, pushing limits that never used to bend. I like that about you. By never settling for my shitty non-answers, you've helped me realize how trapped I've been. I don't wanna be alone anymore, Princess. I'm hoping you're still willing—"

"Yes," she cuts me off before pressing her mouth to mine. "I want it all."

I nibble her lower lip. "No more dodging me, all right? If I screw up, holler at me and I'll try not to yell back. Be patient with me. I've never had a real relationship, but want one with you. I'll probably blow it and have to buy a shitload of flowers. We'll do what works for us."

Her head shifts against me with a nod. "We'll make it work. I happen to really like flowers."

I breathe her in. "Smell like them too."

Raven giggles. "I know how much you like that."

"Damn right. So, no more random trips?"

"I'll tell you first."

I tickle her sides, and she laughs. "Okay, okay. You can come along."

"Hmm, I like the sound of that." I wrap her in a hug, our bodies molding together like a museum masterpiece. Raven nuzzles into my chest, and I hold her tighter, bringing us even closer. "This feels perfect."

"I wasn't sure this would happen for us," she says with a slight wobble in her voice.

"Want another secret?" I whisper in her ear. "Pretty sure I love you."

She peeks up at me through wet lashes. "Well, I might love you back a bit."

I slide my palm along hers, our fingers intertwining on their own. "Just right," I say. Raven's breath hitches, I squeeze her hand.

"My uncle told me about this."

Her face tips up. "What do you mean?"

My heartbeat goes wild, and I'm positive Raven can feel it. "He said I'd find a girl. The one."

"He did?"

Warmth spreads in my chest. "Turns out he was right," I say and nip her chin.

Raven hums. "And what else did Jack say?"

"Mostly nonsense. He only makes sense a small portion of the time."

"Ah, that explains a lot of your behaviors."

I pinch her, and she squeaks.

"Wanna hear a story?" I ask.

"Of course I do."

"There was this guy, super fucking hot, but a total douchebag. You know the type, right?"

"Oh, totally."

"He thought his shit didn't stink until this girl walks into the bar and wrecks house. Stop me if you've heard this one," I say and Raven smiles against my jaw. She motions for me to keep going, so I do. "Right away, he knew there was something different about her. The jerk fought it, really hard. As if he actually stood a chance." I snort, and Raven giggles.

"Maybe he was scared of being weak or appearing vulnerable,

but eventually the dude gives in. He couldn't go on without her, that whole sappy spiel. And I'm damn glad for them. See, this girl, she's so fucking special, Princess. She managed to turn an asshole into a believer. How 'bout that, huh?"

Raven dusts my cheek with soft pecks. I press into her touch, asking for more. Sparks burst along my skin when she peeks her tongue out for a taste. I groan but keep going.

"I didn't know what I was missing until you came barreling into town. Not sure I can tell you what that means to me. Maybe I can show you?" I pull away to stare into her brilliant blues.

Raven bites her lip. "You're adorable."

I slap a palm over my heart. "Don't steal my man-card. I've already given you everything else."

Raven grabs my shirt and drags me toward her. Then, she kisses me sweetly. "I could never take that away," she mumbles into my mouth. "You're far too vulgar for me to tame completely. Not that I'd ever want to."

"Fuck, yes. I'm ready to screw you into next Tuesday." I wag my brows. "But admit it. That first line when I walked in was cute as hell. I'm glad you didn't refuse me."

Raven laughs out loud. "Yeah, I would have folded from that alone."

"Really?" My hands smooth up her thighs. "That's very good to know."

"What can I say? You've got a beautiful soul buried under this armor. Guess I'm the only one to see that," she says and pats my chest. "There's also a relatively huge part of me that likes being your filthy princess."

My dick jerks, ready to join the party. "Oh, yeah? Wanna get real dirty?"

"I've been waiting for you to ask," she purrs.

Grabbing her hand, I yank her off the stool. "My place. Now."

TWENTY-EIGHT

FILTHY

RAVEN

TREY PEELS MY SHORTS OFF, the stretchy denim rolling away without much effort. My legs tremble while he works his way back up. I tighten my muscles in preparation, wanton and waiting. His fingers skim the edge of my panties, a tantalizing tease. I urge him on with subtle shifts, and a husky chuckle greets my efforts. Trey keeps me waiting a beat longer before hooking into the elastic sides. He drags the silk down my thighs, the soft material drifting painfully slow.

"You're so fucking sexy," Trey groans while rocking into me.

"Not so bad yourself," I gasp when he bites my shoulder.

Trey flicks my bra open before sliding it off, the satin rasping against my flaming skin. I push closer, his front to my back, and revel in all the hardness prodding at me. My ass snuggles his dick, but the pesky briefs he's wearing need to go. My core aches, passion thrumming through me. I'm desperate with need while his fingers dance along my hips.

His palms roam up my sides, the friction makes me squirm.

Trey cups my breasts, massaging and squeezing with seductive pressure. When he pinches my nipples, I hiss out a stunned breath.

"How does that feel, baby?" He applies more force, and I almost squeal.

"Good," I gasp. And I'm not lying. The sting is surprisingly pleasurable, and shocks rush from my center.

"How do you want it, Princess?"

"What do you mean?"

"Should I make love to you soft and slow?" he murmurs into my shoulder. "Or you wanna try something new?"

"Oh, Lord," I groan. Trey twists my sensitive tips tighter. "You decide. I can't think straight," I pant.

"So responsive. You'd love more, yeah?"

I nod frantically because it's true. What he's doing is making me hot all over, like a furnace in my lower belly. When he releases me, I choke on a wheeze as the blood rushes back to my tweaked breasts.

His hands travel down before finding a home on my ass. His touch alternates between soft and rough, barely-there rasps before sharp spanks. "This ass, Raven. It's always calling to me," Trey mutters.

"Oh, yeah?"

"Hmm, fucking tempting me." He grips my flesh and drags me in until his length rests along my crack.

I'm a tad hazy and not picking up his clues. My head limply lolls along his chest, Jell-O replacing my limbs. Trey sucks along my neck, gently pulling my sensitive skin between his teeth. My body sags further against him.

"I love how you're touching me," I sigh out.

His tongue flicks my earlobe. "This is only the beginning."

"What're you gonna do to me?" I question softly, my lashes fluttering.

"Something I've never done before."

"That sounds . . . promising."

"Figure our first time as a couple should be special." His thumbs play up my ribs.

A shiver races through me. "I like hearing that."

"I'm hoping you'll love this."

My legs rub together, more than ready. "Enough teasing," I rasp.

"On the bed," he commands.

I glance at him over my shoulder, lifting a questioning brow. "Really?"

Trey juts his chin. "Fuck, yes. Don't question me." This is a surprise, considering we've banged all over town except on an actual mattress. "I want you comfortable and relaxed. Get up there with your ass in the air," he demands before spanking me lightly.

I quiver in anticipation, my brain full of filthy possibilities. My feet stumble in haste, but I manage to scramble onto his king-size without much trouble. I lower onto my elbows and knees, already slick with wanting. Trey has turned me into a doggie-style fiend, and I'm crazy turned-on at the idea of more. I hear him strip, and my breathing becomes more labored.

The bed dips under his weight as he nestles in behind me. Trey nudges my knees, encouraging me to lower further. He grips my ass and pulls my cheeks apart.

"Do you trust me, Princess?" His husky tone has goosebumps breaking out across my skin.

"Of course. Why?" I'm not concerned about his question until wetness drips onto my back entrance.

What the hell? Did he just spit on me?

When he begins touching me there, sparks shoot up my spine. I try scooting away, but he yanks me back.

"Trey, what the fuck?" I gasp.

One hand softly caresses my lower back while he continues stroking around that forbidden area. "Relax, Raven. Stop struggling and let me touch you. It's gonna feel real good."

My head shakes, and I protest, "Not there."

"Yes," Trey purrs. "This type of play will be a first for both of us, Princess. How does that sound?"

When he puts it that way . . .

"Really appealing," I say honestly.

"This'll be something only we share." He keeps circling lightly, spreading the moisture, and the foreign sensation isn't unpleasant. Quite the opposite, if I'm being honest. I love whenever he touches me, so there's no further objection. I decide to open my mind and go with this.

"If I hate it, you'll stop?" I ask softly.

His touch disappears. "Always. I'd never force you into anything."

"O-okay," I agree. My ass wiggles in permission.

"I'm gonna fix that ache, baby. This is gonna be good for both of us."

His finger presses along my rim, and I shudder. When he nudges the tip inside, gentle and slow, my arms collapse. Pleasure explodes from my core as he wiggles the digit back and forth. I moan, embarrassingly loud and drawn out.

Trey chuckles. "Yeah, not complaining now, are we?"

"Holy shit," I whisper into the pillow. This feels good. Like, ridiculous erotic-fantasy good.

As he eases more into me, stars burst behind my lids. There's more moisture, and he slips deeper. Desire races in my veins, and the intensity is a shock, but I don't question it. A climax already looms before me, and I want to reach out. Dark thoughts of more take over, like a hidden corner being exposed, and I want to explore every inch.

Trey sinks that finger in all the way before slowly pulling back out. He follows the same motions again, in and out, until my body seems to adjust.

"Talk to me, Princess," he soothes. "Tell me how it feels."

This man loves being vocal in bed, and until him, I'd always been quiet. Not anymore. That finger keeps working me higher and higher as I try piecing words together.

I twist my head to the side and lick my lips. "I love it. I never knew something there could feel like this."

"You make me so damn hard, Raven. I've never been this turned on." His truth spurs me on.

"I'm so wet. How does your finger have so much power?" My voice is a breathy rasp as he drags out before slipping back in.

"Fuuuuck, your ass is so sexy. Sucking me in like quicksand. You love me back here, Princess." It's not a question. He knows exactly how much I'm enjoying what he's doing.

All I can do is whimper in response.

There's a click, like a lid being opened. Cool drops tickle my hole, and his sunken finger becomes slicker.

"Is that—?"

Trey hums, "Lubing you up. Feeling even better now, huh?"

My brain is too scrambled to answer, but it sure as hell does. The added lubrication allows smooth entrance, my body welcoming his gentle strokes. Trey slides in easily, and there's no resistance.

"Have you been planning this?" I moan.

"Getting into your ass? Absolutely," he growls. "Wasn't sure this would happen, but damn glad I'm prepared. Ready for more?"

I glance up at his handsome face and nod. His eyes burn into me as his finger keeps up the filthy pace. "You're so fucking stunning."

There's pressure as he adds another finger, but it's oddly delicious. I push against him, wanting it deeper and harder. I'm suddenly eager to come with him buried there. I never thought this type of play would work for me, but I'm already becoming addicted.

When he wiggles his fingers, I almost black out. A hungry groan escapes me.

"Who knew you'd be so into this? I would have popped your anal cherry weeks ago," Trey murmurs as his fingers twist inside my forbidden hole. The tightness burns, but not in a painful way thanks to the lube. He's stretching me with each glide and prickles dance along my flesh. Images of taking more filter into my lust-clouded brain. I almost want to try . . . going all the way.

As if reading my mind, Trey drizzles more oil before moving his fingers faster and spreading them wider. The dull ache is fantastic, and my lower belly is tingling in bliss.

"Oh, ohhhh, wow. I could come if you keep going," I murmur softly.

"That's right, Princess. And it's about to get even better."

I look up when he stops moving. I watch him lift a pink object that looks like a big bottle stopper. I squirm just thinking about where that's headed.

"This is the good part," he explains while slicking up the plug. For a moment I'm worried because that object looks a lot larger than his fingers. I unconsciously wiggle away, and Trey's eyes snap to mine. "You okay?"

"It's going to hurt."

He shakes his head. "I'd never do anything to cause pain. This is only for pleasure, I promise. But I don't have to use it."

I take a deep breath and close my eyes. "I trust you, Trey."

"That's my girl," he rumbles as his fingers leave me. In the next moment, he has the plug there. It's cool and stiff as he presses it into me. There's resistance that halt his movements, like my body is fighting the larger intrusion. He adds more lube, the cool drops sizzling on my skin. Trey twists the toy around my rim, getting me ready. He uses gentle force, pushing harder, while whispering, "Don't fight this, Princess. Let me in."

And I do. I breathe out slowly and relax my muscles. The plug breaches past my tightness and lights up my blood.

Fuck, this is pleasure on another level. The texture of the solid object builds me higher, until I'm ready to pop. I'm trembling as he goes farther with it, testing my limits. I don't move an inch, waiting for his lead. Trey drives into me lazily, inch by tortuous inch, and I'm drowning in ecstasy. These feelings are so overwhelming it seems like a dream. The size of the plug amplifies every slight shift, like my entire body is an electric wire. He delves further somehow, making the sensations even stronger.

"Soon my dick will be here," Trey pants while tapping the rubber toy sunk in me. "Would you like that?"

"S-so much," I mumble along my arm before biting down. He drags the plug out before wedging in, leaving it lodged deep.

"You're stretching so far, baby. You'll take me easy, but not today," he says. Trey's slick palms caress my ass, touching me sweetly while talking dirty.

A shudder shakes my limbs, and I can't hold back much longer. "P-please, more," I beg while rolling my hips.

Trey doesn't keep me waiting. His dick circles my center, but I'm too blissed out to process what he's doing. "You think that's good, Princess? You're gonna freak the fuck out over this." When Trey enters me, ecstasy bursts from every pore. His size is difficult to accept with my ass full and he gives shallow pumps.

I feel him in each part of me while silently pleading for these pulsations to go on forever. My world tilts, and a kaleidoscope of color blasts through me. No artificial substance could replicate this type of high. When he pushes further, I'm spread to capacity, yet Trey begs for more.

"I want to own every part of you, Princess. Conquer and claim, like you've done to me."

Somehow, in my muddled brain, I find myself wishing for that too. Shockwaves attack my system before I give up the fight, going limp in his clutches. Trey takes advantage of my surrender, powering forward with a full thrust. He bellows in pleasure, his fingers digging into me. Any moment now, I'm going to rip in half. There's no doubt.

Once he's all the way in and there's no more to take, Trey flips a switch. The plug vibrates to life, and I shatter into unrecognizable pieces.

And what a way to freaking go.

EPILOGUE

HOME

TREY

One month later . . .

I PULL INTO THE DRIVEWAY, a nervous breath easing from my lungs. I glance at Raven in the passenger seat, and the worry washes away. This feels right, like everything does with her. This chick has turned me into a sap, but I fucking love it.

"How's that blindfold, Princess?"

Her face tilts to the side before tipping down. "Very effective. I can't see a thing. Are we there yet?"

I chuckle. "I've lost count how many times you've asked. Are you anxious or something?" I let my finger draw a line around her knee before drifting slowly upward. I smirk at her goosebumps and go a bit further, toying with the edge of her shorts.

"Or something," she says while licking her lips.

"Are you ready for the surprise?"

Raven nods frantically. "Yes, you always give me the best surprises."

My cock twitches at her breathy tone, but this isn't about that.

Maybe after. "Stay there. I'll come to you."

"Oooh, I like the sound of that," she purrs.

I squeeze her thigh. "You're a wicked tease, Princess. Don't tempt me."

She laughs. "Pretty sure you're in charge of this situation."

"Damn straight," I state and hop out of the truck. I stride around the hood and open her door. "Hold onto me." I grasp her hands.

"Is this really necessary? I'm going to fall and—"

I cut off Raven's concern by scooping her into my arms. "Better?"

Her nose presses into my neck, and she inhales deeply. "Much."

I walk up the front steps with her jostling in my grip. She giggles, and I press a kiss to her smiling lips. "I love you, Princess."

A blush tints her cheeks. "Love you, Dirty. Lots and lots."

I struggle with the lock until the telltale click calls out. I maneuver us over the threshold and pause in the entryway. I set Raven down before leading her further into the room. She sniffs the air while blindly swatting around.

"It smells like fresh paint," she points out. Her tone takes on an edge of panic when she adds, "Please don't tell me we're banging in a hardware store."

I link our hands and pull her to a stop. "That's a great idea, but not today." My fingers loosen the knot at the base of her skull. "Ready?"

When the bandana slips off her face, she blinks quickly and catches my stare. She doesn't answer. Instead, she looks around. Without an explanation, Raven might not understand. I wait a few minutes, watching her spin in a small circle, taking in the empty space.

"Where are we, Trey?"

My throat bobs with a heavy swallow. "I figured out what this place was missing."

"Hmm?" Raven mumbles and peers down the hall.

I turn her shoulders until she's facing me. I need her hearing this. My pulse pounds as I reveal the significance. "You, Princess. This house and me, we have been waiting for you."

Raven's sapphire eyes fly to mine, wide and startled. "W-what? We're . . . where?" She rests a palm on her forehead.

I smile at her adorable shock. "When I inherited this place, it felt like a burden. Fuck, it's horrible to say, but it's the truth. I couldn't be here. Never considered stepping foot inside. The memories and ghosts were enough to keep me away. Sure, I eventually wandered into the backyard and the treehouse," I say while wrapping my arms around her waist. "But walking through the front door wasn't something I could fathom. Not until you."

Tears gather in her eyes as my words settle in. "Trey, I don't even know what to say. This is so special."

I nod, stroking her jaw softly. My lips press along hers for a beat before I break away. "That's not all," I admit.

Raven wipes her face. "What else could there be? This is . . . *huge*."

I scratch my temple. "I'm thinking of living here. This hasn't been a home in far too many years, but I'm hoping to change that. They'd be happy to see me exactly where I belong."

She gasps. "Really? That's great—"

"But there's too much space for me," I cut her off. "Thinking of finding a roommate. Would this place be fit for a princess?" Raven's mouth pops open as she stares up at me. I make it official and ask, "Wanna move in with me?"

She bounces on her toes. "Yes! So much yes!" she exclaims.

I hoist her up before locking our mouths in a searing kiss. I slide my tongue along hers and she mewls into me. Our chests press closer and I feel her heart pounding against mine. Damn, we're beating to the same rhythm. We remain intertwined, hugging and just . . . living this moment. The weight of this decision descends around us, but the load isn't unpleasant. Today, I only sense happiness in this house, and that makes me smile.

"What happens now?" she questions softly.

I pull away a little, gazing down at her flawless features. "We should probably christen our home, right?"

Raven's sapphires sparkle. "I love the sound of that."

"And I love you," I murmur and press her against the wall. "Right where we should be to start our happily-ever-after."

Extra EPILOGUE

YES

TREY

THE COOL BREEZE WHIPS FASTER, the gust sending specks of sand flying around us. I bend my neck back and allow the sun to beam down on me. My chest expands with a relaxed breath.

"You weren't lying, Princess. This place is something else." I pull her tighter against me.

Raven's head bumps into my chin when she sways slowly. "Worth leaving Garden Grove?"

"With you? Abso-fucking-lutely," I say without hesitation.

When she hums, the vibration travels through my arms around her. I manage to wrap her impossibly closer, wanting more.

"Told you vacations are a good idea," Raven murmurs.

"You love being right." I grunt. "And this is definitely one of the times I'll admit it. But don't get used to that." Raven scoffs and I kiss behind her ear. "I was stupid to deny this before. Thanks for being patient and showing me the way. Shit is much better with you around."

She laughs. "Such a wordsmith. And I'm always happy to be of service. I'll drag out all over the world."

"Don't mind the sound of that." My fingers dig into her sides and she wiggles into me. The friction gets my blood pumping, as always.

"You and me both," she agrees. "I've never had so much fun getting . . . *filthy*."

My hands roam down to her hips and squeeze. "You love those adventurous parts of me."

"I do," she moans. "Keep it up."

"That's never a problem where you're concerned, Princess." I thrust into her, proving my words.

Raven moans. "You're insatiable. We just left the room after that epic marathon round."

I squint while thinking about her bouncing on my lap. My dick gets harder against her. "Damn, that was hot as fuck. I'll never get enough of your sexy ass, Princess."

"Hmm, that sounds lovely. We should take trips more often."

"I'm down with that."

Her face tilts up to mine, those sapphire eyes lighting up my world. "You're being so agreeable. The beach resort is good for you."

I nip her shoulder. "You're great for me. That's all it is."

"I'm turning you into a romantic gentleman," she giggles.

"That's debatable. And you better not tell anyone," I say. "This is only for you."

Pressure whooshes in my ears as I remember her surprise. The lust flooding my lower half distracted me from the main purpose of dragging Raven out here.

She shifts in my hold. "Dirty?"

I blink rapidly and look down at her. "Yeah?"

"You okay? You're gripping me really hard. I'm not gonna run off." Raven smiles and the tension seeps from my muscles.

"Couldn't be better." I turn her around so she's focusing directly on me, exactly how it should be. My thumb strokes up her jaw. "I love you, Princess. You know that?"

Raven's lips lift higher and she leans into my touch. "I love you more."

I scoff. "Not possible. My life finally makes sense and I have you to thank. Shit finally feels just right, Raven. All because of you." My palms rest on her ass, yanking her into me. Raven's body rises against me with my deep inhale. "You're so important to me."

"Aww, you're being sweet." She stands on her toes, seeking my lips.

I groan into our kiss, getting horny all over again when she melts against me. Raven pouts after I quickly break away. I can't deny her so she gets another swift peck.

Gravel settles in my throat. "I've never been an emotional guy or very good with expressing myself. But for you, I'm trying. Gonna give you plenty more today," I say softly.

I dig in my pocket, rubbing the soft velvet nestled there. My heart hammers a wild beat, threatening to crack a rib. Raven watches while I pull out the small box with a trembling hand. With a flip of the lid, the diamond ring sparkles between us. She gapes, her wide eyes locked on the flawless stone. I remain silent, trying to clear my mind. The words wait on my tongue. I just have to spit them out.

She peeks up at me from under her lashes. "It's stunning," she whispers.

I want to pound my chest at her praise. "Fit for a princess. My filthy one."

I ease down on one knee, the sand sinking beneath my weight.

"Holy crap," Raven gasps. "Is this really happening?"

"Damn straight."

Her palms press against her flushed cheeks. "I can't believe it."

"Want me to pinch you?"

Tears form in her blazing blues. She shakes her head, then nods. I reach out, squeezing the third finger of her left hand. She sucks in a sharp breath.

"Believe me now?" I ask, raising a brow.

Raven licks her lips. "O-okay, yes. Let's do it."

I chuckle at her enthusiasm. "There's a few more things I wanna say, Princess. Let me talk a bit, yeah?"

She blushes a beautiful shade of pink. "R-right. Sorry," she stammers. "I'm just so excited."

"And I'm damn glad."

I can hardly think with my pulse pounding through my temples. But I do my best. I squint up at her through the glaring sun.

"I'm not the sweetest, or most charming. But you get me, Princess. I want you to claim me forever. I'll consume you in return. For today and all our tomorrows. I've kept myself numb, until you. Princess, you've brought me back. Or maybe I was never around to begin with. Either way, whatever joy I have belongs to you. Everything is better, because of you. Say you'll be my filthy girl and marry me," I say without a hint of questioning. There's only one answer I'm willing to accept.

Raven was already agreeing halfway through my spiel, but she makes it official. "Yes, Trey! Of course. Yes, yes, yes!"

I smile and feel the expression cover my entire face. "Best damn thing I've ever heard," I tell her honestly.

Sliding the metal band over Raven's knuckle, I seal the deal. She yelps when I bite down gently on her fingertip.

"So naughty," Raven purrs. I stand up and she folds into my open arms. For a few blissed-out moments, we get lost in a heated kiss. We're a jumble of twisting tongues and reaching hands. Raven's nails scratch along my abs and I growl low, nibbling her bottom lip. I have to force myself to pull back.

"Love you, Princess," I say against her silky jaw.

"And I love you, Dirty. Forever," she promises.

Everything is perfect. Except she's wearing far too many clothes. Will I ruin the moment by suggesting we get naked? Raven beats me to it.

"Let's go back to the room," she suggests.

I tuck some hair behind her ear. "It's like you're reading my mind, Princess."

I scoop Raven into my arms, spinning us around in fast circles, and a peel of laughter escapes her.

"Ready for this to be the rest of our lives?" I ask, jogging toward the hotel.

"You don't have to carry me," she giggles.

"My hands belong all over your body, at all times. Especially now."

"All night long?"

"It'll be my pleasure."

"Such a gentleman," Raven coos.

I brush my nose along hers, resting our foreheads together. "And all yours."

THE END

DELETED SCENES

#1—RESCUE

RAVEN

THIS CAN'T BE HAPPENING.

I watch thick smoke billow from my hood, cursing the check engine light that just started blinking. Oh, really? I couldn't tell. Thanks a ton, Captain Obvious. I roll my eyes. This is stupid. I'm stuck, and arguing with myself won't help.

While wrenching the keys from the ignition, I press my forehead to the steering wheel. The strong burn of rubber permeates the air and claws at my windpipe. Helplessness washes over me and I curse my lack of knowledge in these situations. I never learned how to change my oil or fix a flat tire. My mom's solution was relying on whatever guy was around at the time.

In these moments, I find myself thinking about my dad. Maybe he would have taught me these skills.

I wipe away some frustrated tears. It's silly to cry over something I can't control. I release the air from my cheeks, swallow the tendrils of defeat, and buck up. I reach for my cell and dial Delilah, a reliable support for crisis circumstances.

"Rave?"

"Hey, D," I mumble through pursed lips.

"What's wrong?"

"My car stalled. Again. And I just had it fixed," I say.

Delilah hums. "Well, that beast is almost ten years old. Maybe you should ask for a raise and buy a new one."

"Very funny, but I wasn't calling for jokes."

"Where are you?"

I glance around, trying to find some distinguishable landmark between all the cornfields. "Uh, I dunno. There's no signs out here."

"Are you on 65?"

"Yeah?"

"You don't sound very confident," she deadpans.

I huff, trying not to get frustrated. "I left Greensbarrow fifteen minutes ago. I'm pulled over on the main road that would take me back to Garden Grove. My phone was spouting off directions."

"Okay, that's good. They'll know where to find you."

"Do you have a number for the local roadside assistance?"

Delilah laughs. "Rave, small town remember? That doesn't exist here. You have to call Jacked Up."

"Isn't that where—?"

"Yup. The probability of Trey showing up is pretty damn likely. He tends to take all the emergency calls."

"Dammit," I say. That's not what I wanted to hear. He's been nothing but terrible whenever I have the displeasure of bumping into him. My stomach tightens in knots when I ask, "There's no one else?"

"It's like Russian roulette. Hope for the best, sweets."

"Ugh, all right," I mutter. "Thanks."

"Best of luck. See you soon," Delilah chirps.

"Depends on who they send to rescue me."

"I'll keep my fingers and toes crossed for you. Tootles, Rave."

"Bye, D."

The line goes dead and I slouch in my seat, mustering up some courage. I watch my fingers tremble while searching for the shop on Google. Air freezes in my lungs when I press on the number. My call is answered after two rings.

"Jacked Up Repairs, Jack speaking."

I blow out a relieved breath. "Hi, Jack. This is Raven Elliot. My car stalled off Highway 65. I'm not sure how to describe exactly where, but the map app says twenty-two miles away from town."

"Whatcha doing all the way out there?"

"I was shopping in Greensbarrow."

"Ah, sure. They've got some great spots."

"Uh, huh," I say.

"There's a steakhouse you've gotta try," he adds.

I bite my tongue to stop from asking why we're wasting time with chit-chat. "Okay, great. So, what're the chances you can give me a tow?"

"Absolutely. That's what we're around for. I'll get someone out there right away."

I'm desperate to ask who, but don't want to be rude. "That'd be super."

"Sit tight and we'll be there quick."

"Thanks, Jack."

"No problem," he says and hangs up.

I stare at the black screen and contemplate what to do now. I spend a few minutes scrolling social media and checking my email. After browsing a few sites, I open the Kindle app and select the new romance on top. I try to relax and allow the story to distract me, but my racing pulse won't slow. I'm too keyed up to concentrate.

The unknown is agony. I wait in silence with pins and needles prodding my skin. At least the steam has stopped rising from my hood. That must be a good sign, right? In the next moment, a huge truck comes into view. My restless fingers curl into fists as I wait to see who's driving. I watch with a rock in my stomach while whoever it is pulls in front of me and backs up with effortless ease.

When Trey hops out, a string of expletives flies from my lips. He struts toward me without a care in the world. I strain my ears, pretty sure he's whistling. This ought to be good.

"We meet again, Princess. What a fucking coincidence," he says and leans into my window. "Forget to check your gas tank between shopping stops?"

I rake through my hair, ignoring his snide remarks. "There's something wrong with the engine," I grind out.

He snorts. "You an expert? Why'd you bother calling us?"

"You're such an asshole."

"In the flesh. Glad I'm making an impression."

"Not a good one," I snap.

Trey wipes his brow. "Need help or you gonna keep bitching? I'm a busy man and you're wasting my time."

I jerk in place. "Me? Wha—? Nope, never mind." I gesture to the hood. "Do your thing."

"You need to get out," he says.

"Why?"

"Because I need to load your car onto the flatbed. Can't have you sitting in here while I'm hauling it up. You'll riding back with me." He hooks a thumb to his tuck.

I scrunch up my nose. My heart pounds as I imagine being so close to him for that long. I lick my lips, deciding how to respond. Trey beats me to it.

"Don't look so disgusted, Princess. I keep the cab clean. You won't get dirty. At least not from that." Suggestion is thick in his voice.

"I find that hard to believe," I mumble, tilting my head to the side.

He wrenches my door open and motions for me to get out. I

squint at him, uncertainty tickling my arms. I want to refuse, and the words linger on my tongue, but arguing seems pointless. I unbuckle the seatbelt and slowly ease out. Once my feet touch the pavement, Trey crowds my space with his towering frame. Trey's woodsy musk overpowers the stench of oil, like he's clinging to me in the heated air. The grey coveralls he's wearing are covered in grease and stains, evidence of his hard work. The sight is an unexpected turn-on, and I have to stop myself from touching the stained fabric. I can only imagine his reaction to my fondling.

I glance up and find him staring at me. Static zaps between us, the sizzle hotter than the summer humidity. Trey's brown eyes scorch into mine, searching and seeking.

"Maybe you wanna get dirty after all, Princess." His tone is full of filth.

I gulp but remain silent. I think he might be right.

#2—BARE

TREY

AFTER KNOCKING, I PROP AN elbow against the wood frame.
When the door swings open, the cocky greeting dies on my lips.

Raven stands in front of me, wearing nothing but that damn
pink apron. I blink slowly, gobbling up the glorious sight, and
almost swallow my tongue in the process. Lust pumps into me,
going from zero to sixty in a snap.

Hell fucking yeah.

"Hey, Dirty," she purrs. "I've been waiting for you."

I drag my eyes up to hers, but get caught up in all the exposed
skin. Her bare shoulders and hips are beyond tempting, getting a
serious rise out of my dick. He's saluting her efforts—big time.
I wipe over my brow, the temperature suddenly skyrocketing.

"Damn, Princess." That's all I can choke out.

Seems good enough for Raven because a pleased smile spreads
on her face. "You like?" She holds the bottom edges out, giving
me a peek at what's underneath. When she rocks back and forth,
her curves call out to me in a seductive dance.

I groan into my fist. "You're playing dirty."

"Thank you." Dimples dent her cheeks and I want to bite them.

"Where's D?"

"Not here."

Good enough for me.

I raise my chin and ask, "Gonna let me in or what?"

Raven doesn't say anything while taking a few steps back. Her blue eyes narrow and gleam, beckoning me closer in silent invitation. Desire sparks between us while we continue devouring each other without a word. Raven breaks the connection by turning and walking into the kitchen, her naked ass on full display. My mouth waters, and I get lost in the gentle shimmy of her stride.

When I follow her into the loft, baked sugar and fruit hang heavy in the air. Smells like my girl has been busy. I'm about to give her a huge reward. A single cooling rack sits on the flat stovetop and snags my attention. Six cupcakes rest on the grate, little crowns nestled into the pink frosting. Raven catches me looking and a knowing grin lifts her lips.

"I was experimenting with a new recipe," she explains.

"That doesn't surprise me. You're always inventing something," I say.

"Guess what these are called?" Raven asks. She swipes a finger along the nearest one, making an erotic show of sucking the frosting into her mouth.

A low moan escapes me. "Tell me."

"Filthy Princess," she whispers. "They're cream filled."

"Shit," I cough. "Are you jealous? Because I can change that real quick." I grab my junk.

"I didn't dress like this for nothing," Raven taunts. She twirls slowly, sticking her ass toward me in the process.

"Don't gotta tell me twice," I say.

When I yank a condom from my front pocket, she shakes her

head. "I wanna feel you bare."

I lift my startled gaze to hers. "You sure? I'm clean and always wrap my shit up. This would be my first time going without," I admit.

Raven steps into me. Her fingers brush over mine and take the foil packet. "Same for me. I've never considered it before, but I want this with you. Right here and now."

I smirk. "You been thinking of this, Princess?"

"Uh, huh. I don't typically wear *just* an apron around the house."

"Unless you're sending me pictures."

A blush races up her neck. "That was only for a moment, just for you."

"I like that."

"And this is a special occasion."

"Better make it count," I add.

She nods. "Indeed."

I crash my mouth down onto hers, ending the discussion. My tongue rolls over her lips, tasting and savoring. She's sugary sweet like her cupcakes, and I moan at the flavor. Raven opens wider and I take advantage, staking claim over each reachable inch. I slide my tongue along hers, desperately seeking more. Her nails dig into my biceps, dragging me closer. The damn apron is blocking me from really feeling her.

I rip my mouth away and command, "Turn around. Palms on the counter, legs spread wide."

Raven doesn't hesitate, following my orders in the next beat. Watching her do exactly as I ask makes me harder. I'm more than ready to own her in this way. I unzip and whip out my dick, giving a few warm-up strokes. The need to make this the best yet fuels me. I want to satisfy the desire vibrating off her, and fulfill this fantasy for both of us—completely. I line up at her center and get dizzy from the slick heat waiting for me.

Ready and wanting, Raven shifts when she feels me there. The wiggle of her restless hips is my undoing. In the next moment, I'm slamming all the way home. Her body welcomes me, and I feel *everything*. Stars burst behind my clenched eyelids and I try holding back.

"Jesus, Princess. You're so hot and wet. This bare pussy was made for my cock."

"Yes," she coos. Raven pushes against me, connecting us deeper.

"Fuck, you're hungry for it."

"Please. *More*," she pants.

I slide in and out, setting a steady rhythm. Having her this way, with nothing between us, is detrimental to my stamina. The threat of coming too soon is a very real possibility. I grind my teeth and force the impending release away. My grip tightens on Raven's waist and I bend her forward. This position gives me better access to her g-spot. She lets me know when I hit it.

"Holy shit. There, yes. Oh, God, yes!" Her husky encouragements crank my pleasure up another notch.

Raven shudders in my hold and I know she's nearing the edge. I scoop up some pink frosting and draw a line down her nape. I lick across her seductive skin and strawberry bursts on my tongue.

Filthy has never tasted so fucking delicious.

SNEEK PEAK at MISS

BY HARLOE RAE

Delilah and Zeke are telling their story next in MISS, releasing late summer 2018. Until then, enjoy this snippet . . .

I STORM OUT OF MY father's house for the final time, ignoring the burn blazing up my side. I'm more than ready to get gone and wrench open the truck door. As I toss my duffle across the seat, soft steps sound behind me. I know it's her without turning around. My heart beats wildly, even faster than when he was threatening my life a few moments ago.

Will she understand? Here's hoping.

I turn slowly and my breath falters at the sight of her gorgeous face painted with worry. My beautiful girl looks scared and I'd do anything to wipe the concern away. But I can't stay.

My feet shuffle toward her and piercing pain radiates from my ribcage. I do my best not to wince. He got me good tonight, but never again.

"Where are you going?" She whispers.

"Away. At least for a while."

A quiet sob hiccups from her throat. "W-why? I don't want you to leave."

I cup her jaw and tilt her face up. My eyes devour her porcelain perfect features. "The last thing I wanna do is be without you, Trip. But staying in that house, with him, is ruining me. I don't wanna go but if I stay, there won't be much of me left. He won't stop until he's destroyed me."

"Take me with you," she pleads. "I can't make it without you, Zee."

My shoulders sag under the pressure of her green stare. I hate disappointing her. "You gotta finish school, Trip. And you're so strong. I'm holding you back, feeding off your goodness. You'll do better without me, at least how I am now."

Her bright gaze is fierce and pins me in place. "You take that back. If I'm strong, it's only because of you. Having you here with me is the greatest gift."

I stroke her velvet skin, letting her kindness sink into my soul. I let the memories of simpler times rush in, easing the agony slightly. Our younger selves were full of so much happiness.

"Remember the day we met?" I ask into the darkness.

She nuzzles deeper into my touch. "How could I forget? I still sleep in that ridiculous shirt."

"And you stumbled in the grass rushing over to me. My little Trip." She laughs, and a hint of a smile tilts her lips. "That's right. Think of the good."

"I know what you're doing," she murmurs.

"Is it working?"

Moisture coats her lashes as she blinks rapidly. "No".

"Should I try harder?"

"Does that involve you sticking around?"

I don't respond. Words can't express the war waging in my heart.

Trip sighs. "Okay. I'll be strong. For you."

"For you too. Don't let them win. Keep your head up," I demand. A loud bang shatters the calm around us. I glance at house before focusing on her. "He'll wake up soon. I gotta go now."

My fingers twist a few locks of her blonde hair, committing the silky texture to memory. Her bottomless blue eyes are shining with emotion, and nothing I say will stop her tears.

"No. Please, stay," she cries and clutches onto me tight. I suck in sharply when her fingers dig into the fresh bruises on my torso.

"Trip, baby. I can't. He's gonna kill me if I don't get to him first." I brush away the tracks streaming down her cheeks. Her tears slam into me harder than his fists ever have. With regret pooling in my gut, I lay out the truth. "I can't survive there another minute. But know if I could, I'd do it only because of you."

She stays silent because she knows it's true. Living next door, she hears the constant fighting. When Trip clings to me harder, my teeth grind to force the ache away.

"Where will you go?"

"I have distant family spread all around. No one stays in contact with my dad, but they'll take me in."

"Are you going far?" Her lip wobbles, and my thumb presses against it.

I shrug, helplessness soaking into my bones. "I'm not sure. We'll see when I get there."

"Will you call me? Tell me where you are?"

"Of course. You're all I'll think about. You know that, right? I've always loved you."

She sniffles and snuggles against me. "I love you so much, Zee. It hurts knowing you won't be here tomorrow."

"But it's only temporary. We'll be together again soon."

Silence envelopes us, but my mind is screaming, and time has run out. I can't leave her with nothing but a faded shirt. I fiddle with the chain looped around my neck. As always, my mother's ring hangs from the center. I pull it off and place it over her head.

Trip gasps and grabs the silver links. "No. I can't accept this. It's all you have left of her."

She's right, of course. That necklace is the only possession

I've ever cared about. I tug on the metal strand and tell her, "It's to keep you safe. Like it has for me all these years. I don't need it now that I'm leaving. Wear this and know I'm always with you."

She's crying openly, the tears pouring freely without pause. "I'll never take it off."

"That's right. Hold on to it for me."

Trip nods. "And I'll wait here until you come back."

A knot pulls tight in my stomach at her words. I don't want her clinging to false hope, grasping at a future that might not come, but darn, a life without her isn't one at all. So, I let us both believe.

"I'll come for you soon. Don't worry, baby girl. I'm gonna get a job and save up every penny. I'll get us a cute little place we can share. And when it's ready and you've graduated, I'll come for you."

"I believe in you. I know you'll make this happen for us."

Hopefully she has enough faith for both of us.

ACKNOWLEDGMENTS

HOPEFULLY YOU ENJOYED MY FOUL-MOUTHED mechanic and the girl who stole his heart. GENT was a really fun book for me to write.

I need to start off by thanking the readers. Whether you finish a couple books per year or read nonstop, I greatly appreciate you. Time is precious and any piece you carve out for reading is very meaningful.

It's been a whirlwind of a year since I pressed publish for the first time. Here I am, twelve months and four books later. Wowza. I wasn't sure this would ever happen for me and I wouldn't have survived without the support of these amazing people in my corner.

To my husband and family for being the greatest gift a woman could ask for. I thank my very lucky stars each day that you're in my life. You're allowing me to fulfill my dreams and follow my passions and I couldn't do this without you.

Talia is not only the most talented cover artist, but also an outstanding friend. She is patient when I don't deserve it and always listens to me ramble about crazy ideas. Thank you for understanding my insanity and always knowing just what to say. Our random chats are my favorite!

Sunniva is a wonderful author and talented wordsmith. Her skills are boundless. Thank you for taking time out of your busy schedule to edit my book. I love talking nonsense and extremely important business with you. I'll never be able to express my level of gratitude for all you do. I owe you a million.

Michelle is bloody brilliant. You're the most selfless person

I've ever "met". I always look forward to our chats and listening to your accent. Day after day, your encouragement keeps me going. I could never ask for a better cheerleader. I would be lost without you, my sweet friend. I'm really hoping to see you soon!

There aren't enough words or adequate space to explain my gratitude to Ace. She's been a constant from the start and has made me a better writer each step of the way. Thank you for talking me off the ledge and always answering my texts. Maybe I'll visit you in Vegas.

Anne is a genuine and lovely soul. Also, she's a kickbutt author. I'm so happy we're friends. Your knowledge and wisdom are endless, and I'm so thankful you share it with me. Give Walter extra pets, okay?

Tijuana is an extremely bright spot in this beautiful book world. I'm talking blinding sunlight. I'm still pinching myself that you agreed to help me. Be my friend? That's a bonus I didn't see coming. You're stuck with ME! Get ready for an epic swag pack. in awe of you.

Kate is one of the sweetest gals I've met in this magical book world. Thank you for always being there for me when I need a friend. You're fabulous!

Suzie writes swoony-alpha rock stars like no one else and she loves fiercely. Thanks for rooting me on! I'm a lucky duck to call you friend.

Victoria is one of the first authors I bonded with way back when. She's fantastic and sweet and all the goodness. Have you met her sexy alphas? You're an amazing support and I'm very thankful!

Sarah is a sensational blogger, reviewer, and beta. She's a jack of all the trades. Your creative ideas made all the difference and I appreciate every moment you spent making my story better.

Lauren knows all the things and doesn't let me slip. I'm so excited to see you soon. I miss your face! Thank you for all you do, for everyone.

Leigh makes me want to be better and work harder. You're the greatest inspiration and truly extraordinary. Thank you for encouraging me. I hope we get to hang out one day for some Shen-anigans!

Nicole is always there with a listening ear. Your humor and drive are two things I need more of. Thanks for always being a true friend.

Madison has become a much-needed force and gives me the greatest motivation. Thanks for always being there with helpful advice and encouraging words.

Bobby is crazy amazing with ads and data and all the ways to build marketing success. Thank you very much for sharing your skills with me!

This book is dedicated to Megan, Shauna, and Jacqueline for a reason. They're a fierce trio that I'd be lost without. I'm beyond words by your endless effort and selfless work for authors. I don't know what I did to deserve all your help but I'm extremely grateful for it. Thank you!

Cindy is a wonderful friend and true confidant. I'm so grateful to have you in my life, friend! Thank you for always sticking by me and giving me positive words when I need them most.

Melissa knows just what to say to make me smile. Your graphics are almost as gorgeous as you. Thanks for being a genuine and reliable friend within all the madness.

Eric is an extremely talented photographer and he works so darn hard to promote us. GENT has a very gorgeous cover image because of you. I'm beyond words thankful that I saw your story that morning and snagged it up. You're wonderful and I can't wait for the next one!

Crystal and Maggie took a chance on a new author last year. In this industry, there are so many book and too little time. These two didn't hesitate when I asked them. I love you ladies something crazy. Thank you for everything, from my bottom of my happy author heart!

A huge shout out to Tia, Devney, Cora, Lauren, Penelope, Kahlen, Luke, Leigh, Auden, Jess, Andi, Ella, Alyson, Haylee, and Dylan.

To my Hotties, you're the greatest reader group EVER! Thanks for always interacting and being around for me. I love our special place on social media!

To the Harloe's Review Crew, thank you so very much for wanting to read and review my words. You're the bestest and I'm forever grateful.

To my fellow DND authors, I owe you all a huge hug for all the motivation and support. I love our little family and would be lost without your encouragement.

To The Squad, you're all lovely and fantastic and beyond words phenomenal. Nicole, Jane, Jess, JL, Kim, Liv, Paige, Meg, Ava, and Brooke rule for always!

Bobbie, Margie, and Jen are my besties forever. We started years ago and are still going strong. BS&BS strong!

I'm extremely grateful and honored to have such fantastic blogger support. You know who you are and I'm sending a big hug your way! I wasn't sure what to expect when first publishing but so many sensational people stepped up to help. Even when social media cuts off visibility and organic reach, you all still power through. You're in this for the love of books and I love you all so much for it. Thank you for sharing and spreading the word.

To Eva and Emily for making gorgeous teasers and GIFs.

A huge thank you to Christine with Type A Formatting for always making my books beautiful.

And last but certainly not least, thank YOU for reading GENT. I'll never be able to thank you enough for that. Keep reading and loving books, yeah? You've made me a very, very happy author!

About the Author

HARLOE RAE IS A MINNESOTA gal with a serious addiction to romance. She's always chasing an epic happily ever after.

When she's not buried in the writing cave, Harloe can be found hanging with her hubby and son. If the weather permits, she loves being lakeside or out in the country with her horses.

Harloe is the author of Redefining Us, Forget You Not, Watch Me Follow, and GENT. These titles are available on Amazon.

Find all the latest on her site :
www.harloe-rae.blog

Made in the USA
Columbia, SC
10 January 2024

30233128R00169